Tracks
Of
A
Pigeon-toed
Horse

Also by J.T. Fleming

Tracks of a Pigeon-toed Horse

The Obsidian Serpent

Mouriel
{Coming soon}

Tracks
Of
A
Pigeon-toed
Horse

BY
J. T. Fleming

Tracks of a Pigeon-toed Horse
Copyright © 2010 by John T. Fleming

Cover Art & Photos
Copyright © 2010 by John T. Fleming

Library of Congress # TXu001735419 / 2010-09-24

ISBN: 978-0-9832461-0-7 (PBK)
ISBN: 978-0-9832461-2-1   (mobi)
ISBN: 978-0-9832461-4-5 (e-pub)

This novel is a work of fiction. Names, characters, places, and incidents are the product of the author's imagination or are used fictitiously. Any resemblance to actual events, locales, organizations or their doctrines, or persons, living or dead, is entirely coincidental and beyond the intent of either the author or publisher.

FORTRESS PUBLISHING, LLC
www.fortresspublishing.net

*Dedicated to my wife, Gail,
proofreader, critic, typist, and
best friend.*

With special thanks to all those who took the time to read and comment on this project while it was in progress.

Tracks
Of
A
Pigeon-toed
Horse

Skin Walker

Uintah Mountains—August 1857

*T*he ghost slipped nearly unseen through low-lying clouds that lay on the mountainside like the shifting tendrils of a thick fog. At the edge of a rocky cleft in the mountain, the ghost resolved itself into the bulky shape of an old man clad in a worn and dirty buffalo coat. Frost from the cold of the morning air and the moisture of his breath crusted his whiskers like a winter frost on a forest of twisted pines. He was tall, lanky and thin in the face, and though the dim light of the rising sun did not show it, he was baked dark as a native and wrinkled with age.

He was late. He should have been here sooner. Somehow, he had been detained. For that, he blamed himself. Now, he gazed into the rocky ravine where the snow-melt was already hard at work removing the softer soil that had covered the body.

"Skin walker," he hissed angrily, knowing instantly how the man below had been murdered.

Quickly, as though expecting an attack at any moment, the old man searched for recent evidence of the skin walker's presence. The search revealed little, except the old and hardened tracks of small animals that had passed the site in the dampness left by the last rain—nothing large enough to be connected easily with the skin walker. Yet, there was something—a feeling that something watched—something the old man must find and destroy before it could kill again. He had little love for these men. They were whites who had taken a native American legend and twisted it for their own purposes—purposes that the old man was only now beginning to understand, and there was nothing for it but to hunt the skin walker.

The trail was cold as the old man began the hunt—cold as the frozen ground of the narrow deer trail he followed. He knew the murder was recent. In fact, it could not have been more than a day or two since the thin layer of loose earth had been thrown upon the body, for the runoff was swift and it wouldn't have taken long to erode the burial. Still, there had been no sign of the killer, and the old man followed the deer trail only because it afforded easy walking. So, when he heard the shots as he topped a ridge five miles to the west and saw the smoke of a burning camp, he knew he had found his prey. Three hundred yards away, three bodies lay quietly ignoring the killer as he systematically looted the ruined camp.

Quietly, the old man tied his horse among a sea of sagebrush and began working his way down the slope. At a hundred yards and still above the camp, he stopped and dropped to one knee. He eased the heavy Hawken rifle to his shoulder and took aim on the figure below. Between the iron sights, the killer bent over his victim and with quick slashes, removed the dead man's scalp.

The old man growled deep in his throat and tightened his finger on the trigger. There was no mercy in his heart, no thought of ignoring the situation below, for the killer was no Indian, and the scene below had been repeated far too often. It had been pure chance that the old man had heard the shots, but he had not made it in time to lend aid to the three men who now lay butchered among the small cluster of aspen below.

The old man eased his finger from the trigger. Something was wrong—something he had not noticed until the killer shifted position, revealing the long barrel of a muzzle loading rifle. The situation had changed—or rather the old man's understanding of the situation had changed.

Three men were dead, but there was only one slow loading rifle to do the job.

"It might be," he muttered quietly, "but not likely. More likely, you ain't alone."

The old man felt the hair rise on the back of his neck. He had been tracking this killer for nearly fifty miles, and there had never been any indication that the man had partners. Now it was all too clear that, somewhere along the way, the killer had collected companions, and the old man had become the hunted rather than the hunter.

The old man smiled. Hunter and prey—he remembered that game. He remembered the jaguar stalking the serpent deep in the brakes at the river's edge—the jaguar's attack and death as the serpent struck with a speed that left the jaguar ruined upon the ground. The old man pushed the memory aside. Quickly, he squeezed the trigger. A sullen boom thundered across the mountain, rushing up canyons and dry gullies until the reverberation dwindled and died in the distance.

The old man was on his feet in an instant. He did not attempt to load the rifle; he simply turned, lashing out with the barrel, taking the first of his attackers in the face with the heavy octagon barrel. The man went down without a sound, lifeless. Two more charged from the tall sagebrush, intent on combining their strength to take down the old man. But the first crashed to the ground with a broken knee, and the second died as the barrel of the rifle stabbed forward, splintering his ribs and puncturing his heart.

The old man looked down on the wounded man and smiled. "I was once an eagle," he said quietly. "They called me Obsidian Serpent."

The wounded man looked up in agony and grabbed for his knife. The barrel of the rifle lashed out.

Hours later, the old man stood quietly at the edge of the ravine, knowing that a friend lay beneath the rocks and earth now being washed away by the spring run-off. It was an untimely death that would cause untold ripples in a vast ocean of probabilities. Unhappily, he steeled himself for the grisly job of removing the body and burying the friend he had known for so long.

"If only it could be undone," he murmured unhappily.

As though responding to his half-spoken thought, the wind gusted across the mountainside, laying the tall cheek grass to the ground and buffeting the old man until his heavy coat seemed ready to drag him across the hillside like a small ship under sail.

"Mouriel," he whispered suddenly. "I hear. Time ain't a stream… an' some things *can* be fixed.

Murder

Utah Territory
Ogden, 31 August 1868

No one was the least amused when the mongrel bitch guarding the alley door of Jake Farney's store ravaged the quiet of the evening. The day had been hot and windy, and by dusk, nearly everyone in town had deserted the streets and hid in their homes feeling humorless and irritable. To the west, clouds boiled and lightning flashed over the Great Salt Lake.

Lester Reynald ignored the barking dog, fumbled for his key, and opened the door of his small shop. Reynald was elated. For six years, he had collected antiques, ancient junk, artifacts, and an assortment of odds and ends, hoping for a time when someone in town would buy the stuff. Finally, something was going to pay off. Someone wanted the mummy. Well...it wasn't really a mummy, but it was old. At least it looked old. Reynald wasn't much of a hand at judging that kind of thing, but he liked to think of himself as an expert on things ancient and worth collecting. Still, the mummy had to be something special. He had a buyer who wanted the thing *right now*. His dreams of wealth were about to take a step closer to reality. In some ways, Lester was a bit naïve—too naïve for a grouchy little man who generally got along with as few people as possible.

Inside the shop, Lester locked the door and lit a lamp. The mummified remains of the Indian woman lay on a canvas-covered table in the center of the room. Lester trimmed the smoking lamp, and began checking the artifacts that would go with the purchase. Mostly, they were an odd assortment of trivial items—a few small pots, leather moccasins, brittle with age, and a few teardrop-shaped pieces of shell that might have been part of a necklace. Groesbeck claimed that most of the artifacts had been crammed into the larger pots, which had been carefully arranged near the body.

The body itself was dried and stiffened by desert heat. The head lay twisted sharply to the right, the left arm thrown awkwardly across the upper torso. To Lester's naive eye, the clothing seemed strangely out of place, as though not truly suited to the woman. Still, Groesbeck had assured him that everything was just as he had found it. Cautiously, Lester touched the brittle doeskin dress. "Strange," he muttered. Surely the clothing was drier.... Suddenly apprehensive, he shifted the body. Matted hair fell back from the side of the face. He reached out and touched the small earring still attached to the leathery ear. Lester backed toward the door, gagging. He vomited before he could turn the key in the lock and push his way into the alley. Finally, he stood in the alley, half bent, trying to catch his breath. The night was silent, the only sound the *creaking* of crickets and the soft scuffing of a boot behind him—his client. Lester turned at the sound, and felt a stabbing pain deep in his chest. Someone pushed him hard against the wall of the store. He felt himself choking. The sound of the crickets grew shrill for a moment; then the night grew oddly silent.

Everyone dies. Some folks die peacefully in their sleep. Some are awake and see it coming. And some, a rare few, deserve a bit of a surprise—a knife in the heart—a bullet between the eyes.... Lester Reynald may not have been all that deserving, but he was surprised.

CHAPTER 1

Utah Territory
Ogden —1 September 1868

Sarah Mitchell stood with her back to the window of Jon Browning's firearms store and watched the slow moving traffic on the muddy streets of Ogden City. Water pooled in footprints, ran down the deep ruts gouged by wagon wheels and turned into miniature rivers. At a poorly fashioned corner, the rivers slowed and built to a flood. Her father claimed to have seen a full-grown mule washed down Fifth Street and into the Weber River, but her father was known to tell a tale now and then, so she was inclined to believe that the mule had really been a goat or a small pig.

Sarah shifted the revolver in her hand. The butt of the navy Colt was slick from the rain, but it was loaded and ready to fire. From within the store, her sister's laughter sounded strained and unnatural. Sarah risked a quick glance through the rain-spattered glass. Her husband stood at the back counter, inspecting a revolver. Her sister, Susan, stood close beside him. Collin Mitchell spoke quietly to the man behind the counter. The man nodded, took the revolver, and turned away. Sarah watched as her husband drew Susan close and quickly kissed her. Hurriedly, Sarah wiped the dampness from the palm of her hand. It wouldn't do to have the thing slip from her hand when she fired it.

She turned from the window, and again watched people and animals alike slug through a street turned to mud by a cool September rain. Some of them might understand when she killed the man, but a goodly number of those people had come from the East and harbored the grand illusion that they were now the cream of society. There was no doubt in her mind that they would be the ones demanding her life when her bullet tore a hole through the man's chest. She tensed as two men stepped onto the boardwalk. Their muddy boots left a trail as they stepped to the window and peered through the glass. They passed her with barely a nod, and entered the store. Sarah was close on their heels.

"Help you fellers in just a minute," said the clerk. "About done here."

Sarah slipped to one side of the room, standing partially hidden behind a rack of new rifles. No one seemed to notice as she slipped the revolver from the pleats of her skirt.

"Brother Mitchell," said the clerk, "those are the two finest Colts we have in stock. Jonathan test fired the both of 'em, and they both print a mighty fine group at fifty feet."

Carefully, Mitchell tested the action and cylinder timing of each pistol. Both worked smoothly and locked tightly.

"You'll trade for both?" he asked.

The clerk eyed nearly a dozen, used firearms lying on his counter. "Sure," he said, looking at Mitchell as though fighting the urge to ask how he had come by so many of the things.

"Jon won't mind?"

"No sir. He told me you were coming, Brother Mitchell. He said, I was to take good care of you."

Mitchell nodded. "Good. I also need powder, caps, and a hundred rounds for each one, including holsters, and a set of tools for the forty-four."

"Tools and a spare cylinder come with 'em, Brother Mitchell."

Sarah watched as her husband wrapped Susan's hands around the butt of one pistol.

"Well?" he asked.

"Feels heavy," she said quietly.

Sarah caught Susan's eye, and saw a faint trembling of her sister's lips. Less than ten feet separated them, and she could see Susan's eyes widen.

The store was damp and muggy from the storm. The smell of oil and gunpowder hung faintly on the air. Sarah brought the Colt up—just like Collin had taught her. She stared at the man's chest, instinctively pointing the barrel toward his heart.

The gun bucked in her hands. She felt the hard recoil, saw the blast of smoke and fire. She saw the spot of blood under the man's arm—the arm that held the pistol. There was no time to do more. The .36 caliber in Susan's hands shot fire and lead, and Sarah could almost feel the lead ball as it struck with a hard *thump*. The second man staggered and fell.

For a moment, the clerk stared at the men lying on the floor. "Those fellows were going to shoot you in the back, Brother Mitchell," he stammered.

"They surely were," Mitchell replied. "They followed us from the hotel, and they were watching us last night at dinner. Have you seen 'em before?"

"I don't know.... I better send for the Sheriff."

"You're sure you haven't seen 'em?"

"The one...maybe. I think he was in here once before. Seems like there was a rumor goin' around—said he was one of those fellows wastin' time up in Corinne."

Mitchell nodded. The two women came to him, and he wrapped an arm around each one. Both were trembling.

The clerk shook his head. "Lucky man havin' two wives that ain't afraid of handlin' a pistol when it's needed."

"I don't plan on makin' a habit of it," Mitchell muttered.

"I suppose I ought to send for a doctor and the County sheriff." The shopkeeper muttered again, thrusting shaking hands into the pockets of his homespun trousers.

"I don't think you'll need to do that," Mitchell replied. "Looks like a deputy headed this way now."

The deputy, slickered and dripping rain, entered the store. He was a middle-aged man who didn't look hardened enough for a job that threw him into an association with society's less desirable members.

The deputy stared at the two bodies on the floor, while the storekeeper stumbled through an explanation of the attempt to shoot Mitchell in the back. Finally, the deputy shook his head.

"Don't look like a doctor can help them none," he growled, looking at Mitchell. "You the Mitchell that was a deputy for the Territorial Marshal?"

Mitchell nodded. "I was, 'til I come back from chasin' Utes down south."

The deputy frowned. "Heard about that. Heard you was good at trackin' folks that didn't want to be found."

"Some," Mitchell admitted.

The deputy stood quietly for a moment then hitched his head toward the door. "Come with me." He nodded to the two women. "Bring your women with you."

Outside, the deputy pointed to a wagon and team standing at the front of the shop. "That your outfit?" he asked.

"It is," Mitchell admitted. "We bought the wagon and the team this morning. Got a bill of sale, if you want to take a look at it."

The deputy tromped down the boardwalk, shaking his head. He grabbed up the reins of a hammer-headed nag and unhitched it from a nearby rail. "I don't need to see your bill of sale, Mitchell. Just gather up your outfit and come with me."

Rain pelted the canvas top of the wagon as Mitchell helped the two women inside. Sarah took the reins. Mitchell mounted and rode beside the deputy.

"Name's Becker," the deputy announced when they had ridden for some time in silence.

Mitchell, now wet and irritable, said nothing.

"You're a lucky man," Becker continued.

"So I've been told," Mitchell replied.

"Both of those fellers were no good. I've got fliers on both of them." Becker wiped rain from his face. "I figure the Federal government owes you and your women about three-hundred dollars—give or take a little for the cost of burying those boys. But, I wouldn't count on seeing that money very soon. Things move a bit slow out here."

Becker turned down Fourth Street and headed west. Rain and wind buffeted Mitchell in the face. He looked back. Susan had pulled the canvas down. It was small protection, but kept most of the rain out of the wagon and off of the two women.

"Is this leading somewhere, Becker?" Mitchell asked finally. "This weather is getting worse, and the hotel is back the other direction. I'd like to get my wife and her sister inside."

"Listen, Mitchell, I knew those two gals before they ever met you. They got more gumption between the two of 'em than any five women I've ever seen. They won't complain about a little rain. And I know you're plural married to the both of them. Don't matter to me. I want you to come with me and look at a body. Feller was stabbed last night, and I got to go down to Salt Lake for a few days. Folks say you're a good tracker, and you seem able to take care of yourself. I want to offer you a job. Might be temporary, but it'll earn you some money while you, your wife, and her *sister* are finding a place."

Mitchell thought of the thirty-five hundred dollars he had locked in the hotel safe—better not to touch that if they didn't have to, and a temporary job with the sheriff might be a useful pretense for coming to Ogden. Finally, he turned to Becker. "Alright… but we take my wife and her *sister* to the hotel first then I'll take a look."

Becker's face hardened briefly in anger. Finally, he shrugged and turned his horse and headed back toward Main Street and the White House Hotel.

CHAPTER 2

Utah Territory
Ogden—September 1868

Susan Mitchell sat quietly beneath the protective canvas of the wagon. She let her body sway to the broken rhythm of the jouncing vehicle and listened to the hammer of raindrops on the canvas. She loved the rain. Living in a desert had made her appreciate the thunder, the lightning, and the freshness of the air when the storm was gone. But she hated the mud, and worse, she hated Ogden City. She hadn't always hated the mud, but she couldn't recall a time, even when she was young, that the ratty little town had appealed to her.

She had grown up with heat, mud, and grasshoppers. Today, it was mud and grasshoppers. Yesterday, it had been dust and grasshoppers. Tomorrow, it would be heat and grasshoppers. The valley was awash in a plague of grasshoppers. Heat, dust, and mud she had learned to accept, but Ogden City and the hordes of invading ironclads had been tried and condemned long ago.

When the ironclads came, crops disappeared as though a starving horde had been invited to a poor man's dinner table. They devoured everything in their path, and the crops weren't enough. The ironclads clung to everything and ate anything. They ate the gardens, the flowers, the bark from the trees, and the paint on the houses. Worst of all, they would eat the clothing right off your back, if they liked the color.

After ten wonderful years of reprieve, returning to her hometown simply reinforced her original resolve to avoid the town and the invading ironclads at any cost. Now, she was trapped.

When Collin had informed her that he was taking them on holiday, she had been surprised and elated. Zion might be a holy gathering place for the Saints, but in an everyday sense, it was a land of hardship and unremitting toil. Going on holiday was something done by the rich folks up in the avenues, and the Mitchells were certainly not in that class. Nevertheless, on holiday they were, and somehow she intended to enjoy it.

Susan looked at her sister, wondering how this morning's events had affected her. Sarah was a tall, blue-eyed, redhead—a strawberry blond in the summertime when the summer sun had time to bleach the color from her hair. At five-feet seven inches, she had been a tall, lanky girl who had grown into a stunningly beautiful woman—a woman who knew her own mind and was not afraid to let anyone know what she thought. 'Both my girls have guts.' That's what Papa would say if none of the women were around. What he meant, Susan wasn't always sure, but when she really considered it, maybe it was just Papa's way of saying he was proud of them and that he loved them both.

Like enough to be mistaken for Sarah's twin, Susan was a woman completely secure in her sense of self-worth. She was as beautiful as her sister, and had no doubts that Collin Mitchell loved both of them equally well. There were differences however. She did not like being mistaken for Sarah. She was her own person, and prided herself on the fact that she was as talented and competent as her sister, and in some ways, even more capable. She had never felt the need to compete with Sarah, though there were times when she would have enjoyed giving her older sister a good hair pulling.

She watched one of the ironclads crawl across the trunk that had held her clothing. Irritated, she leaned forward, snatched the five-inch insect from its perch, and flipped it headlong toward the back of the wagon. The ironclad slammed the edge of the tailgate and tumbled to the mud of the street, dazed and unable to fly.

One down, she thought. *Ten million to go.*

"I hate these grasshoppers," she grumbled.

"I'm not overly fond of the things myself," Sarah answered.

"I wonder what made Collin bring us here on holiday." Susan said quietly, not expecting an answer.

"Maybe he thought we would like to see home," her sister offered.

"I think he knows by now that neither of us likes this town all that much," Susan replied.

Sarah reached out and adjusted the canvas front of the wagon. "Yes. I guess he does," she replied.

"I thought I heard him say something about looking for land," Susan confided.

"Here?"

"That's what I heard."

Sarah frowned and looked back at the younger woman. "I hope not," she protested.

"Me too."

Ten minutes later, the two women stood on the hotel's veranda and watched Mitchell and Becker ride west in the driving rain. Lightning flashed amid the thunder's boom, shaking the hotel and sending both sisters in a rush for the front door.

"That was close!" Susan exclaimed when they were inside.

"Right on top of us!" Sarah agreed.

"Hit the cottonwood out back," said the owner, as he entered the lobby. "Split the tree right down the middle."

The owner was a heavy man with a balding head. He seemed genuinely pleased that the Mitchells had taken rooms in his hotel, and he had done everything he could to make them comfortable.

"Lightning's a strange thing," said a voice from near the window.

Sarah turned her attention to the old man who sat watching the rain batter the glass.

"I remember watchin' a storm come in one time. I was down to my place in Provo, just sittin' under an old cottonwood watchin the clouds churnin' out over the lake. It was a pretty sight too. Not a soul around but me.... That old cottonwood was thrashin' around in the wind a bit, but it wasn't anything to worry about, so I was just sittin' on my favorite bench, watchin' the lightning.

"It was just startin' to sprinkle when I heard this voice plain as could be, sayin' 'Jasael, get away from the tree.' 'Course there weren't nobody around but me, so I figured I was imaginin' things. I just sat there, dummer'n a rock. The wind come up a bit more, and the rain got a bit worse, and I heard that voice again sayin' 'Jasael, get away from the tree.' But bein' a stubborn sort, and not real experienced at payin' attention to such things, I just sat there a bit confounded. 'Course about then lightning struck that old cottonwood, and half of that darn tree come crashin' down and knocked me right off my bench. I reckon I'll have to pay more heed to that voice next time." The old man turned back to the window and the storm, leaving Sarah to wonder if every stranger she met could hear voices.

Sarah let her eyes wander through the lobby and into the large connecting dining room. "This hotel wasn't here last year, was it?"

"No," the owner replied. "Just finished building it this spring.... First hotel in town."

"There is the Prairie House," Susan offered.

The owner nodded then smiled. "Yes, but it's clear out in Harrisville. Besides, I figure folks will need a nice hotel right here in town, when the railroad comes through."

"What if the junction goes to Corinne?" Susan asked.

"That just wouldn't make any sense," Goodwin replied. "But even if Corinne gets the junction, I think business will continue to grow."

"I suppose it will," Sarah responded. She settled herself on the sofa near the entrance, watching the rain through the open doorway.

Susan watched expectantly, wondering how long her sister would remain seated. She had tried that sofa the previous evening and judged it to be the sofa from hell, an uncomfortable arrangement of cloth and coiled springs. She smiled when Sarah stood a moment later, and looked down on the offending object.

"Terrible, isn't it?"

"Awful," Sarah agreed.

"I've named it 'the sofa from hell,'" Susan admitted.

"I believe it is," Sarah agreed.

"Everyone hates that seat," Goodwin said morosely. "I bought it because they had one just like it in the Huntsman Hotel."

"We've never had occasion to stay at the Huntsman," Sarah replied.

"Just as well," Goodwin answered. "I learned later that no one likes the one at the Huntsman either."

"I see," Sarah acknowledged.

"Mind if I close that door?" Goodwin asked. "The cool air feels nice, but the grasshoppers are as bad as ants—one of 'em gets inside and a million of 'em follow."

"I'd rather that didn't happen," Susan confessed. "I hate the things."

"Can't say I blame you," he replied. Goodwin turned as if to leave then stopped. "Someone left a letter at the desk for you."

"Thank you," Sarah replied. "We'll pick it up on our way to our rooms."

Susan watched the man struggle for words. "Is there something else?" She asked.

"I just wanted to let you know that everyone in town is talking about what happened at Browning's place."

"That certainly didn't take long," Susan observed.

"It's still a small town," Goodwin answered. "Anything unusual gets about like a streak of lightning."

"I guess we should have expected that," Sarah murmured.

"Don't take it wrong," he objected. "Both of them boys was wanted, and everyone in town thinks it was a fine thing, standin' up for yourselves like that."

Susan stood at the rain-spattered window and watched the muddy street below. She wanted to purge that experience from her memory and somehow cleanse her soul of the killing. She had never dreamed of finding herself in such a position. She realized now that the duty of defending family, home, or country was a chore she had always expected someone else to perform. Now, she was smack in the middle of it, and no matter how justifiable her actions had been, she still needed a good cry and time to make peace with God and with her own conscience.

"I need a walk," she said, still gazing through the window.

"Yes ma'am," Goodwin replied. "It's a bit wet for walking around town. The streets will be a regular swamp of mud, and the walks between the shops won't be much better. But if you don't mind waiting, I think this storm is about finished. In an hour or two, things might be dried up enough for a nice walk."

Susan looked south, to the point where the Oquirrh Mountains nearly touched the tip of the Great Salt Lake. She couldn't see the mountains or the lake. The flat-topped ridge south of town blocked that view. But she knew where to look, and the skies in that direction were clear and blue.

"I think you're right, Mr. Goodwin," she replied. "Maybe I'll just sit on the veranda for a while."

"You do that," he replied congenially. "I'll send someone to bring whatever you want."

"Thank you." When he was gone, Susan looked at her sister.

"I believe I'll go up to our suite," Sarah announced. "I'll see you later," she added, as she started up the stairway.

Susan watched her sister until she was out of sight then walked out on the veranda. The wind had calmed. The rain still fell, but it had changed to a heavy drizzle without the malevolent bursts of horizontal moisture. For several minutes, she paced the length of the veranda until finally she sat and stared at the street, watching the raindrops strike in the pools of water.

CHAPTER 3

Utah Territory
Ogden—September 1868

*M*itchell stood quietly in a muddy alley near the middle of town and pondered the circumstances that had brought them to a place he knew neither Sarah nor Susan had any desire to visit. In a way, he was running—running from memories of the Nauvoo Legion and a year of his life wasted chasing Antonga Black Hawk and his renegade Utes. Indeed, the need to run from those memories had prompted the trip, but it was the letter in his pocket and a personal request from the Prophet to find a missing girl that had brought them to Ogden. Neither woman knew of the letter or his reasons for dragging them away from their home. And if he didn't tell them soon, he was sure to be in hot water. He'd intended to tell them when they left Browning's place, but Becker's sudden request had forestalled the explanation. Already, he felt a growing dislike for the deputy, and a rising irritation that the man kept sizing him up from the corner of his eye. What Becker expected to see, Mitchell wasn't sure, but he had a feeling that it had more to do with the navy Colt strapped to Mitchell's leg and the fact that its rosewood grips were worn and darkened from plenty of use. Some folks noticed the gray beginning to streak his light brown hair or the hardened set of a square jaw, but no one ever missed the hazel eyes and a gaze that seemed to bore into their heads and lay bare their every thought. Men tended to turn away, or gear-up for a fight. Women, on the other hand, blushed and avoided his eyes, or on rare occasions gave as good as they got and sized him up as a potential mate. For the most part, he sized up pretty well. Most folks, however, just took note of the tall, hard-muscled fellow riding a line-back dun and decided he was safe enough, if unprovoked.

Becker frowned at the body. "I can't tell whether he was killed comin' or goin'," he admitted.

Mitchell knelt beside the body. It lay sprawled in the mud, against the wall of the building. Only a little blood remained. Most of it had washed away with the rain. Beneath the body, the ground was still dry. He rolled the body slightly, away from the wall, and stared in disbelief. There, perfectly preserved beneath the dead man's body was the track of a horse—a track he knew as well as he knew the critter that made it—the track of Sarah's pigeon-toed horse. "Killed before the rain started last night," he suggested grimly, trying hard to ignore the tracks.

"Probably about eight o'clock last night," Becker replied. "Some of the neighbors heard a dog barking about that time. The fellow who owns the shop next door keeps an ornery little bitch tied up at the back door every night."

Mitchell glanced at the door to the neighboring store. It lay about ten feet farther toward the back of the alley. "Who was he?" he asked, turning back to the body.

"Lester Reynald," Becker replied. "He lived here about five or six years. He sold antiques. Didn't do too well. Folks out here don't have a lot of money, so they tend to buy what they need, not some rickety old piece of junk." Becker pointed toward the mountains east of the city. "A few rich folks live up toward the bench. Reynald probably sold some things up that way, but I'd guess he wasn't doing too well."

"Knife went between the lower ribs—probably tore up the left lung," Mitchell suggested. "A long blade might have nicked the heart or cut an artery, if the angle was right."

Grim faced, Becker nodded as water drizzled from the brim of his hat. Mitchell studied the body. Reynald lay on his right side, his left arm outstretched as though reaching, his right arm twisted backward beneath him. Both fists were clenched, and there was a dark smudge, like a birthmark across the dead man's forehead.

Mitchell pried the left fist open. Dust sifted through the curled fingers. The right fist opened more easily, and a small earring, shaped like a silver cuff, fell to the mud. Mitchell retrieved the earring and the leathery flesh it gripped.

"That looks like a piece of an ear stuck in that thing," Becker muttered.

"It is," Mitchell agreed, "but it's dried-out like a piece of jerky." Mitchell checked the pockets of his jacket. "Got any paper?" He wasn't sure what good it would do to save the ear, but he felt certain the silver cuff was important.

Becker fished around in his pockets, and finally produced a crumpled handbill. Carefully, Mitchell wrapped the earring and its grisly partner and dropped them in the pocket of his jacket. He searched the dead man's clothing while Becker watched. A sour smell clung to the dead man's shirt and face.

Finally, Mitchell stood, wondering what he should look for next. He was a fair hand at tracking a horse, or other animals, but tracking a murderer was something less familiar. The tracks were completely different in nature. He studied the alley. The back door of Reynald's store stood slightly ajar.

"No keys, and no marks on the door or the frame," he noted. "Did you go inside?"

Becker shook his head. "Somebody could have gone in, but I don't think so."

Mitchell pushed the door open. Inside, the sour smell grew to an overpowering reek. "No mud on the floor, but it looks like Mr. Reynald was ill before he could get outside," he suggested.

"He didn't die from sickin' up," Becker grumbled.

"I know," Mitchell replied, "but it tells us he was killed as he left the shop."

"How's that?"

"No key on the body," Mitchell answered. "No marks on the door, or the door frame—and the vomit. Body still smells a little of the vomit when you get close enough. I'd guess that Mr. Reynald used his key, came in the back door, did whatever it was he came for then got sick and tried to run outside."

Mitchell pointed at the wall beside the door. "Looks like he was standing at the door—probably trying to get it open and just couldn't hold back."

"Maybe he got sick as he came inside then backed out afterward," Becker argued.

"He could have just turned around in the doorway," Mitchell replied. "Why spew your guts all over the floor when all you need to do is turn around and do it in the alley? No.... I think he was inside and had to get out quick. I'd guess he had a habit of locking the door. Locked it when he went in.... Maybe locked it when he left. The killer took the key and went inside."

Mitchell pushed the door closed. It rebounded from the frame and stood slightly ajar. Mitchell closed it again and turned the latch by hand.

"The killer must have been in a hurry," he offered. "He closed the door, but it didn't latch."

"What about the key?" Becker asked.

"The killer probably dropped it in his pocket and just forgot about it."

Mitchell walked through the store. It was dingy and small. The alley door connected with the main room of a shop that was a jumble of odds and ends. Shelving lined every wall from floor to ceiling. Only the doors and the large window looking out on the street were clear of the stacks of old books, furniture, and other oddities. Every surface was coated with dust, except the surface of a large table near the center of the room and a counter near the back wall. On a shelf beneath the counter lay three cigar boxes, each containing an assortment of expensive-looking jewelry.

Becker wiped a hand across the table's surface. "No dust," he said. "You think the killer took whatever Reynald had on the table?"

"Maybe...." Mitchell leaned close, looking for anything that might suggest what Reynald had kept on the table, but there was nothing, only the rough surface of a cheap pine table and oddly, the faint smell of smoke.

"Listen, Mitchell," Becker said finally. "I got to go. I'm supposed to meet the Sheriff in Salt Lake tomorrow. I'll be gone at least a week, maybe two. I'll tell the city constable you're deputized, and he won't interfere. He's got other things to worry about, but if you run into trouble, you get hold of him. Keep notes on everything you find. When I get back, we'll go over everything and see what you've got."

Becker laid a badge on the table. "I'm deputizing you. You got authority to make an arrest if you think you got the right man, but you be darn sure you got the right one."

Mitchell dropped the badge in his coat pocket. Becker looked around the room. "Reynald was nothing big around here," he said, "but he never caused any trouble, and he minded his own business. Folks don't like it when somebody gets murdered, but they really get upset when people like Reynald get killed right on their own doorstep. Makes 'em worry they might be next."

Mitchell agreed. But he had known, from the moment he had seen the boxes of jewelry, that Reynald had not been killed as part of a simple robbery. Something more had happened here.

When Becker had gone, Mitchell wandered through the clutter of the store, searching for anything that might identify the missing contents of the table. Nothing changed.

Finally, when the dust and the jumble of the store became oppressive, he left the store, and stood in the alley.

The rain had slowed to a drizzle, but even the mud and the rain seemed fresh compared to the gloom of the dead man's shop. The body was gone. Becker had mentioned something about moving it, but Becker had said a lot of things, and Mitchell was certain he had missed several points of their conversation. Mostly, his mind had been on the two men in Jon Browning's store.

Why were they following us? He wondered. He had never seen either of them before, and he could think of no reason for them to want him dead. Yet, there was no doubt of their intent—no doubt they would have shot him in the back.

When Mitchell left the alley, the drizzle of rain had almost stopped. The sky was still dark, but the wind was now high off the ground, pushing the clouds northeast over the top of the mountains, and for the moment, life was a little less wretched.

Ogden, or Junction City as some called it, was a miserable, nothing of a town. Mitchell was sure it would grow quickly, once the Union Pacific and the Central Pacific railroads finished laying their track. But at the moment, nothing was certain, and everyone from Corinne to Salt Lake was willing to argue about it. Some favored Ogden as the depot for the railways, while others pushed for Corinne, or the "Burgh on the Bear," as some called the little *gentile* town that lay thirty or forty miles north of Ogden.

But Mitchell's money was on Ogden. It was closer to Salt Lake, and better situated for a southern spur into the Capitol of the territory. Mormons had entered the Great Salt Lake Valley in July of 1847. Now, twenty-one years later, the only place with any real growth was Salt Lake City, and it needed the railroad badly.

Everyone knew Brother Brigham wanted the railroad in Salt Lake. He had done everything he could to convince the powers behind the Union Pacific to run their track over Emigration Pass, through Salt Lake City, skirting the south side of the Great Salt Lake then northwest to meet the Southern Pacific somewhere west of the lake. But railroad officials had opted to follow the Weber River, placing the rails nearly forty miles north of the capitol.

The sun was finally out, pouring its heat into the streets and quickly baking the muddy streets into a stiff, hardened crust. Mitchell walked the half-block to the shop just east of Reynald's store. He took a deep breath and entered. The man behind the counter was rail-thin, and nearly a head taller than Mitchell. "Are you Jake Farney?" Mitchell asked.

"Only one I know of," the man answered.

"I'm Collin Mitchell. Harold Becker deputized me this morning. I'm looking into the death of Lester Reynald."

"Lester's dead?"

"Appears so."

"Probably choked on that cheap rot-gut he kept stashed in the back room."

"Did you know him well?" asked Mitchell.

"Hell no."

Mitchell smiled disarmingly. At least he tried for disarming. What he got was something less than friendly. "How did you know about the whiskey?"

"Hell, you don't need to snarl like you're gonna tear my throat out," Farney growled. "I seen him tippin' the jug more than once."

"Once ain't likely to kill a man," Mitchell offered.

"No, but I smelled it on him every time I was anywhere near him."

"You're not partial to folks that drink?"

"Hell, I don't care much what folks do, as long as they don't hurt me or mine."

"Where were you last night?" Mitchell asked, hoping for some reaction.

"I don't like the sound of that," Farney growled. "You said Reynald was dead. How?"

"Someone shoved a knife between his ribs," Mitchell answered.

"And you're asking me where I was last night?" Farney's face was quickly flushing red. "I didn't kill the little weasel. I didn't like him much, but I didn't kill him."

"So, where were you?" Mitchell prodded.

"Darn it," blustered Farney. "I was here till about seven … then I went home."

"Becker said folks heard your dog barkin' around eight," offered Mitchell.

"Now how in the world would I know that, if I was home?"

"Guess you wouldn't," Mitchell replied.

"Dang right." Farney moved to a small table and pulled out a chair. "Sit down Mitchell." He shoved a chair at Mitchell with a booted foot. "Sometimes I wish I never got that dog. Never could train her for nothing. She was too old. The little bitch barks all the time. Anyway, nobody complains much. Mostly, folks are gone home by the time I put her out. Reynald didn't mind.... Said it kept folks out of the alley after dark."

"Did the dog ever bark at Reynald?"

"She barks at everybody."

"So the barking at eight last night could have been when Reynald went into the alley?"

"Sure."

"Did Reynald use the alley entrance much?"

"All the time."

Mitchell looked around the shop. "You build furniture?"

"I do."

"Prices reasonable?"

"Some folks think I charge too much, but I have to earn a living too."

"Reynald ever have late visitors at his store?" Mitchell asked, returning to business.

"Some.... I don't often stay late, so he could have had a brass band and a chorus line every night, and I'd never know."

"So you went home at seven last night," Mitchell responded. "What time did you come in this morning?"

"About eight."

"Anything out of the ordinary happen at Reynald's place lately?" asked Mitchell.

"No."

"What about folks with a grudge against him? Or money? Did he owe money to anyone?"

"Well...."

"Who?" Mitchell prompted.

"Really, I...."

"Who?" Mitchell urged.

"Well, he owed me a bit."

"Anyone else?"

"Tolson."

"Who's Tolson?"

"The blacksmith... across the street—on the north side."

"Did Reynald owe Tolson much?"

"I reckon."

Mitchell looked around the shop again, realizing that Tolson was probably the man who had written Brother Brigham about his missing daughter. "Tell me about Melinda Tolson," he suggested.

"Hell, I don't know much about her," Farney complained defensively. "She was just a kid. All I ever done was say hello once in a while. She had real dark hair, and I think she was growin' up to be a real handsome woman."

"She have many suitors?"

"I don't know! Maybe.... Reynald anyway. I never paid no attention."

"Who might know who she was seein'?"

"Tolson might, if she wasn't givin' him too much trouble for him to notice."

Mitchell looked around the shop again. He'd about exhausted all the questions he could think of, and for the moment it looked as though he'd pried everything he could from Farney. "I'll probably need to talk with you again," he said as he opened the door.

"Fine," Farney muttered unhappily as the door closed.

Outside, Mitchell took the rein from the hitching rail, and led the gelding into the alley between the two buildings. The alley was quiet. Farney had caged his dog somewhere, leaving Mitchell free to search the area without distraction. He wasn't at all sure what he was looking for, but he needed something to go on, and so far he had a big nothing. He didn't expect anything obvious, but there had to be a reason for the killing, and he was certain anything missing from the shop was important. That might be a big stretch, because nothing of real value seemed to have been taken. The jewelry behind the counter was certainly worth more than anything in the shop; yet the jewelry had been untouched. The shop had certainly been robbed; yet the only thing missing was whatever had been on the table. Nothing else had been disturbed.

The alley was bare, not even a stack of broken crates—nothing. It was nothing more than a narrow slot between the two buildings, hardly wide enough for a horse to pass, and certainly much too narrow for a wagon. If the killer had passed this way, he had probably done so on foot.

At the mouth of the slot, Mitchell paused. The alley opened into a vacant expanse that stretched out until it reached the backs of the buildings facing south on Fifth Street. The entire center of the block was a field of grass, weeds, muddy patches of earth, and shoulder high sunflowers. Resigning himself to a prolonged search through a weed patch that would resist his every move, Mitchell started out into the field.

The sunflowers were tall and beginning to shed their seeds. The grass underfoot was thick except for the paths that had been trodden bare by neighborhood kids and anyone else looking for a shortcut through the block. Half an hour later, he was sick of kicking his way through a tangle of weeds. He had seen nothing other than a stray dog prowling through the sunflowers, sniffing the ground in search of food.

He had one foot in the stirrup when he saw it—a flash of reflected sunlight caught in the thickness of the weedy undergrowth of the field—sunlight and a paw print. For a moment, the track grabbed his attention. At first it looked like the track of a dog. But the thing was unusually large—more like the track of a large wolf—an animal no one would want prowling a town where children ran loose like cattle on an open range. Cautiously, Mitchell dismounted, his hand shifting to the butt of the Navy Colt. He drew the pistol as something moved within the thickness of the weed field.

"You again," he grumbled as the multi-colored dog poked its nose from the tightly packed leaves of the weed patch. For a moment, the dog stared at the human, then grinning, it nosed its way out of the weeds to sniff at the track that was at least four times as large as its own. Instantly, the hackles rose on its back and the motley-colored animal stiffened and growled ominously.

Somewhat nervously, Mitchell shoved the growling animal out of the way and carefully retrieved the blood-stained knife and wrapped it carefully in a clean white kerchief.

CHAPTER 4

Utah Territory
Ogden—September 1868

*B*y noon the streets were nearly dry. Susan dodged the scattered puddles of water and made her way down the west side of Main Street. Collin had suggested that she take some money and go shopping, and she'd started out with the thought of buying a new pair of riding boots, but now, in front of Ericson's bookstore, she changed her mind. Across the street, Browning's store beckoned like a flame, and she was the mesmerized moth.

Inside the store, she waited near the window while the clerk talked with another customer. She glanced nervously about the shop. The events of the morning were still printed on her senses—the smell of burnt powder, the men lying on the floor, the blood....

"Dangedest thing I ever saw," the clerk told a man at the counter. His voice yanked Susan from the pain of the memory. "Those fellows waltzed in here smooth as you please. Never said a word. Just hauled out them Colts and made ready to shoot Brother Mitchell in the back. They never figured on them Flitton girls though. Rock solid them girls was. Sarah off to one side and Susan facin' both them killers like a guardian angel. I ain't married, but I'd give everything I own for a woman like that."

"Fellows like us don't get that lucky," the man answered.

"Reckon not."

"I heard that one of those boys was wanted for killing a girl down in Arizona," the customer offered.

"That's what they say," the clerk responded. "A couple of mean ones, but they tangled with the wrong bunch today."

"Mitchell's a lucky man."

"That's what I told him," the clerk replied. "There ain't a man in town that wouldn't be struttin' like a rooster bein' married to them gals. I hear that every bachelor in town was riled when Mitchell married the both of 'em. I was a mite put out myself."

"I can imagine," admitted the other.

Susan stood quietly, trying to disappear among the racks of rifles standing about the room. She was embarrassed at overhearing the conversation, but inwardly relieved, even pleased to hear that her actions were not condemned. She couldn't help feeling that if these people, who could often be judgmental and unforgiving, could justify her actions then perhaps God, who was infinitely more merciful, could forgive her.

When the customer was gone, and the clerk had disappeared into a back room, Susan stepped from the cover of the racks and stood at the counter, waiting. When the clerk returned, he stared at her in surprise.

"Sister Mitchell," he stammered. "I didn't hear you come in. What can I do for you?"

"Brother Larson, I wondered if you could tell me anything about those men, and if you've heard anything about why they were trying to kill my husband."

"I don't know much about any of it ma'am. Only what I've heard around town the last couple of hours... mostly talk from folks passin' by out front."

Susan watched the sweat bead on Larson's forehead. "That's what I want to know," she prompted. "People aren't saying much where I can hear, and I'm at a loss—I don't understand why those men came after my husband. He says he didn't know either of them." Larson took a large kerchief from his back pocket and wiped the sweat from the back of his neck then dabbed at his forehead. "I don't think it was just Brother Mitchell they was after," he confided. "The talk I heard says they figured to get him first then kill both his womenfolk."

For a moment, Susan stood in shocked silence. "But why?" She asked finally.

"All I heard is that they was paid to do it. I ain't heard nothing about who paid 'em or why."

"But we didn't even know those men," she protested.

"I reckon you didn't," Larson replied, "but whoever paid 'em knows you and wants you dead."

"It seems so senseless," she objected. "Collin has made a few enemies; we've known that for long time, but we've never heard of anyone wanting to harm the whole family."

"I don't know how to help you, Sister Mitchell," Larson conceded. "All I know is what little I've heard, but if I was you, I'd be real careful. And I'd practice with that new Colt 'til I could pop a running jackrabbit every time."

Susan stood quietly, but her thoughts moved at a gallop. Suddenly, she understood a little of the sadness that seemed so deeply rooted in her husband and his reticence when discussing his past. She realized now that some memories brought with them the sufferings of perdition.

Five minutes later, she turned away from the counter. Something moved at the window, a face and a dark hat—both pulling back from the window before she could distinguish anything. She walked to the door and looked down the boardwalk.

"Something wrong?" Larson asked.

"I'm not sure," she replied. "Did you see someone looking in at the window?"

"All the time," Larson answered, "but not in the last few minutes."

"Someone was there," she asserted.

"I wish I could tell you more, but I really don't know anything more." Larson said anxiously as she stood at the door. "You might ask some questions over to the drugstore. Aaron Calder owns the place, and it was him tellin' me that them fellers had been paid to kill all of you."

"And where is Mr. Calder's drugstore?" She asked.

"Across the street and two blocks down," Larson answered, pointing north toward the unfinished Tabernacle.

Aaron Calder's drug store was a small, clapboard structure on the west side of Main Street. Calder had built the place three years earlier, stocked it with every herb known to man, or so he claimed, and did a booming business from the day he opened. Calder was a born salesman, and he had seen the possibilities for a well-informed Doctor of herbal medicine the day he had heard Brother Brigham preach against the medical practices of the so-called Doctor's of Medicine. Consequently, Calder concentrated on herbal treatments and avoided anything to do with bloodletting, or treatments of arsenic and mercury. Those three methods seemed to be the core of Brother Brigham's dispute with the medical community, and Aaron Calder had calculated, and rightly so, that any business that could tie itself to Brother Brigham's coat tails had a fine chance of success.

Susan entered the store, noting the cans, bottles, and bags of herbs filling shelves from floor to ceiling.

"Afternoon ma'am." The man behind the counter stooped, rearranging the bottled herbs decorating the countertop and looked at Susan expectantly.

"Are you Brother Calder?" She asked.

"I am," he replied congenially.

"I'm Susan Mitchell," she announced. "Brother Larson, over at Browning's shop, said you could help me."

Calder seemed to pale. "I'll do what I can," he answered.

"I just have a few questions," she said, placing her finger atop one of the bottles. "Brother Larson told me that you overheard a conversation between two men this morning."

"It wasn't really a conversation," Calder said defensively. "One of them came in here first thing, when I opened up— asked if I had anything could cure a runny nose and itchy eyes."

"He was a rough looking character, but he was civil enough, so I was explaining about how the different humors of the body could get out of balance and lose heat. He said he didn't know about any of that, and just wanted something to fix him up. I told him that what he needed was to restore that body heat and get his humors balanced again. He said fine, what did he need? So I told him he needed some lobelia and some cayenne for starters. He asked how I knew that."

"And what did you tell him?" Susan prompted. She could tell that Calder was just warming up, and she wanted every detail the man could remember.

"I told him that Dr. Samuel Thompson recommended lobelia treatments to clean out the stomach and the intestines then doses of cayenne to bring back the body's heat. I was just starting to explain which herbs might work best for his particular problem when another fellow opens the door, pokes his head inside and says 'Let's go. They're over to Browning's place right now.'

"The fellow inside was a little put out and hollers 'Just a Dang minute Kyle.' Then the one at the door gets this mean look on his face and kind of snarls back at him. 'They want it done now. You wanna get paid.... We do it now.'

"After that, the one inside slaps his hat on his head and leaves without another word.... 'Cept he was a grumblin' to himself.... I couldn't make out what he was mutterin', but he wasn't happy.

"I didn't like the way any of that sounded, so I went out the back way, got on my horse and rode down to the courthouse lookin' for the city police or a county deputy. I found Becker and told him that two hard-cases were headed for Browning's place and they looked to be causin' trouble."

"You're sure neither of them mentioned who was paying them?" Susan asked.

"Not a word."

"Did you see them talking with anyone?"

"No, but I saw the one fellow over to Doc Wadman's place yesterday afternoon. Maybe Wadman knows something."

Susan stared thoughtfully at the large glass jar of lobelia beneath her hand. "The man with the itching eyes?" She asked.

"No. It was the other fellow, the mean one."

CHAPTER 5

Utah Territory
Ogden—September 1868

*S*arah Flitton Mitchell read a verse from Elizabeth Browning's *Aurora Leigh* for the third time. She closed the book, realizing that she hadn't really read any of it at all. Oh, she had read the words, but not one bit of it had penetrated the turmoil of her thoughts. She laid the book aside, realizing that what had begun as a simple holiday had quickly devolved into something clearly different. She had pondered the situation and spent more than an hour on her knees, asking God to either confirm or refute her appraisal of the situation and her plan of action. She had come away from that communion with the certainty that both her appraisal and her plan were faulty and that she lacked essential information—information she must gather herself, if she wanted to know the truth and adjust her plan accordingly.

She was certain the incident at Browning's store was no coincidence. Collin hadn't known either of the men, and that ruled out the possibility of spontaneous revenge. The lack of spontaneity relegated the incident to the category of a premeditated and planned assault by someone who would hire the job done. Actually, she couldn't think of anyone who hated Collin enough to kill him, and that opened a whole new can of worms.

Suddenly, she remembered a few of the words she had read. She snatched up the book, and opened to the page.

She had lived, we'll say,
A harmless life, she called a virtuous life,
A quiet life, which was not life at all....

A sort of cage-bird life, born in a cage,
Accounting that to leap from perch to perch
Was act and joy enough for any bird.

It was a perfect analysis of her own life, before she had met Collin Mitchell. After that, life had changed, grown deeper and more satisfying. Again, she laid the book aside, resolving that no one would spoil that satisfaction. No one would send her back to that "cage-bird life." Her handbag was on the table, beside the book. She took it and held it in her lap. She looked at the book. Romance lay there—the "cage bird life," a life of feminine charm—the expected, the prescribed. In her lap weighed reality—the living of life—not the dreaming of it. In an instant, she chose between the two. Quietly, she opened the bag, removed reality, and reloaded its empty chamber.

Later, when the sun was high and the suite hot enough to try a camel's patience, Sarah deserted their rooms and ensconced herself in the shade of the hotel's veranda. She swatted an ironclad from her table, drew a chair up beside her own and dropped her handbag on the seat. Several minutes passed before Goodwin noticed her sitting near the window, gently fanning herself. Several more moments passed before she noticed the multi-colored dog sitting in the dust of Main Street, panting and watching.

Goodwin returned. He set a glass and a pitcher of water on the table. "It's cold ma'am—fresh out of the well."

"Thank you Mr. Goodwin." Sarah glanced at the long-haired animal sitting in the street. The dog licked its lips. Without rising, it scooted a little closer to the veranda. "Mr. Goodwin?" she asked suddenly. "Would you bring me another pitcher and a large bowl as well?"

Goodwin gave her an odd look. "Certainly Mrs. Mitchell."

Minutes later, with the bowl of water near her chair, Sarah made kissing noises at the dog.

"I don't think she'll come near you," Goodwin offered, giving the dog his best scowl.

"And why is that Mr. Goodwin?"

"She's a stray. Been hanging around a couple of weeks now. I keep running her off, but she keeps coming back. Real skittish animal.... Won't let anyone get near her."

"I see." Sarah looked at the dog again. The animal had scooted a little closer. "Mr. Goodwin?"

"Yes."

"Mr. Goodwin, why don't you go inside and have your cook fry a very large steak?"

Goodwin looked at the dog then back to Sarah. "Yes Ma'am," he replied.

When Goodwin had gone, Sarah watched the dog scoot a little closer, still panting from the heat. "He's gone now," she told the animal. "You can come have some water."

The dog tipped its gray and white ears forward at the sound of her voice. It hesitated a moment longer then bounded up the steps. Sarah sat quietly as the animal came cautiously to the bowl and drank. Sarah held out her hand. When the dog lifted its wet muzzle, it sniffed at her fingers, licked them once and went back to the water.

When the steak arrived, the dog was at her side, its head against her thigh as she rubbed the gray and white ears. Goodwin looked down at the animal, shook his head, and left quietly.

"That steak for you, me, or the dog?"

Sarah looked up at the sound of Mitchell's voice. "The dog," she answered.

"Hmm. Wouldn't want to split it three ways, would you?" He leaned over, kissing her on the cheek.

"I might be persuaded," she answered, "but my friend might object."

"She didn't object to sharing a piece of jerky with me an hour ago," Mitchell observed.

"A piece of jerky is hardly a fair trade," Sarah responded.

"True," he acknowledged.

"So slice it up," she prompted. "You can't expect a lady to gnaw her food like a wild animal."

Obediently, Mitchell sliced the steak into small pieces. "I've been nosing around where that fellow Reynald was killed last night. Mostly talking to a fellow named Farney. His shop is next door to where they found Reynald's body. I still have a couple of people to talk with. It might take a while," he added, tossing a piece of steak to the dog. The animal whipped its head to one side and snatched the meat from the air. "Nice catch," he acknowledged.

"I don't understand why you got involved in this," Sarah complained. She felt slightly put-out that her vision of a holiday had been transformed considerably. "I thought you were finished with the Marshall's office."

"I am," he replied, "but this is something I couldn't ignore."

"I expect an explanation," she insisted.

"I know," he replied, "and I promise to explain everything."

"Before Christmas," she advised.

"Before Christmas," he agreed. He tossed another piece of steak to the dog, deliberately making the catch difficult. The dog lunged, snapped the tidbit from the air, and quietly returned to its place at Sarah's side.

"Looks like your little lady is part crocodile," he suggested.

Sarah smiled coquettishly. "Just talented," she replied sweetly.

"Listen," Mitchell said softly. "Be careful." He slid the plate of sliced beef in front of her.

"Is there something I should be concerned about?" She asked.

"I don't know," he answered. "I'm just worried about what happened at Browning's this morning. I didn't know those men, and I have no idea why they came at us like that."

"I wondered if we weren't all at risk," she answered.

"That's what bothers me," he admitted. "I heard rumors that they were paid to kill all three of us. That's why I'm here now." He hesitated, knowing she would resist his next statement. "I want you and Susan to pack your things. I'm going to send you back to Salt Lake."

"No."

"How did I know you would say that," he muttered.

"You knew it, because you knew it was unfair to ask," she retorted.

"I don't think I'm being unfair," he argued.

"But you *are* trying to send me home without even asking if I want to go."

"I only wanted to keep you safe."

"Brother Mitchell," she hissed. "I am not a pet bird in a cage, and I will not be treated as though I am."

Mitchell remained quiet. He knew her mind was made up, and there would be no changing it. In private, she seldom called him *Brother Mitchell*. When she used that form of address, he knew he was about to catch it. She'd spoken purposely, hoping to put an end to the idea immediately.

Sarah took a piece of the steak and held it near the dog's muzzle. Gently, the dog took the offering from her fingers. "You see... She is a lady," she pronounced.

"Yes, she is," Mitchell admitted.

"I understand your worry," Sarah assured him quietly, "but I've already considered the possibility that Susan and I are at risk, and I've made my decision." She took the revolver from her handbag and laid it on the table. "I have this," she pointed out. "And now I have a dog."

"That pistol won't save you from a bullet in the back," he argued. "And that dog ain't gonna snap lead out of the air like she grabs that steak."

"Hiding in Salt Lake won't stop a bullet either," Sarah retorted.

Mitchell hung his head, shaking it slowly. "Dang it, Sarah," he groaned.

"Are you going to hide in Salt Lake?" She demanded.

"I have some things to take care of here," he admitted.

"Very well," she conceded. "When *you* go to Salt Lake and hide in the house, I'll go with you. I'm sure Susan will agree. But if you leave the house for any reason, I will take the same privilege for myself and so will Susan."

"You're not making this easy."

"No cages, Collin," she said softly. "I want to be a real person.... You've always given me that, and that has made me love you more every day." She watched as he leaned forward, head hanging, eyes closed. She knew he was thinking. He was trying to decide whether to pressure her more or let it be. She knew how much he loved her, but she also knew he could be a hard and practical man. It wouldn't be easy for him; yet she knew she had already won the battle.

Finally, he looked up. "You're right. Forcing you to go would be an unrighteous dominion."

"Yes, it would," she agreed, recognizing his reference to a verse from the Doctrine and Covenants.

"I won't say it's a good choice," he complained, "but it ain't my place to take away your agency."

Sarah smiled. "No, it isn't," she answered gratefully.

"Stubborn redhead," he muttered.

Sarah smiled, knowing his liking for stubborn women and his passion for the redhead seated beside him. After a while, he stood. He leaned down, kissing her on the lips. She felt herself responding to him—wanting him.

"When will you be back?" She asked softly.

"Two hours, maybe three," he answered. "I want to talk with Matt Dalton and a doctor over on Third Street."

"Watch for Susan," she suggested. "She's gone out, but she wasn't handling things very well when she left."

"She's upset over those fellows at Browning's?"

"I'm sure she is," Sarah replied.

"I'll watch for her," he promised. "While I'm gone, keep that long-nosed coyote close. Maybe she'll make a racket if trouble gets too close."

When he had gone, Sarah looked down at the dog. The animal's chin now rested on her knee. "Are you going to protect me, Lady?"

The dog raised its head, its black lined mouth grinning, waiting for more of the steak.

"You doin' okay ma'am?" Goodwin asked as he came to her table.

"Yes, Mr. Goodwin. I am."

"Would you like anything else?"

"Yes, I would," she answered. "Do you have someone who can run an errand for me?"

"You bet. I'll send the Grange kid... Mark Grange. Just tell him what you want."

"Thank you Mr. Goodwin. I'll make a list." She looked down at the dog. The animal's ears were laid back, its hackles raised. "I've been adopted," she said. "I'll need a place for Lady to stay, and enough meat scraps from the dining room or the kitchen to keep her fed."

"I think we can take care of that, Mrs. Mitchell."

"I'll expect you to add any extra expense to our bill," she advised.

"Scraps just get thrown out anyway, Mrs. Mitchell."

"I suppose that's true, Mr. Goodwin, but when there are no scraps; I'll want meat for her anyway."

"Yes, ma'am."

An hour later, Sarah was still on the veranda, absently stroking the dog's ears and contemplating the open packages on the table.

"That's a fair sized collection you got there," Goodwin observed. He took the empty picture of water from Sarah's table, replacing it with one that was full.

"Yes, it is," Sarah admitted. "I'll need a place to work with it."

"There's a cut-bank out back," Goodwin replied, staring at the side-by-side. "I'd recommend you don't pull more than one trigger at a time on that thing."

Sarah smiled disarmingly. "Thank you, Mr. Goodwin. I'm sure that's good advice."

CHAPTER 6

Utah Territory
Ogden—September 1868

*M*atthew Dalton had lived at Fourth and Young Street since 1851. He had bought or claimed three lots on the block, built a two-room log home, and started raising a garden. Before long, he had added a shop and was building furniture for anyone willing to pay. Mitchell entered the shop and closed the door.

"Afternoon," greeted the owner.

"Afternoon. You Matt Dalton?"

"I am."

"I'm Collin Mitchell."

Dalton brushed his hands on an apron covered with wood chips and dust. "How can I help you?"

"Deputy Becker asked me to help look into the death of Lester Reynald," Mitchell replied. "I'm just asking the neighbors if they saw or heard anything that might help us find the killer."

Dalton nodded thoughtfully. "Monday night, wasn't it?"

"Or any other time," responded Mitchell. "Anything unusual...."

"I don't think I've seen anything that would help," answered Dalton.

"Folks say they heard Jake Farney's dog barking around eight that night," prompted Mitchell.

Dalton shook his head. "I don't think there's anything unusual about that." He leaned back in his chair and pointed Mitchell to its mate. "Farney's dog barks at anything. I've seen her bark at people, horses, dogs, even flies."

"Did you hear anything Monday night?"

Dalton shrugged. "I heard the dog barking."

"I've been wondering about the dog," Mitchell confided.

"How so?"

"Did the dog bark when Reynald went into the shop, or when he came out?"

"I don't understand."

"We know Reynald locked up and left the shop around five-thirty or six. Folks saw him leave. But no one saw him come back. The dog went crazy around eight, and it started raining at nine. Reynald was killed before the rain started. I think the dog barked when he went in, but not when he came out."

"I think I see where you're going with this, but I don't think it will help any."

"Maybe not."

Dalton sighed. "All right. Reynald always used the alley door. And the dog barks at everyone—except Jake Farney." Dalton leaned back in his chair. "Is that what you wanted to hear?"

"I reckon so." Mitchell paused and glanced around the shop. It was similar to Jake Farney's place, but not so cluttered. "Did Mr. Reynald have any enemies?" He asked finally.

Dalton looked at the ceiling. "Tolson hated him, I guess. And Jake Farney punched him in the face and broke his nose on the twenty-fourth of July last year. I didn't like him much either. I think he was stealing my chickens every now and then. Doc Wadman and Nephi Clarke had some kind of disagreement with him a few years ago, but they've been on speaking terms as far as I know."

"Anyone else?"

"Probably, but I can't say I know everyone who disliked the man. He was just disagreeable. Folks said he didn't pay what he owed, or he tried to change the deal and weasel out of paying the whole amount. That's probably why he never did very well with his business. Folks didn't trust him."

"How did he survive this long?"

"I don't know."

"What did he sell from his store?"

"Antiques—I think. The wife was in there once or twice, but never found anything she wanted."

"What about jewelry?"

"She never looked for any."

"No. I was wondering if Reynald sold any jewelry."

"No. Just Furniture and the like."

"Do you know why he had several cigar boxes of fancy jewelry stashed under a back counter?"

"No idea. Probably stole the stuff—like he did my chickens."

Mitchell hauled out the knife. "Ever see this before?"

"Might be Tolson's. He has one like it."

"That might account for the *A.T.* on the handle."

"It might."

Alfred Tolson's smithy faced south on Fourth Street, directly across from Reynald and Farney. Mitchell pushed the tall double doors open and entered. Tolson was shoeing a blue roan. The old man dropped the hoof and straightened slowly, arching his back.

"I hate workin' on that animal," he muttered.

Mitchell watched as the older man hung a heavy rasp and hoof nippers on wall pegs near the forge.

"He leans on me," Tolson explained. "After about an hour, it feels like I've got a ton of lard pressin' up agin' my shoulder."

Mitchell noted the size of the roan and was glad the animal's big rump wasn't trying to press him into the ground. "Seems like a good sized animal," he commiserated.

"He's fat," Tolson replied, "and he's lazy. If I thought I could get away with it, I'd knock him in the head with a rock and shoe him while he was unconscious."

"Reckon that wouldn't do," Mitchell agreed.

Tolson smiled wickedly. "Reckon not, but it's tempting."

"Looks like he's well fed."

"He is," Tolson replied, "but Doc Wadman don't ride him enough. They tend to get a little fat when they ain't exercised regular."

"Doc Wadman come around much?"

"Off and on. Not regular like, but he's here now and then. Says he likes horses."

"So he comes here to see your horses?"

"Naw! I figure he comes here to watch Reynald's store. Though I can't figure why. The place ain't much to look at."

"I found a knife over yonder," Mitchell said suddenly. "Mat Dalton seemed to think it was yours."

Tolson looked at the knife. "Yep, she's mine. Somebody stole it a couple of days back. Been lookin' for it since."

Tolson held a hand out, but Mitchell kept the knife back.

"Reckon I'd better hang on to it for a spell. Appears like it might be the knife that killed Reynald."

"Damn!"

I guess you don't know how it got over to Reynald's place?"

"Like I said, I ain't seen it for days."

"You've been here a few years," said Mitchell. "At least that's what folks say."

"I been here eight years—since 1860."

"Ever have any dealings with Reynald?"

"Some."

"Such as?"

Tolson frowned. "Well.... I sold him a couple of horses one time. Since then, I ain't had much to do with him."

"Mind tellin' me why?"

"As a matter of fact, I do mind. Besides, you can get my whole life-story laid out for you. Just ask around. There's plenty of busybodies that'll bend your ear just so they got something to talk about. Got nothin' goin' on in their own pinched-up little lives, so they got plenty to talk about when somethin' happens to other folks. You go talk to them folks. I got no time for it."

Mitchell left the smithy feeling sorry for the old man. He knew exactly how Alfred Tolson must feel with the whole town ready to talk about his family at the drop of a hat. But somehow, he had the feeling that Tolson would take another emotional beating before things were done.

By the time he re-crossed the dusty street, Mitchell was ready to chuck the whole thing—just pack up his women and kids and head north. He wanted time to concentrate on his own family. Time to find some land, and build a couple of houses. And it didn't help his attitude one bit that the ground in front of Tolson's smithy was literally covered with the tracks of a pigeon-toed horse.

The hinges on Jake Farney's front door squawked in pain.

"You oughta oil those hinges once in a while, Jake."

"You back again? You was here just an hour ago."

"I'm back. I got nothin' better to do than wander around askin' stupid questions."

"Find Reynald's killer yet?"

"I'm still gatherin' the pieces," Mitchell answered. Farney said nothing.

"Can you build furniture like that fancy stuff from back east?" Mitchell asked.

Farney looked surprised. "I can build anything you want," he answered.

Mitchell took two neatly folded sheets of paper from his shirt pocket, and handed them to Farney.

Farney unfolded the sheets and studied the drawings on the two pages. A moment later he nodded and looked up at Mitchell. "I can build all of it," he said. He held up both sheets. "Which one do you want?"

"Both," answered Mitchell.

"Both!" Farney shook his head. "You want two full sets of fancy, back east dining room furniture?"

"Both sets," Mitchell agreed. "Eight chairs each—not six."

Farney looked at both drawings then his eyes seemed to roll back in his head.

"Good grief! You got two of 'em." He laid the drawings on a large worktable. "You gonna end up buildin' two of everything?"

"Appears so," Mitchell replied.

"Don't envy you none," Farney concluded sympathetically.

"How much for the job?" asked Mitchell.

Farney looked at the drawings again. His forehead furrowed with concentration. Finally, he looked up. "Eighty dollars for the lot of 'em."

Mitchell nodded. "How soon?"

"Thirty days," Farney said quietly.

"Fine," Mitchell replied. He dropped four ten dollar gold Bees atop the drawings. "Half now," he said, looking directly into Farney's eyes. "Half when they're done."

Mitchell looked carefully around the shop. Furniture of all types and styles lined the walls, but there were no examples of anything as fine as that in the two drawings.

"We don't know each other very well, Jake," Mitchell said quietly, "but I expect this stuff to be fit for a queen— no plain old wood—no oak. You shop around and find some of that exotic hardwood I saw in Boston one time. Make one set from light colored wood and one from something darker, but I want plenty of burl and grain in all of it. You find something that looks like the good Lord dipped his finger in some color and twisted it around inside that tree. I'll pay extra for the wood. I'll pay extra for your time."

Quietly, Mitchell laid ten, twenty-dollar gold eagles beside the four gold bees.

Farney swallowed loudly, staring at the coins.

"You up to it?" asked Mitchell.

Farney nodded. "Might have to go to Denver," he said finally.

Mitchell laid another gold eagle on the table. Farney picked it up, hefted it then handed it back to Mitchell.

"Wood ain't that costly," he said. "Might take more than thirty days though."

Mitchell nodded "I can give you three months...maybe six," he answered. "I still have land to buy and two houses to build."

"Like I said," Farney grumped. "Two of everything."

Mitchell smiled, and took Farney by the hand. "Deal?"

"Deal," Farney agreed.

"Now," said Mitchell, "tell me about the wagon that unloaded at Reynald's place on Monday."

"Forgot about that," admitted Farney.

"So tell me now," prompted Mitchell.

"Not much to tell," Farney began. "About two in the afternoon a buckboard stopped in front of Reynald's place. Reynald came out and talked with the driver for a minute or two then the two of them unloaded a bundle and took it through the alley and into Reynald's shop."

Mitchell looked toward Reynald's shop. From Farney's store window, it was almost impossible to see the street in front of Reynald's store.

"You saw the buckboard from here?" asked Mitchell. His face was nearly against the glass before he could see the area where the buckboard would have stopped.

"You can't see much from there," Farney admitted. "Most of what I saw was from the alley door. The dog went crazy when that buckboard stopped. I went out to shut her up just as Reynald and the driver unloaded the bundle and hauled it into the store."

"Who was the driver?" Mitchell asked.

"Don't know him," answered Farney. "I've seen him around once or twice, but I don't know him."

"Did you see what was in the bundle?"

"Nope.... It was all wrapped up. Kinda looked like a canvas army tent... long and narrow—all tied up with pieces of twine."

"Anyone else see them unload the bundle?"

"There was a bunch of fellows over at Tolson's. They were all watchin'"

"Tell me who they were."

Half an hour later, Doctor Harold Wadman watched quietly as Mitchell unwrapped the ear-cuff and the dried flesh clamped in its jaws.

"Ever see anything like that?" Mitchell asked.

Wadman held the thing in the palm of his hand, turning it and peering at it from several angles. His jaw tightened for a moment, as though remembering something unpleasant.

"Once," he replied, "back in Nauvoo, more than twenty years ago. Joseph had a mummy. He set it up and let folks come and look at it. I went one afternoon, and Joseph let me look real close. The flesh on that mummy looked just like the piece you have here—dark and dried out."

"You think this came from a mummy?" Mitchell asked.

"I don't know," replied Wadman. "It looks about the same, except this piece doesn't seem as dry. This piece is dried out, but it's not bone dry and brittle like the one Joseph had."

"Where would you find a mummy around here?" Mitchell asked.

Wadman shook his head. "I'm not sure. I've heard rumors that a few mummified remains have been found in some old Indian ruins, or in caves, but I don't think I've ever heard anything that was definite."

The doctor shook his head. "It would take more than just a hot, dry place to dry a body out that way. Salt might do it. Lord knows there's plenty of that here."

"Anywhere close by?" Mitchell asked.

"I don't think so," the doctor replied. "I think it would be too damp around here. You'd have better luck with preservation someplace out west. Maybe in the desert on the other side of the lake.... Someplace that doesn't get much rain. Someplace protected from the weather."

"Like a cave?"

"I suppose."

"What do you think of that silver earring?" asked Mitchell.

"I'm no expert," Wadman replied, "but I've seen Indians around here wearing fancy silver like that."

"You think this piece was made by Indians?"

Wadman looked closely at the earring. "I don't know. Somehow, it gives me the impression that it was made by Indians."

Mitchell looked at the small ear-cuff. He could see nothing about the piece that identified it one way or the other. It was nothing more than a simple band of silver, like a tiny bracelet.

CHAPTER 7

Utah Territory
Ogden—September 1868

Sarah stopped with her back to the big glass window of the millinery shop.

"You're not going in?" Susan asked.

"I'd like to look around at the dry goods store," Sarah replied.

"I doubt it will be as well stocked as the mercantile in Salt Lake," Susan advised, glancing at the dry goods store on the east side of Main Street. "Besides, we should be looking for that bolt of cloth."

"They may have some cloth," Sarah replied absently.

"We could go there after we finish here," Susan suggested.

"I'm not in the mood to look at cloth," Sarah answered suddenly. "Why don't you look here, and I'll look at the dry goods?"

Susan looked at the boardwalk and bit her lower lip. She was no fool. She had seen the well-dressed man standing in front of the dry goods store. It took every ounce of self-control she could dredge up not to take Sarah by the ear and give her a good tongue-lashing. She felt her face flush and anger flared. "You told me you needed a bolt of cloth," she said. "I don't like shopping for cloth anyway, and if you aren't going in here, neither am I!"

"What has gotten into you?"

"You stand there making eyes at that fellow across the street and then ask what's gotten into me?"

"I am not making eyes."

"Like fun you're not!"

"I am not." Taking Susan's arm, Sarah turned into the millinery. "He's been watching us and pacing us for more than a block. I'm just very curious."

Susan frowned with irritation. "A dangerous pastime, I think."

Both women peered cautiously from one side of the millinery's front window. The man had taken a seat on the wooden bench in front of the dry goods store and was quietly watching the millinery.

"You see," Sarah insisted. "He's watching us."

"Maybe he is, and maybe he isn't," Susan replied. "I don't see what you can do about it in any case."

"I don't know," Sarah answered in a whisper. "There must be some way to find out why he's following us."

Susan glared at her sister in irritation. "I suppose you thought you'd just walk over and introduce yourself like some woman of ill repute?" She accused.

"Not so brazen as all that!"

"Brazen enough, I think."

Sarah frowned. "And what do you suggest, dear Sister Mitchell?" she demanded indignantly.

"He's probably some kind of cutthroat," Susan muttered.

"He doesn't look like a cutthroat," Sarah observed quietly.

Susan glanced out of the window. "I see what you mean," she agreed. "No scalps tied to his belt, no bloodstained dagger in his boot-top, and no one with such broad shoulders and handsome features..."

"You have a very sarcastic wit," Sarah grumbled.

"Sarcastic, yes," Susan agreed, looking through the window again. "But wit enough to know that you don't just walk up to a complete stranger and say: 'Hello, I'm Sarah Mitchell. Are you following me?'"

"I can be more subtle than that."

"Yes you can. And you will," Susan advised. "You would die of shame if anyone knew you'd done such a thing."

"I know it," Sarah replied testily, "but what else would you suggest?"

"We'll have someone we can trust ask a few discrete questions," Susan replied.

"Whom do you have in mind?"

"That fellow coming up the walk will do nicely."

Sarah let her eyes follow Susan's pointing finger. "Yes," she agreed. "He will do nicely."

Susan left Sarah at the millinery. She had no interest in the dark haired fellow who sat quietly on the bench in front of the dry goods store and watched her sister. It bothered her that the man was blatantly watching Sarah. She was painfully aware that men seemed to enjoy looking at her tall, elegant sister. She was equally aware that somewhere inside her there lurked just a tiny bit of envy.

Nevertheless, she was perfectly willing to ignore the situation and let that gun-toting Brother Mitchell assure the fellow that any romantic inclinations were extremely ill-advised.

Across the street, Doctor Harold Wadman's sign caught her eye. Impulsively, she headed toward the doctor's office, hoping to ask him some questions about the behavior of her eight-year old daughter. Immediately, she forgot the man at the dry goods store.

Instead, a minor curiosity had piqued her interest for the moment, and she was intent on discovering why the good Doctor Harold Wadman had ushered such a disreputable looking fellow into his office, closed the blinds, and hung a 'Closed for the Day' sign in the office window. A moment later, the door had opened and the doctor emerged from the office alone and locked the door behind him. Wadman turned, touching his fingers to the brim of his hat as Susan stepped onto the boardwalk. "Good morning, young lady. May I help you?"

Susan looked up at the doctor, noting the sallow face and the pale blue eyes. The man looked tired, physically exhausted, perhaps even ill.

"I was hoping for a moment of your time, doctor," she answered. "I have a question of a medical nature that I hope you can answer for me."

Wadman tugged his key from the lock. "I would be happy to help you, my dear." He dropped the key into a vest pocket and stepped to the edge of the boardwalk. "Is it an emergency, young lady?"

Susan glanced at the office window. "No, it isn't an emergency, just a curiosity."

"Then perhaps we can talk about it at a later date."

"It really wouldn't take much of your time," Susan protested weakly.

Wadman unhitched his horse from the rail and hooked the handles of his medical bag over the saddle horn. "I'm not trying to be rude, young lady, but I have a patient on a farm ten miles west of town. The little girl is quite ill, and I have a long ride. I will be happy to speak with you when I return in a day or two."

The doctor smiled, climbed into the saddle, and rode away, leaving Susan more than a little irritated at his briskness and even more curious about the man who had gone into Wadman's office and not returned.

"Why did you run off like that?" Sarah called out as she climbed onto the boardwalk beside Susan.

Susan shrugged. "I didn't run off. I had a question to ask the doctor, but before I got here, he closed up his office. He said he didn't have time to talk."

"A rather inhospitable attitude," Sarah replied.

"He did say he had a ten mile ride to see a patient," Susan admitted quietly. "Did you notice that your admirer has disappeared?" She asked.

Sarah glanced toward the dry goods store. The man had indeed deserted the bench and was nowhere to be seen. "Thank goodness," she sighed in relief. "He was beginning to make me nervous."

CHAPTER 8

Utah Territory
Ogden—September 1868

Mitchell reined up in front of the White House Hotel and dismounted. The dun gelding snorted, shaking its head like a big, wet dog.

"Dang it!" He pushed the animal's wet muzzle away from his shoulder. He tied the reins at the rail and swiped horse spit from his sleeve onto the ground.

"You never do that unless I'm standin' where you can spit all over me," he growled at the animal. "It's a dang bad habit."

The gelding dropped his head and peered at Mitchell with a big, dark eye. Mitchell ignored the ploy, stomped the dried mud from his boots and climbed the front steps of the hotel. Inside, the air was motionless and hot.

The White House Hotel stood on the southeast corner of Fifth and Main. It was a two-story structure of adobe brick that had been painted white. It was the only hotel in Ogden, unless the Prairie House Hotel in Harrisville could be counted. But most of the locals viewed the Prairie House as a tavern, or if they were feeling exceptionally generous, a way station.

When Mitchell entered the second floor suite, Sarah and Susan were entertaining a young woman whom he had never met. Mitchell removed his hat and nodded to the women.

"Ladies," he said quietly.

Sarah raised a hand in greeting, and Susan merely nodded in his direction. For a moment, Mitchell looked at both women. Sarah was a tall redhead with a temper that could flash as suddenly as lightening from a clear sky, but she had a smile and a personality that would make a man happy to let her fry him to a cinder. Yet, she had never turned that volatile temper on Mitchell, and somehow, he knew she never would.

Susan, two years younger than her sister, was so much like Sarah that they could have been twins. Mitchell hadn't mistaken one for the other as yet, but he knew a number of their friends who had given up hope and resorted to addressing either of them as *Sister* Mitchell.

Sarah stood and made introductions. The woman, Mitchell learned, was Eliza Richards. Reluctantly, he took the woman's outstretched hand.

"I am so glad to meet you, Mr. Mitchell. Mr. Farney spoke highly of you."

Mitchell withdrew his hand from the woman's grasp. He stifled the urge to wipe the hand on his pant leg, and finally hooked his thumbs in his belt. "Good afternoon Miss Richards."

"Mrs.," she prompted.

"Mrs. Richards," parroted Mitchell.

"Mrs. Richards has come to visit about Ogden's suffrage movement," Sarah said quietly.

"I see."

"Yes," Sarah continued. "It seems that your friend, Mr. Farney, told her that we were staying here, and that we would most certainly want to talk with her about the movement and the effort to rid the territory of that barbarous practice of plural marriage."

"I see," Mitchell replied, "and I suppose Mr. Farney mentioned that your *sister* was traveling with us?"

"He surely did," Susan interjected.

"Well, don't let me ruin your conversation ladies. I just dropped in to let you know that I have several people to talk with this afternoon, but I don't expect to be late. So, I wanted to invite the two of you to dinner this evening."

"I would love to have dinner out," Sarah replied.

"I would too, Collin," answered Susan.

"Good,"

Mitchell hung his hat on the rack near the door and turned back to the drawing room of the suite.

"If you will excuse me for a moment ladies, I need to change."

Sarah covered a smile with one hand, but Susan couldn't contain herself. "The gelding?" she laughed.

"Every time."

Mitchell winked at his younger wife, knowing how difficult the visit would be for her. It wouldn't be easy playing the part of the spinster sister, and for some reason neither of the sisters had deigned to inform Mrs. Richards of their marital situation.

"Susan, would you entertain Mrs. Richards for a moment?" Quietly, Sarah followed Mitchell into the adjoining room.

"Tread lightly," she said softly. She laid a hand on his arm. "That woman's a witch, and we don't trust her." Then she was gone, leaving the lingering scent of lilacs behind her.

So, they didn't trust the woman. That didn't say much for the character of Mrs. Richards. Generally, Sarah was a bit too trusting and willing to give anyone the benefit of the doubt. But something had created an almost immediate distrust, and it would pay to follow Sarah's advice. When Mitchell reentered the drawing room, the three women were in deep conversation.

"We were just discussing Mr. Reynald's murder," Susan offered.

Mitchell let himself sink into a chair near the window.

"An unpleasant subject to take with your tea."

"Yes, but very intriguing," simpered Mrs. Richards. "But we've also been discussing the suffrage movement."

"An intriguing subject," suggested Sarah.

"Indeed," agreed Mrs. Richards. "And it's a subject that the people of this territory can no longer ignore. I have it from a reliable source that the women of this territory will be the first to obtain the vote. It's a proposition that good Methodists like you should eagerly embrace."

Mitchell kept his face straight, but only with difficulty. Jake Farney had told the woman one hell of a whopper.

"What we need is a solid contingent of men and women who will spread the word throughout the territory. Prime the pump, you might say."

"And these good citizens will do what?" asked Susan.

"They will talk with the oppressed women living in these barbarous plural marriages, and convince them to cast their vote against the practice."

"And how do you propose to convince them?" prompted Sarah.

"We must help them see how they are being exploited in these loveless relationships and give them the courage to walk away from an unholy bondage."

"That might prove difficult," suggested Mitchell.

"Then we will employ every possible means to liberate them!"

Susan frowned unhappily. "You would use force?" she asked grimly.

"We will make use of force in its most practical form," answered Mrs. Richards. "We will use the government. These Mormons are a minority, despite all their numbers in this territory. I have sources who tell me that we can pass laws that have some teeth—laws that will put an end to this disgusting religion." Her conversation rose to a fevered pitch, and Mitchell fought an overwhelming urge to throw the ranting witch from the room. Silently, he fumed, his thoughts growing darker and angrier with the unending tirade.

Suddenly, the room was still, the silence hanging uncomfortably until Mitchell realized that the woman's eyes were locked with his own, and her hands were trembling.

"I have to go," she announced abruptly. With that warning, she noted the time, grabbed her parasol, and left the room without another word.

Sarah breathed a heavy sigh. "Thank you," she murmured, taking Mitchell by the hand.

"What did I do?"

Susan smiled and closed the door. "I think you terrified her," she responded.

"I did no such thing!"

Sarah squeezed his hand and looked up into Mitchell's eyes, her mouth an angry line and her eyes squinting.

"What's that look for?"

"It's the look you get whenever you're angry," she answered. "I've seen grown men back off when you look that way."

"You terrified the woman," Susan repeated.

"I was just sick of listening to her rant about things she knew nothing about," Mitchell defended.

Sarah smiled. "We're not angry with you dear. We were tired of it too. I've never met anyone so rabid," she murmured.

"Do you think they can do all she says?" Susan asked.

"I don't know," Mitchell replied, "but even if they don't accomplish everything, they are going to make our lives miserable."

"What are we going to do?" Sarah asked calmly.

Mitchell shook his head. "I don't know. I guess we just live our lives as though freedom means something. Her kind doesn't really care about anything but power and prestige. They'll do everything they can to destroy relationships like ours then once they've made the kill, they'll take their fill and walk away. They won't care about the broken families they leave behind. They'll leave those wounds for someone else to bind."

"So we stay together?" asked Susan.

Mitchell saw the tears in her eyes. "I never considered anything else," he said, "but we need to think things through and make a plan of some kind."

"Can they act that quickly?" Sarah asked.

Mitchell shook his head. "I think we have some time to prepare, but we can't fool ourselves into thinking things will smooth over and go away."

"You don't think we can win?" asked Susan.

"I'd like to think we can," Mitchell replied. "But this isn't about what's right or wrong, and it's not about freedom. This is about power and control. I think there are folks that don't like Mormons having control of the territory. And there are others who don't like our religion and want to make us live by *their* moral values. I reckon both groups are trying to use the government as a weapon to get what they want."

"It's not fair," Susan murmured.

"It's not," Mitchell agreed.

"So, we plan for the worst?" asked Sarah.

"I think we should," Mitchell answered solemnly.

"What about the murder?" Susan asked suddenly.

"I wanted to discuss that with both of you," Mitchell answered.

He removed the silver ear-cuff from his pocket and handed it to Susan. He had separated the silver cuff from the leathery piece of ear and cleaned it. The silver cuff was important—that much Mitchell was sure of.

"What is it?" wondered Sarah.

"It's an ear-cuff," Mitchell answered.

"It's like a tiny bracelet," Susan suggested.

"It is," Mitchell agreed. "It clamps on the outer ridge of the ear."

"And this is part of the murder?" asked Sarah. She handed the silver cuff to Susan and settled herself in the chair opposite Mitchell.

"I found it clenched in the dead man's fist."

"Mr. Reynald?"

Mitchell nodded. "Yes," he replied. He took a moment and explained what he had discovered and how little he had to work with. "So far," he admitted, "no one, except Alfred Tolson, seems to have any reason for killing the man."

Susan was about to fit the silver cuff to her ear when Mitchell looked up.

"Please. Don't do that," he objected.

"It's quite pretty," she answered. "I was only curious how it might look."

"I'm sure it would be beautiful on your ear," Mitchell replied, "but when I found it, it was attached to a dried out piece of human ear. Somehow, I can't stomach the idea of you wearing it."

Susan laid the silver cuff back on the table. "I'm not sure I like the idea myself," she replied.

"It's silver," asserted Mitchell. "I'm sure of that, but I'm not sure of anything else about it."

"And Mr. Reynald was holding it when he died?" asked Sarah.

"Yes."

"Do you suppose his killer was a lunatic woman with very dry skin?" Susan asked softly.

Mitchell stared at the girl for a moment. "Ah! You rotten wench." He tossed a small cushion at the girl.

"You are *terrible!*" Sarah cried.

"But I think you have a point," Mitchell confided. "The silver cuff and the ear are probably from the body of a woman."

"Another body?"

"Seems likely," Mitchell answered. "Unless Reynald kept them as a *souven—ear.*"

Susan tossed the pillow back at Mitchell. "Now that's tactless."

"I know."

"Why do you think there's another body?" Sarah asked.

"Yes, why?" echoed Susan. "You didn't find one?"

"No. But on Monday, Reynald took a delivery at the alley door of his shop. Jake Farney says that he saw Reynald and the driver unload a long narrow bundle that looked like an army tent."

"You think the bundle was the body that goes with the ear?" asked Sarah.

"If the bundle wasn't a body, then Mr. Reynald collected that ear some other way," Susan answered.

"So, we have a dried piece of an ear, a silver cuff, and a missing—dried out body," Sarah concluded.

"That's about it," Mitchell replied. He took a moment and described what he had found at Reynald's store. When he finished, Sarah seemed distant, as though puzzled by something he had said. "The jewelry...," she said at last. "Was it boxed?"

"Mostly, no—just jumbled in a couple of cigar boxes."

Sarah frowned. "That's odd."

"Yes, it is," added Susan.

"I don't understand?"

"Anything new would be boxed individually," Sarah replied.

"And nothing was on display," added Susan.

"That's right," Sarah agreed. "If Mr. Reynald was selling jewelry out of his shop, why wasn't it on display?"

Mitchell smiled. It was interesting how the two women looked at things so differently. He had been concentrating on the silver ear-cuff, and the driver of the wagon. Now, in less than ten minutes, Sarah and Susan were following a new set of tracks.

"This is quite interesting," Sarah confided.

"I do like puzzles," Susan agreed.

"Maybe we should go down to the shop and look around," Sarah suggested.

"We could look at the jewelry," Susan offered brightly.

"I don't think I like the idea of the two of you poking around where someone has just been murdered," Mitchell protested. "The murderer is still out there, and he might...."

"Or she," corrected Susan.

Sarah grinned mischievously. "Yes," she agreed. "We mustn't forget the lunatic woman with very dry skin."

"Your dry skinned woman may get violent if she sees too much interest in Reynald's affairs."

"We could be unobtrusive," Susan argued defensively. "We could visit Mr. Farney's furniture shop, and when no one was watching, we could go into Mr. Reynald's shop through the alley door."

"We could be back in Mr. Farney's shop in ten minutes," Sarah added.

Mitchell considered the proposition. Both women had quick minds, and he wasn't about to let them trick him into an agreement before he had thought things through. Finally, he nodded.

"I'll let you look around Reynald's shop," he said, "but I don't want anyone to know you were ever there."

"You trust Mr. Farney?" asked Susan.

"I think Mr. Farney is someone who can be trusted," Mitchell replied. "But I'll decide *when* and *if* either of you go anywhere near Reynald's place.

CHAPTER 9

Utah Territory
Ogden—September 1868

*E*arly the next morning, Sarah Mitchell knocked at the front door of a small, log home. She brushed nervously at the imaginary wrinkles in the dress that Collin had bought for her only two weeks earlier in Salt Lake City. She loved the dress. It was the first *store-bought* dress she had ever owned, the first she had not made for herself, and she felt utterly spoiled. Collin had taken her to a seamstress in Salt Lake City where she had spent hours choosing cloth, looking through patterns, and finally standing to be fitted. But, that wasn't what earned Mitchell a place in her heart. It took a lot more than a dress, but Mitchell knew how to make a woman love him—and *keep* loving him.

"Hello."

Sarah looked up quickly. Sister Dalton was a kindly looking woman with skin dark from hours in the sun and hair beginning to gray with age.

"Sister Dalton," Sarah replied, "I'm Sarah Mitchell. I was passing by and thought I might stop for a visit, if you have the time."

"You're one of the Flitton girls, aren't you?"

"I am."

"Well, you just come inside, and give me a minute to put some dishes away."

Sister Dalton closed the door behind them. Sarah took the offered chair and glanced quickly around the room. It was a large room and typical of its time. It served as kitchen, dining room, and living room all rolled into one. The walls had been chinked and plastered, the wooden floor planed and sanded smooth, giving the room a quiet sense of home that put Sarah instantly at ease.

"You said, Sarah Mitchell?" Sister Dalton prompted.

"Yes."

"So you're married now."

"I am."

Sister Dalton shelved the last few plates and came into the sitting area.

"Anyone I know, dear?"

"I don't think so. He came through Ogden about ten years ago. That's when we first met, but he's been working in Salt Lake and south as far as St. George. His name is Collin."

"Collin Mitchell?"

"Yes. You know him?"

"No, dear. But I know of him. Lorin Farr and Isaac Goodale used to come and visit with Matthew quite often. They told Matthew how they found your young man in the brakes of Ogden canyon while they were surveying for the road. Brother Farr claimed they found him in the remains of a grisly gun battle, with a bullet crease in his head and raving about Sarah Flitton. I've never known Brother Farr or Brother Goodale to tell an untruth, but they were hard pressed to believe their own story. Brother Goodale said your young man shot it out with four killers then tracked down another and killed him just as the man tried to shoot you down." Mrs. Dalton took a deep breath and looked Sarah straight in the eyes. "That my dear is a man and a romance that I will not easily forget."

"Nor I," replied Sarah.

"So, you married him."

"Ten years ago."

"Children?"

"Two, they're staying with my parents for the summer."

"I haven't seen your parents for over a year. Are they doing well?"

"They're doing fine."

"And your sister?"

"Susan is doing very well."

"Has she married too?"

"She and I married Collin in the Endowment House the same day."

"Children?"

"A girl. She's staying...."

"With your parents for the summer," laughed Mrs. Dalton.

Sarah smiled. "Yes."

"So tell me why you're in Ogden."

"Well, Collin has saved a bit of money and wants to buy or homestead some land for a cattle ranch. He's gone out of town for the day to talk with a man who lives out in Plain City."

"I see. So you had the day to yourself, and you're out doing some visiting."

"In a way," Sarah replied. "You see... Collin is also looking into the death of Mr. Reynald. We were discussing things yesterday, and Collin asked Susan and me what we knew of the man. Of course, we were little help. We knew that he had a shop and dealt in antiques or something, but we never had any dealings with the man. Then, as I was passing your home today, I realized that you might know something that could be important."

"I doubt I know anything that would help Brother Mitchell find a murderer."

"Perhaps not," Sarah admitted, "but it could be something that's not even directly related. I just have the feeling that something odd was going on. Collin went to Mr. Reynald's shop yesterday. Everything was covered with dust. It was as though he hadn't sold anything in years. And he had cigar boxes filled with jewelry, under a counter. Collin says it was all just tossed haphazardly into the boxes."

"That is odd. I don't remember any jewelry."

"That's why I was wondering what you could tell me about his business dealings," Sarah prompted.

"Very little, I believe."

The older woman arose and hurried to her sink. A moment later, she returned with two glasses of cold water. "I went to his shop twice. It was too cramped. You could hardly move, and I really saw nothing I wanted or needed. After that, I never saw any reason to go back."

Sarah waited while the other woman sipped her water.

"There were never any strange happenings over there—just normal comings and goings."

"No strangers visiting?" Sarah asked.

"I couldn't say. You can only see the back of those two shops from here. So I never saw much of anything. Mostly, I've had no contact with the man since Alfred's daughter, Melinda, ran away."

"I don't remember those names," Sarah admitted.

"That's not surprising. You married and moved away before the Tolsons came to town. Melinda was six or seven years younger than you. And they were only here a few months when she and Alfred quarreled. She ran away that same evening."

"How is that connected with Mr. Reynald?"

"Mr. Reynald wanted to marry Melinda. That's why she and her father quarreled. Her father wouldn't hear of it."

"So they quarreled, and she ran away," concluded Sarah.

"Yes, but that wasn't the end of it. Alfred thought Melinda was going to run off with Mr. Reynald, so he went to the shop—Mr. Reynald lived in the back room then. Alfred was fit to be tied, but Melinda wasn't there. A week later, Doctor Wadman went to Alfred asking if Melinda was finished with his horse, because he was going to Salt Lake and didn't want to take his buggy."

"Melinda borrowed the Doctor's horse and never came back?"

"That's right."

"I suppose Mr. Reynald and Mr. Tolson were enemies after that."

"Wouldn't speak a word to one another."

"Do you think Mr. Tolson hated him enough to kill him?"

"After all these years? I wouldn't think so."

"It *would* seem rather odd," Sarah agreed. "And no one heard from Melinda again?"

"Six months later, Doctor Wadman received some money and a letter from Melinda. He said she was living in Denver and wanted to make things right by paying for the horse."

"She never wrote her father?"

"Not that I know of."

CHAPTER 10

Utah Territory
Ogden—September 1868

*I*t was late afternoon when Mitchell returned to Ogden. The ride out to the Sharpe farm had been a complete waste of time—at least as far as the death of Lester Reynald was concerned. The day had begun hot and dry, but by mid-afternoon, dark clouds had formed over the lake and wind gusted through the streets spattering grit against buildings and windows. Mitchell stabled the dun and entered the hotel just as thunder rolled in the distance and rain filled a soot-colored sky.

Sarah opened the door of their suite and drew Mitchell into the room. They were alone. He drew her close and held her. Her breasts were firm against his chest, her body warm and urgent against his own.

"Susan just left," she murmured. "She'll be gone for a while."

Mitchell didn't need to be asked twice. Sometimes he was a little slow on the uptake, but he wasn't dense, and when her petticoats fell to the floor, Mitchell knew that a hard day was about to become much better.

Susan entered the mercantile shop on Main Street. Inside, the shop was small, clean, and neat, but more importantly, it smelled of new leather. She was drawn immediately to the saddles, bridles, and other tack occupying one corner at the front of the shop.

"Looking for a new saddle?"

Susan turned from the saddles and their heady aroma. The owner of the shop towered over her.

Nephi Clarke was a bear of a man. Corpulent, bearded, and nearly six-and-a-half feet tall, the man dwarfed Susan, who was slender, fair, and barely an inch over five-and-a-half feet.

"Howdy, Susan. You ain't been in for awhile."

"Hello, Mr. Clarke," she replied. "I got married, and we've been living in Salt Lake."

"Well, don't that beat all?"

"I'm looking for some earrings."

"I can't recall a single time you've come in here when you weren't looking for earrings."

"I'm looking for something different this time."

"Different I got."

"These look like tiny silver bracelets that clip on the outer ridge of the ear."

"Ear-cuffs?"

"Yes."

"I only got a few right now. Gals up here seem to want the *dangly* kind that hang from holes in their ears, but I got a few of the ear-cuffs."

Susan followed the massive silver smith to the back of the shop. There, the huge man tipped back the lid of a small, velvet-lined case and stood back.

"These are nice," she said quietly. She touched one silver cuff with her finger.

"Gold inlay," Clarke replied.

"Where did you get the idea for making these?"

"I think they've been made before, but the first time I made any was when Sister Miller come to me six or eight years back. Said she had sensitive skin or some such—didn't like the way some of 'em pinched, and she wasn't about to punch holes in her ears. So, she had me make up something for her."

"Have you ever seen Indians make anything like this?"

"Don't reckon I have, but I'm no expert on what kind of earrings Indian women are wearing this season."

"How many pair have you sold that were just plain silver?"

"Countin' Sister Miller?"

"Yes."

"Only the one. After that I tried inlays and dangly things on some. Never made any plain silver ones after that."

"Does Sister Miller still have hers?"

"Reckon so. 'Course she died six or eight years ago. But she liked 'em so well, her old man put 'em on her at the viewing, and they buried 'em with her."

"How much are you asking for these?" Susan asked, touching the pair with the delicate gold inlays.

"Nothing," he replied.

"They're not for sale?" She asked.

"They belong to a friend," he answered.

"Oh."

Nephi smiled. "They're yours, you goose. A fellow came in here this morning. Picked out that exact pair—said they were a present for a pretty redhead. Said he expected you would be along presently, 'cause you couldn't resist lookin' at jewelry. When he told me who you were, I wouldn't take his money...wedding gift.... For all those times you came in here pestering me."

Susan smiled at the big man. "You know you liked having me pester you."

"That I did," he answered.

Susan hurried back to the hotel. She was anxious to talk with Sarah about her visit with Mrs. Dalton. She was nearly inside the hotel when she heard a voice call her name. Suddenly, strong hands pinned her arms and forced her down the steps.

Mitchell woke to an insistent pounding at the door and a voice bellowing his name. Sarah was awake in his arms. She lay half across him, her hair damp and tangled. The door rattled again. Mitchell threw on his trousers, strode to the door of the parlor and threw it open.

"What the blazes do you want!" he snapped.

"It's your wife," panted the attendant from the hotel lobby. "Two fellows rode up and took her right off the hotel steps!"

"They did what!"

"They took her and rode off!"

Mitchell had his boots on when Sarah entered the room. She pulled at her robe and watched as Mitchell dressed.

"They rode north," sputtered the lobby man. "One of them hung back and said you could come get her in Corinne—if you still wanted her when they was done with her."

Mitchell was mad enough to shoot the lobby-man and half the people in Ogden by the time he belted on his pistols.

"You tell that stable boy to saddle the dun *and* the grulla," he growled.

The man sensed the anger and backed hurriedly into the hallway. He was gone when Mitchell took Sarah in his arms.

"You bring her back safe," she demanded.

Mitchell brushed her hair back and kissed her forehead. "I've got only five people in the world that care for me," he replied. "If she's hurt, those men will wish I never found them."

Sarah looked up at her husband. "You come back safe too," she advised.

Ten minutes later, Mitchell spurred the grulla and headed north in a pouring rain. Susan and her three kidnappers had less than an hour lead and a forty-mile ride to Corinne. If they had remounts, he would never catch them on the trail, but they couldn't stop, or he would overtake them before they could set up camp. They had to know he was close, and he could only hope that taking Susan was nothing more than a ploy to get him to Corinne.

Corinne was a sinkhole of ill repute; at least that was what most of the locals thought. Folks claimed that the *Burg on the Bear* was a wide-open town—except on Sundays. Every day of the week there was fighting, gambling, or a *soiled dove* to keep a man company, but on Sunday, the town shut down while the "doves" went dancing, and the men went fishing. Given a choice between Corinne, dancing, or fishing, Mitchell preferred fishing. But his life had changed since meeting the Flitton girls. Somehow, the things that had been so important when he was a kid seemed less significant now. He still liked fishing, but a quiet evening at home had become more desirable. Susan was part of what made life good, and Mitchell was mad as blazes that anyone thought they could use his family to get at him. He wanted Susan home and safe, and he wanted out of the danged rain.

After three miles at a lope, Mitchell reined the grulla to a trot. The animal still had its wind, and the sound of its breathing was steady and strong. The dun was a better mount, but the grulla was a close second in Mitchell's book. Actually, the only thing he didn't like about the animal was its color. In fact, when he thought about it, the grulla had plenty of bottom and worked just as hard as the dun. And it didn't spit on him. That had to count for something.

An hour later, Ben Lomond peak loomed in the growing dimness. The sun had dropped below the mountainous islands of the Great Salt Lake, leaving the sky dark with clouds and the western horizon streaked with a red-orange glow. Mitchell stopped. The rain had slowed to an intermittent, windblown drizzle, and the grulla needed a rest. Under the protection of a few straggling willows, Mitchell shifted his gear to the dun, watered both animals and hit the trail at a fast walk. Both animals were tired, but if they kept to the road, it was still light enough to ride.

Already, he was bone-tired and more than ready to get out of the rain, but Susan's kidnappers would make only brief and necessary stops, and he hoped to overtake them if he could push hard enough. It was likely that the men he followed would soon stop, and there was still a chance he could close the distance between them.

An hour later, clouds filled the entire sky, and darkness blotted out the trail. Mitchell dismounted and led the animals to a small stand of trees. He shucked his gear from the dun, watered, grained, and rubbed down both animals then tossed a tarp and his bedroll beneath the nearest tree.

The ground was rock-hard and laced with tree roots. He wouldn't sleep worth a hoot—that much was certain. But that was what he wanted. He wanted a short night and a mean disposition when he woke. Normally, he was hard to provoke, but he wanted none of that when he caught up with these men. He wanted to be as hard as the ground he lay on and as unforgiving as the root jabbing him in the spine.

It was midnight when he woke. He was stiff, cold, and hungry. Hot anger had turned to cold fury. He saddled the dun and with the grulla in tow, started north.

Less than a mile down the trail, the dun rounded an outcropping of rock, and Mitchell slipped from the saddle. Firelight flickered in the trees ahead. Cautiously, he moved forward. If it was Susan and her abductors, he wanted to catch them off guard. Mostly, he wanted to catch them asleep, giving no one a chance to grab for a gun. Finally, the camp was in view.

"Hullo, Mitchell!" Bellowed an old man near the fire— an old man who was ragged and dirty as sin.

Mitchell dropped the Colt back in its holster. "Dang near shot you!" he growled. "What are you doing out here?"

"Waitin' fer an old friend... feller called Mouriel. Ain't seen 'im have you?" The old man held up a stick with a chunk of dripping, half-burned meat skewered on its end. "Want some rabbit?"

"Hell no! The last time you fed me rabbit you tried to shoot me!"

"Hardly knew you back then, Danite. Don't be holdin' that against me."

"I ain't no Danite," Mitchell muttered, resenting the insinuation that he had ever been part of Sampson Avard's pack of retribution seekers. The Prophet, Joseph, had excommunicated Avard for that bit of nonsense. "I was never part of that. I was only six years old, and I never liked Avard anyway."

"Sorry." The old man pointed the skewered rabbit to the north. "You might as well get some rest," he suggested. "Them fellers rode past here an hour ago, an' they was goin' to beat the band."

"They have to stop sometime," Mitchell argued.

"They had fresh horses waitin'. They won't be stoppin' 'til they fetch up to Corinne."

"How do you know they had fresh horses waitin'?"

"They stopped over yonder—off the trail. They was talkin'. Two of 'em wanted to stop.... The young feller said they otter stop 'cause your little gal was gettin' tired. But the lead feller—he just hollered at 'em. Told 'em they was a gettin' paid to get that gal to Corinne—so her old man would follow. Said he would tie her to the saddle if he had to."

"If they have fresh mounts, I'll never catch them before they reach Corinne."

"That young feller acted a mite upset. Seems the other two never told him they was a goin' to grab your gal. He didn't like the deal one bit."

"He's thrown in with them," growled Mitchell. "I'll give him the same as I give the others."

"Voice says: 'Spare the boy,' Collin Mitchell."

"Still hearin' that voice, are you?" Mitchell hunkered down near the old man's fire and gazed into the darkness beyond the camp. "Still think you're the angel of death?" he asked finally.

"Yep."

"I suppose this voice told you to take the boy yourself."

"Nope. Voice says I'm to take you—if you kill the boy."

"Dang it!" hissed Mitchell. "You're makin' this too complicated."

"Reckon so. But there's more to this than you know. There's skin walkers out there."

"Skin walkers?"

"Fellers who think they got some kind of contact with spirits or demons that can give them powers other folks don't have. Shape changers...stuff like that."

"Navajos believe something like that," Mitchell responded.

"Maybe so, but these fellers ain't Navajos. These fellers are whites, and they've gone bad...real bad."

"And how does that involve me?"

"Well... I ain't sure, but I think they might be lookin' to kill you."

Mitchell stood and walked to his horses, wondering if the old man was as crazy as he sounded. Deliberately, he stripped and watered both animals then hitched them near the old man's roan. The roan nuzzled against his shirt pocket.

"I'll be switched," he muttered. He strode back to the fire and dropped his gear opposite the old man. "How'd you come by that horse?" he demanded.

The old man squinted through the firelight.

"Like 'im, do ya?"

"Hell, I ought to. He's mine."

The old man lifted the half-burned rabbit and gnawed at a greasy hindquarter.

"Yeah.… Well, Sarah didn't mind none," he argued congenially.

"Sarah let you take her horse?"

"Shore did. She ain't mean an' distrustin' like some folks. 'Sides, she took a likin' to me."

"I've been seein' his tracks everywhere," Mitchell growled.

"Reckon I get around some," the old man replied, "but I don't keep real good track of where I been." He tossed the remains of the rabbit into the fire. "He's a mite pigee-toed though; you oughta have 'im reshod."

"Hell," grouched Mitchell, "I filed them feet flatter than a pancake a dozen times, and he just grows 'em out crooked again."

"Hmm.… Well, he seems like a decent critter. An' he rides good." The old man picked at his teeth with a twig. "He got a name?"

"Sarah calls him Milo."

"Milo! Sounds like somethin' you'd call a dog!"

"Reckon so."

"Milo? Who'd a thought.…"

Mitchell slapped his tarp and blankets on the ground then settled down for the night. He glared at the old trapper. "What is your name?" he asked suddenly.

He'd met the old goat more than once, but had never learned the man's name. The old coot was crazy and thought he was the *angel of death*, but Mitchell figured the old geezer could be *Michael the Archangel* if he wanted, as long as he didn't keep taking potshots at one Collin Mitchell.

"You shot at me," he growled, remembering a night ten years earlier. "The first time we met, you offered me a piece of rabbit then took a shot at me before I even got a bite out of it. Now you're ridin' Sarah's horse.… After all that, I think you could at least tell me your name."

"Ah, well…You can call me Mort."

"Mort?"

"Why not? Sounds like a good name for a feller like me."

Mitchell rolled on his side and yanked a blanket over his shoulder. "Don't let me over-sleep," he told the old man.

"An' who's a goin' to wake me?" Mort answered.

"Reckon the *angel of death* don't need any sleep," Mitchell replied.

"Smart mouthed kid." The old man stomped to the edge of the camp. "I like sleepin'," he muttered.

CHAPTER 11

Utah Territory
Ogden—September 1868

Susan slumped against the tree, feeling the rough bark bite into her hands and back. Twenty feet away, flames roared from pile of broken branches, twigs, and dry grass. She watched the movement of her kidnappers as they shuffled about the fire in an attempt to warm their hands and dry their clothing. They were a miserable lot. But Susan felt more miserable than any of them. They had taken her from the steps of the hotel, slammed her into a saddle, and made her ride nearly twenty miles in a wind-blown rain.

She was wet, cold, and miserable. Her wrists were tied behind her, and the ropes had chaffed her wrists and hands. At this moment, she would gladly have strangled each of the men warming themselves at the fire. In her book, they deserved much worse, but she was feeling a little dazed at the moment and strangulation was the only suitable torture she could think of. Mostly, she was concerned with finding a way to get free of the ropes and get away into the trees or anywhere else that might provide shelter and a place to hide. She was tired of being wet, and she was tired of being tossed around like a sack of potatoes.

The ground beneath her was hard and unyielding. She shifted her weight, searching for any bit of comfort, but moving only uncovered more rocks, and even that effort gave her more pain than she cared to handle.

There were three men and a boy now. She watched as they built up the fire and hunkered down close to the flames. The boy held back a bit, standing behind the others, staring across the fire at her. The three men muttered at one another and tried to keep the wind and the drizzling rain from killing the flames.

"Come over here and block some of that wind, kid." The leader of the bunch looked over his shoulder then turned back to the fire. "You look like you ate somethin' that didn't agree with you, boy."

"You told me we was guardin' a special shipment goin' up to Corinne," the kid said quietly.

"Looks right special to me," one of the others replied.

"You didn't say nothin' about kidnappin'," the kid muttered.

"Look, boy… you asked me for a job. This is it. You don't like it, ride out. But don't figure you're in the clear. Her old man will come after you too."

Susan watched as the boy moved closer to the fire. He stared sullenly at the flames, rain dripping from the brim of his hat, until two of the outlaws stretched a blanket between them and stood as a windbreak between the wind and the fire.

Without a word, the kid stalked away from the warmth of the flames and took a blanket from his saddle. A moment later, he walked across the small camp and hunkered down on his heels in front of her.

"Lean forward," he said, shaking out the woolen blanket and draping it around her back and shoulders. He wrapped the edges of the blanket tightly at the front then quickly wedged something between the laces of her shoe.

"It'll cut rope like butter," he whispered softly. "If you can get loose, hide somewhere. I'll try and get you back to town somehow."

A moment later, he was gone, leaving her to the growing warmth of the blanket and the dimly reflected firelight glittering on the obsidian flake tucked between the laces of her shoe.

CHAPTER 12

Utah Territory
Ogden—September 1868

Sarah Mitchell spent a restless night. Lightning ripped the sky, thunder rolled across the heavens, and rain pelted the windows and walls of the hotel in a rhythm that changed with every blast of the wind. Windows rattled, and the wind howled through the streets, dragging grit, leaves, papers, and anything else weighing less than a good sized laying hen. More than one unwary bird had slammed the wall of the hotel hard enough to wake her during the night.

She knew that Collin would be miserable. He would push himself relentlessly until he found Susan. She prayed that he would find Susan unharmed, but her concern was not for her sister's welfare alone. Collin was not easily provoked, but he was deadly serious about his family, and he wouldn't hesitate to shoot Susan's abductors if he felt it necessary. She had hoped that this trip would prove to be the means of shifting Collin into a less violent way of life, but somehow trouble seemed to follow him. That thought pestered her and filled her dreams with a quiet, yet growing apprehension.

In the deep solitude of the night, the rain stopped. And when morning came, she was tired but restless. Something in their discussion of the murder bothered her, something Susan had said—a joke about a dry-skinned woman. Yet it wasn't the joke that bothered her. It was the *idea* that it provoked. The ear-cuff had belonged to a living person, a person with family and friends... a person who may have lived in Ogden—or perhaps nearby.

Who was the woman? She wondered. And more importantly—*why wasn't she decently buried like any other dead body?* That question held only two answers for Sarah. Either the woman had never been buried, or someone had taken the body from its grave. Suddenly, she was convinced it was the latter. She found it impossible to believe that the body had not been buried somewhere. She was certain that exposure to the elements would have hastened decomposition and possibly some disarticulation. And there were always scavengers. Left exposed, a body would soon decompose, be scattered and the bones lost. No, the body had been buried—of that, she was convinced, but she was unsure how it all connected with the death of Lester Reynald.

She ate a leisurely breakfast, offering occasional tidbits to the lady-dog, but by nine a.m., she had reached the conclusion that the ear-cuff was important enough to investigate. But she knew that Susan had already chosen the ear-cuff as her own portion of the puzzle, and while Susan might welcome discussion and a few suggestions, any encroachment on that territory would only stir trouble.

For Collin's sake, Sarah wanted to avoid contention, yet deep in a treacherous part of her personality resided a spark of resentment, a spark that on occasion prodded her to needle her younger sister. Susan had been pampered and spoiled from the beginning. She wasn't a bad person, but she had learned how to get what she wanted and wasn't above using a little feminine charm to get her way. Somehow, Sarah had never learned that trick.

As children, Susan had been their mother's favorite. For Susan, dolls and dresses had always been new, store bought, and covered with frills. For Sarah, dolls had been few, and dresses, though finely made, were generally the castoffs of a wealthy cousin in Salt Lake. Consequently, the years had planted a small seed of resentment that had only been assuaged by the efforts of their father, who had seen the disparity and had done his best to counter the hurt. Yet, now and again a judicious bit of needling was enormously satisfying.

Less than an hour later, with the lady dog trotting at her heels, Sarah marched happily away from Nephi Clarke's mercantile and headed for the home of Vernon Miller. Nephi had been uneasy when he learned of her intent to visit Miller, saying, "You ought not to go there."

Nevertheless, after exercising a little feminine charm—a pale imitation of Susan's methods—she had weaseled the information from the reluctant silversmith.

Miller's house was a small, squatty box of whitewashed adobes. The roof needed repairs, and weeds choked what had once been a flower garden at either side of the door. Miller obviously cared little for appearances, and Sarah expected the interior of the house to be as unkempt as the exterior, but she was pleasantly surprised when she knocked on the door and a young woman led her into the well-kept interior.

Cow-eyed and furtive, the girl motioned toward a chair. "Sit down," she said quietly.

The bearded Miller entered the room and with a slow, carnal gaze, stripped Sarah from head to toe. The thin, ferret-like man glanced briefly at her face then let his eyes rove her body.

"What can I do for you, young lady?"

Sarah stiffened. She was instantly offended and outraged that the man had the nerve to stare at her as though she were a whore.

"Mr. Miller?" she asked.

"I am he." For a moment, his gaze lingered on her hips.

"Mr. Miller, I'm Sarah Mitchell."

"Pleased to meet you. Sit down please."

Already, she was anxious to leave. *I should have listened to Nephi*, she thought. But Miller had her by the elbow, guiding her to the chair. "I can only stay a moment," she protested.

"How can I help you?" he asked, letting his hand slide from her elbow to her wrist.

Sarah took the offered chair, positioning herself for maximum distance from the man. "I have a few questions I'd like to ask you."

"I'll answer them, if I can."

Sarah took a deep breath and steeled herself for a conversation she wanted to end before it even began. "My husband is working for the county sheriff."

"A less than ideal position," Miller offered, watching the rise and fall of her breasts.

"He's looking into the death of Lester Reynald. Did you know him?"

"No."

"I see." Sarah fought the urge to run from Miller's presence. "A silver ear-cuff has turned up, and I understand that your wife, Ruth, owned a pair made by Nephi Clarke."

"Ear-cuffs?"

"Yes. They are somewhat unconventional. They attach to the outer ridge of the ear—like a small bracelet."

"Indeed."

"Nephi Clarke says he made a pair for your wife before she died."

"I recall something like that."

"Nephi says that he never made anything like them again, but he doesn't think the one my husband found can be one of the set that belonged to your wife."

"He's right. Those were buried with my wife." Miller's gaze lingered at the hollow of her throat. "Are you new in town?" he asked suddenly.

"We arrived this week," she admitted reluctantly. Miller's lust was like a cloud fogging the air. She wanted out—she wanted out now. "Well.... Thank you for your time," she said, rising.

Miller was at her side in an instant. "You needn't leave so soon," he complained. "Stay awhile. I'll have Deborah fix something to drink."

"Thank you, but no. I do need to be going."

"You know, I do seem to recall someone asking about those earrings," he offered.

Sarah hesitated. She was certain Miller was lying, but there was always the possibility that the man really knew something helpful.

"Recently?" she asked.

Miller raised one hand and stroked his chin. "No. It was, soon after my wife started wearing them."

"Do you remember who asked about them?"

"No. Only that they were surprised to see her wearing them."

"Man or woman?" she asked.

"A woman, I believe."

"Someone your wife knew well, or just someone making a comment in passing."

Miller hesitated. His eyes shifted then continued their appraisal of her figure. "A stranger, I think. Just asking where she bought them."

"I see," she responded, feeling the urge to bolt like a frightened rabbit.

"Perhaps I should contact you if I remember anything else," Miller suggested.

"I suppose you should," Sarah admitted reluctantly.

"You're staying at the hotel? I could contact you there," Miller suggested.

"Yes." Even as she spoke, Sarah caught a glimpse of blue eyes peering through the crack of a partially open door and the frantic shaking of the woman's blonde head.

"Excellent."

Sarah turned to the door as Miller took her elbow in a pincer-like grip.

"I look forward to seeing you again, Sister Mitchell."

Sarah nearly ran from the house. The man was an animal, and she was desperate to escape his attentions. Yet, she wanted more than anything to go back and slap the man.

Punch him in the mouth. He deserves that much.

The man had told her little she hadn't already learned from Nephi Clarke. The ear-cuffs had been buried with his wife, and that had seemed final enough. But it was still possible that Ruth Miller's body had been in Reynald's shop. Someone could have dug it up.

But why?

It was mid-afternoon when Sarah re-entered the silversmith's shop. Like Susan, she took a moment to enjoy the smell of new leather and the touch of several bolts of new cloth stacked on a table near the front window. She worked her way slowly toward the back of the shop and the bench where the big silversmith worked.

"Back already?" Clarke asked. "You ain't been gone more than an hour or so."

"I was here this morning, Mr. Clarke. It's nearly three now."

"Hmm.... Reckon I don't keep good time when I'm workin'." He placed a small silver ring on the bench and wiped his hands on a rag. "What brings you back so soon, Sarah?"

"Questions."

"Reckon I knew you would be back sooner or later."

"I went to see Vernon Miller."

Clarke scowled in disgust. "Not a nice visit, I'll wager."

"Not nice at all," she replied. "You were right about that."

"I never liked him much," Clarke admitted. "Guess I shouldn't be so open about it, but there's something about the man that makes me want to stomp him into the ground."

"Tell me about Ruth," Sarah interrupted.

"Nothing to tell."

Sarah shook her head. "You gave her the ear-cuffs, didn't you?"

Nephi Clarke looked down at his workbench.

"She didn't commission them and neither did her husband," Sarah insisted. "Mr. Miller never discovered who gave them to her. But you made them, Mr. Clarke, and either you gave them to her, or you know who commissioned you to make them."

For a moment the big man looked trapped then he raised his head.

"He treated her like something less than human," he grumbled. "I know he beat her. She was always bruised. She used to come in here to look at the jewelry and the cloth.... Kind of like she just wanted to look at something she knew she could never have. She never had any money. Old Vernon had plenty, but he was always a skinflint. He'd spend on himself if he had a mind to, but he never bought her anything, and she never spent any money on herself. I never wanted to cause trouble. I just wanted her to have something nice; so I gave her the ear-cuffs."

"She wanted a divorce," Sarah responded. "Was she in love with you Mr. Clarke?"

"I never meant it to go so far.... We just became good friends. She wanted the divorce all right, but only because she figured she would be happier alone."

"And when Miller refused the divorce, she took rat poison?"

"I never believed that," Clarke growled.

"It wasn't poison?"

"She didn't kill herself. I always thought that Miller poisoned her, but there ain't no way to prove it."

"Miller says she was wearing the ear-cuffs when she was buried."

"Miller lied."

"She wasn't wearing them?"

"I was there when they closed the casket. She was wearing them. But someone must have taken them, and the only one mean enough to do that was Miller."

"So, the ear-cuff Collin found is one of the pair?"

"Mitchell showed it to me. It was hers, but I couldn't make myself admit it. It was too much like living it all over again."

Sarah frowned. "You think that Miller opened the casket and removed the ear-cuffs?"

Clarke frowned and threw his hands up. "How else could your husband get hold of it?"

Sarah shrugged and was quiet for a moment. "I wonder?" Something about the situation seemed odd, yet the answer evaded her. "If Miller didn't take them then someone robbed her grave," she announced suddenly.

"Don't be ridiculous," Clarke chided. "No one has robbed a grave around here since Jean Baptiest was convicted and exiled back in sixty-two."

"Jean Baptiest?"

"Grave digger in Salt Lake City. He looted over three hundred graves before they caught him. They exiled him to Fremont Island for life. Just took him out there and left him. 'Course he was gone when they come back three weeks later. Tore down the little shack he was to live in and built himself a raft. They figure he drowned out on the lake. They never found his body."

"You see," Sarah argued. "Baptiest could have survived. Fremont Island is only a mile or two from the shore out west of here. He could have come here and started all over.

Clarke shook his head. "I doubt it. Someone would have recognized him. Someone drew a real good likeness of him and it was in every paper in the Territory. And when they exiled him, they wrote the words *grave robber* across his forehead with indelible ink. No, if anyone did it, it was Miller."

"But why? If Miller didn't want them buried with her, why go to all that trouble?"

"Miller wouldn't. But her friends knew that she liked those ear-cuffs, and they wanted her to wear them. They pestered Miller until he agreed. Once they were satisfied, he probably did as he pleased and removed them."

"So, how did Mr. Reynald get one of them?"

"Who knows? He was an antique dealer. Maybe he bought them from Miller."

Sarah studied the silversmith for a moment. "You're probably right," she agreed. But she was certain that Miller had never sold the ear-cuffs to Reynald. Collin had found the ear-cuff still attached to a piece of human ear. No decent person would every buy such a thing, if they knew. *There must be a better explanation,* she thought.

"Thank you, Mr. Clarke. I'm grateful that you would take the time to explain the situation to me."

"I always worried people would get the wrong impression," Clarke replied. "We were only friends."

Sarah was thoughtful as she left the store and walked southward along Main Street. Ogden was a growing town, and it was a far cry from the quiet place she had known as a child. Just having a hotel was something of a novelty. Only a few months earlier, the Prairie House in Harrisville had been the only thing resembling a hotel, and barely five years had passed since the Morrisite War had rocked the county. That had been a poorly handled situation as far as she was concerned. But no one had felt it necessary to consult her, and she had been more than happy to leave town when the territorial Militia surrounded the Morrisite fort and turned an argument over personal property into a gun battle. The debacle had left six men and women dead and a young girl with half her face ripped away by a Militia cannon ball. Sarah had always considered the use of the Militia as an excessive measure. But, of course, she wasn't running the Territory.

Still, the town might eventually become more refined... perhaps even as stylish as Mrs. Richards demanded. That day was probably far in the future, especially if the Railroad made Ogden its junction. If that happened, Sarah was sure the town would become much like any other rail stop—mean, disorderly, and more complex than ever before. She definitely wanted a different environment than that for her children, but Susan didn't seem to agree.

Susan wanted a place in town. At least, she argued for a place in town. It was entirely possible that her opposition to a more rural location was driven by something other than her real desires. She had always talked about living on a ranch, and like Sarah, she had always wanted some distance from their neighbors. Ten years in Salt Lake City had sharpened that desire for Sarah, but apparently not for Susan. Still, there was a possibility of working things out, but at this moment, she had no idea what Susan really wanted.

By the time she reached the hotel, she was tired of thinking about Lester Reynald, tired of thinking about Ogden, and tired of trying to solve the puzzle of an ear-cuff that should have been decently buried for more than half a decade.

For a moment, she wanted to put it all out of her mind. *Just for an hour or two. Then I'll try figuring it out again.*

CHAPTER 13

Utah Territory
Ogden—September 1868

Mitchell was tired and feeling mean enough to fight anyone. Sweat ran down his back. His collar ground dust into the back of his neck, and for five hours, he had listened to the story of Mort's life as the *Angel of Death*. Either the old man was mentally unbalanced, or he was older than dirt. Mitchell could almost believe the latter. Either way, Mitchell felt ornery. The old man hadn't slept a wink, and he had kicked around camp, making just enough racket to keep Mitchell tossing until the sun came up. Now it seemed as if he would talk forever.

"Corinne's just ahead," the old man pointed out.

Across the flats, toward the lake and the Promontory Mountains, a few gray, weather-faded buildings squatted amid a cluster of tents, dry sagebrush, salt grass, and a scattering of trees that paralleled the slow moving waters of the Bear River.

"Ugly little place," Mort added grimly. "I don't think I'm gonna like Corinne."

The town was small and sagebrush dry. Two small but busy saloons faced each other across a dusty main street. On the north, a general store and a mercantile stood nearly side by side. On the south a boarding house, a blacksmith, and a scattering of white canvas tents paralleled Main Street, stretching out until they blurred into the surrounding desert.

Mort slapped his hat against his dusty shirt. "You remember not to shoot that kid."

"What if he tries shootin' me?"

"You just pay attention to them other two fellers."

Mitchell frowned. "And if I don't?" he asked unhappily.

"You won't live long enough to regret it."

"You're dead set on this?"

"Generally, I don't give folks much warnin', but that there voice tells me to look out for you, 'cause your women folk keep a pesterin' 'im day an' night."

Mitchell smiled. "I reckon they do."

"Well.... I gotta look out for them gals too. Voice says there's a feller naggin' about both of 'em."

"Glad to hear it."

"Voice says you already knowed it."

Mitchell smiled. "Reckon that's between the voice and me."

"Reckon so."

Horse hoofs kicked up small swirls of dust as they took possession of the town's narrow main street.

"Looks like we're expected," Mort observed.

Mitchell looked down the deserted street. Nothing moved, save a few horses hitched in front of one saloon and a little dust stirred by gusts of intermittent and restless wind. Slowly, they walked their horses west, watching for signs of Susan and her captors.

Finally, Mort stopped. "I seen that horse before. They must be waitin' inside," he suggested. He slid out of the saddle and tossed Milo's reins around an end post of the hitching rail.

Canvas doors swung away as Mitchell entered the huge tent that served as a saloon. Mort was close on his heels, shifting quickly to the left. Mitchell squinted into the room, his eyes adjusting slowly to the dimness.

Inside, the structure was a cross between the beginnings of permanence and a portability that suggested the need for a quick removal, should the county sheriff decide to interfere with business. Wooden floors creaked ominously under the shifting weight of men and women. Feet churned sawdust into small heaps and twisted ridges. Dingy, smoke stained walls sucked light from the room, and in the dimness, the air reeked with the stench of stale tobacco, spilled whiskey, and old vomit.

Mitchell's gaze searched the room—crossed tables, card players, drinkers, whores—and lighted on the bar at the back of the room. Two dusty riders stood hipshot at the bar, downing their drinks. Far to his left, nearly hidden in the dimness, sat a sullen-looking kid.

Mort shoved his chin toward the bar. "Reckon them's your meat," he prompted.

Mitchell advanced a few feet and stepped to the right. The men at the bar were primed and set their drinks aside.

"You fellows took my wife," he growled, directing the accusation toward the two at the bar. In the dimness, the entire room grew silent.

"Don't reckon we know what you're talkin' about," answered the taller of the two. He was a swarthy, dark haired man, and carried a pistol in a worn holster tied low on his right leg. He was a gunman, or thought he was. The second man—shorter and heavier than the first—shifted a step to Mitchell's left.

"I tracked three of you from Ogden," Mitchell replied. "The hotel man described you, and I reckon someone here saw the three of you ride in with a woman."

"I seen 'em," offered someone behind Mitchell.

"Where is she?" growled Mitchell.

"Like I said—don't know you or your woman. Harlow and me just rode in, but there ain't no woman."

The denial stopped the conversation in it tracks. Mitchell knew these were the men, but he waited.

"It's them, Mort said suddenly. "I recognize his voice. He's the one that was gonna tie her to the saddle if he had to."

Both men stiffened. Their denials meant nothing now. They were caught, and they knew it. "Now wait a danged minute!" the short man bellowed, dragging at his revolver.

Suddenly, the room shuddered with the explosion of gunfire. The tall man lurched backward, his spine smashing against the edge of the bar. He sagged, and the pistol in his hand belched fire and lead into the sawdust covered floor.

Harlow staggered back a step then thumbed the hammer of his revolver. Powder flashed at the bore, smoke fogged the room, and the thirty-six-caliber bullet punched a hole through Mitchell's pant leg. But the gunman was down, struggling to lift himself from the floor when the muzzle of Mitchell's gun centered on the forehead of the kid standing in the dimly lit corner. Every instinct prodded Mitchell to pull the trigger, but he held off.   Then,   the   kid   fired. Like a blue-gray flower, flashing a heart of flame, the kid's pistol jolted the room. In the silence that followed, Mitchell and the boy faced each other through a cloud of sulfurous smoke. Mitchell heard a choking cough behind him and knew the kid's bullet had gone home.

"Feller was goin' to shoot you in the back," Mort observed. "The kid shot him."

Twenty feet away, the *kid* in question dropped his pistol on the table.

"Where is she?" Mitchell demanded.

"Across the road," the boy answered. "Dickson hog-tied her and left her in one of those tents out on the edge of town. Fellow named Beazer is runnin' the outfit, and he's out there guardin' her now. "

"Show me," Mitchell ordered.

Urged by the snout of Mitchell's revolver, the boy marched to the edge of town and threw back the door flap of a ragged, empty tent.

Susan fought the ropes that held her hog-tied and struggled to reach the sharp flake of obsidian wedged behind the laces of her shoe. Her fingertips touched the smooth surface of the razor-edged stone, but the laces were too tight, and the flake refused to budge.

She struggled angrily, sucked furnace hot air around the dirty handkerchief stuffed in her mouth and wondered how long she could stand the suffocating heat of the enclosed tent. Every moment, the tent grew hotter and the air more insufferable. Sweat poured from her body, soaking her dress until she wanted to scream with frustration and near panic. Her side ached where the rocky ground pressed against her ribs, and she shifted for the hundredth time, hoping for a little relief. The movement brought her face closer to the wall of the tent where she lay panting and frustrated.

Several minutes passed. Susan arched her back, reaching for her shoelace. Again, her head brushed the canvas, and a faint stirring of air touched her cheek. A tiny slash of light glared at her. For a moment, she stared numbly at the bright line. She had watched Dickson and Harlow trench around the base of the tent, burying the lower edge of the canvas walls with a heavy layer of dirt and rock. Harlow had complained with every shovel-full of the hard packed soil, but Beazer had insisted. Twenty minutes of hard digging had left every inch of the tent's edge covered.

Suddenly, she didn't care how or why the two had missed that tiny strip. She was just plain relieved to feel the touch of the outside air and see that little strip of light. She bumped her head against the canvas and felt the opening grow wider.

"Settle down in there, missy."

The voice at the front of the tent surprised her, though she had half expected someone to stay behind, ready to stop her if she tried to escape, someone resting in the shade of the canvas, watching.

Irritated, she reached for the laces of her shoe. She tugged angrily and the knot came loose with a sullen pop. A moment later, the stone flake sliced through her bonds like a freshly honed razor. Quietly, she sat in the semi-darkness of the tent. The tent was an oven, and sweat soaked her clothing, but she could breathe easier now that her hands and feet were no longer cinched up behind her back. Her first instinct was to slice the tent wall and run. Yet, anything, the slightest noise or even a chance impulse could move her guard to check on his captive. It would do no good to escape, only to be rounded up like a stray calf before she could find help. Joe Beazer was certain to be watching the way back into town, and she had little confidence, given the town's reputation, that she could find help once she got there.

I need a horse.

The thought was barely the flash of an idea, but the more she considered it, the better she liked it.

Collin would be following. She knew that just as she knew the sun would rise in the morning. Some things were that certain in life. But right now, she had a chance to escape and she was willing to risk it.

Carefully, using the razor thin edge of the obsidian flake, she sliced the wall of the tent.

"You're awful quiet in there, missy."

Suddenly, sunlight streaked through the tent's open door. "You been makin' a racket in here for over an hour. Now, you're all quiet." Susan felt her heart pound with panic. She was barely half-way through the cut in the canvas when Beazer's callused hand clamped down hard on her ankle. She kicked at him and felt the heel of her shoe smash against his groping hands.

"Damn it, woman!"

Beazer grabbed at her again. She clawed at the rocky soil heaped at the edge of the canvas, clenching dirt and stone in her fists.

"Got ya!"

Suddenly, she was dragged back into the tent and slammed to the ground.

"Stop squirmin' or I'll beat the sass out of ya!"

Yanking at one arm, Beazer threw her over, straddled her and pawed at the front of her dress.

"Might as well enjoy the wait," he sneered.

Buttons popped. Beazer leaned forward then froze as the fist sized rock in Susan's hand smashed the side of his head. For an instant, he seemed to waver, then he fell forward with his full weight pinning her to the ground.

"Get off me," she snarled. She shoved at Beazer's limp form, struggling beneath the man's weight. Finally, she staggered to her feet. Rock in hand, she stood over the man, ready to bash him again. But Beazer lay still.

Frustrated, she dropped the rock and strode angrily out of the tent and into the glare of late morning sunlight and the pungent odor of sagebrush and cattle. Beazer's gun belt dangled across a rotten tree stump near the tent. His horse was hobbled less than ten feet from the stump. Susan snatched up the gun belt, pulled the old navy revolver from a stained holster and spun the cylinder. Every chamber was loaded and capped.

Ten minutes later, she was a half mile south of town with a chunk of canvas and fifteen feet of rope rolled and draped across the pommel of Joe Beazer's saddle, and Joe Beazer's bay mare was running flat out for Ogden.

The town was just over a mile behind her when she slowed the mare to a trot—then finally to a walk. Thirty minutes later, she was five miles out, and Corinne was no longer visible. The sun was high and hot enough to blister the hide on a camel's hump when Susan reined in the mare and dismounted.

"Good thing I stole Beazer's hat," She told the mare.

The animal flicked one ear and stood quietly.

"Don't look at me like that," She muttered as she poured water from Beazer's water bag into the hat and shoved it under the mare's muzzle.

"He isn't dead," she informed the mare as the animal lapped greedily at the water. "I knocked him plenty hard, but he was breathing fine when we took out of there. Besides, he'll wish I *had* killed him if Collin gets hold of him."

The mare finished the water, and Susan slapped the damp hat on her head. Inwardly, she cringed at the thought of horse spit and Beazer's sweat-fouled hat touching her hair, but Beazer's saddle bags were poorly stocked with anything that would keep the sun from frying her brains, so she was stuck with the hat. Thoughtfully, she gathered up the reins and started walking south. She needed a plan. Ogden was still nearly forty miles south.

A full day.

If she pushed the mare and could keep up a good pace, it would take at least a full day. She tried to remember what she knew of the area, but it was too little.

Brigham City was to the east, near the canyon leading into the mountains and north to Logan City. Sooner or later, if she kept riding south, she would probably have to cross one of the meandering curves of the Bear River and if she wasn't careful, she could end up wading through the marshy wetlands near the shores of the Great Salt Lake. That path might throw off any pursuit, but it would surely add another miserable day to the ride. She would have to veer east eventually or take a chance of running right into the lake.

"We can't do that," she told the mare. "We can't waste that much time. As soon as Beazer finds another horse, he's going to gather up some help and come after us."

She looked south-east to where the western cliffs of Ben Lomond Peak sloped downward to form a boulder strewn ridge that stabbed like a finger pointing at the belly of the Great Salt Lake.

That's where I need to go, she thought suddenly.

It was the fastest route, but it was also the route Beazer would expect her to take, and he would ride hard to catch her before she could cross the point of the ridge near the hot springs.

She thought of riding east to Brigham City, but immediately discarded the possibility. A small dust cloud moved in that direction already, and if Beazer had sent riders in that direction, they would cut her off and corner her before she got anywhere near the town.

Suddenly, she doubted her decision to leave Corinne. She might have found help there, if she hadn't given in to her fears and run away. Now, she had no choice but to go on and hope she could stay ahead of Beazer and his men. Reluctantly, and painfully aware that Beazer's saddle fit her like a pair of worn out, hand-me-down shoes, Susan climbed into the saddle.

She looked back toward Corinne. A small cloud of dust now rose between her and the town, drifting slowly eastward on the breeze.

That settles it, she thought.

"I hope Collin is somewhere near the hot springs," she muttered, "because that's about where Beazer will catch up with us."

Ten miles south of town, Susan suddenly reined the mare to a stop.

They're not going to track me. It would take too long, and they might not be good enough to find my trail and still close the gap between us.

No. They would try something else. They *were* trying something else. The first dust she had seen must have been several horsemen riding east to Brigham City to force her away from that route while the second group of riders followed her and forced her south. The first bunch would

surely try to outdistance her and wait for the second bunch
to herd her like a dumb animal. If she tried to outrun them,
she would be herded right into their trap. No matter how
badly she wanted to run straight to Ogden City, that option
would only get her caught.

She looked back to the east, toward Brigham City,
wishing now that she had ridden there as quickly as she
could. She might have made it, and she might have found
help with the town's sheriff, but she had let her fear of
Beazer and his men cloud her thinking and fill her with
distrust and doubt of anyone she didn't know. She knew it
was an unreasonable fear. She had known it when she
turned away from Brigham City and headed south. But
now, she was cut off from that possibility. Her own fear had
turned her south, and now she would pay for that fear with
a forty-mile ride that could easily turn into several days of
dodging Beazer and his men.

It's not fair, she thought, feeling as though the world had
suddenly turned against her. "I should be home taking care
of little Sarah and doing my chores," she muttered angrily.
But she did like riding and camping, and she could
remember the family outings they had taken and the time
Collin had let her shoot a mule deer while they were
hunting in Little Cottonwood Canyon. She hadn't enjoyed
the killing, although she had felt a certain thrill of
accomplishment over a fine shot. But she had enjoyed the
meat that winter and venison had become a favorite very
quickly in the Mitchell home.

But this was no family outing, no quiet ride through the
foothills north of the Avenues. It would be a hunt and she
was the rabbit, with a dozen wolves on her trail. That was
something she couldn't afford to forget for even one
moment.

Toward Corinne, dust continued to rise into the sky. She
watched over her shoulder as the breeze carried the dust
cloud.

"I refuse to let them herd me until I have nowhere to go," she told the mare grimly. "So, we'll go southwest instead. There must be nearly five-hundred square miles between here and Ogden. There's no way Beazer can have men hunting every foot of it."

Yet, Beazer held the high ground, and a single man on a high point could see for miles across the relatively flat ground of the ancient lake bed. Somehow, she must make Beazer and his men complacent enough to sit still and wait for her to come to them.

The sun had reached its zenith. She could feel the furnace-like weight of its heat bearing down on her shoulders. The thin breeze from the west did nothing to cool the air and brought with it nothing but the odor of rotting vegetation.

Reflexively, she covered her mouth and nose with one hand. The odor reminded her of a place where too many dogs had done their business. It was the kind of odor a man might grow used to, but neither she nor any of the women she knew had ever become accustomed to the smell. It assaulted the senses at its first touch, and only by conscious effort could it be ignored. Luckily, the odor arose only when the winds of a storm agitated the waters of the lake and carried the stink towards the mountains where anyone could judge how badly it reeked. It reeked now, but she knew that it would soon dissipate with the wind; so, she fought her offended sensibilities and ignored the odor.

She nudged Beazer's mare and reined the animal onto a narrow trail heading to the southwest. The land was dry and nearly barren of vegetation. It was a seemingly desolate place to anyone familiar with the lush greenness of Missouri and Illinois—places she hardly remembered but had heard of often enough.

For Susan, however, the land was as starkly beautiful as it had been when she was a child. She loved the desert dryness, the ubiquitous sagebrush, and the sparse covering of salt grass. She loved the wind and the thunder and the lightning of a storm rushing over the lake and into the valley. She loved the farms and the smell of cattle and horses. But mostly, she loved how the evening sun seemed to sink into the lake and set the sky ablaze with the fires of heaven. If she had been an artist, she could have painted it every evening; if a poet, she could have written it every evening. As it was, she simply watched in awe when the lake swallowed the sun and the sky flamed with red-orange fire.

Now, the sun was at its apex and though she wanted rest and shade, she knew Beazer and his men would not stop, and they would not rest until they finished what they had started. They would not relent and neither must she.

Unexpectedly, the trail disappeared, and the ground fell away, down a steep embankment to the slow, meandering waters of the Bear River. The mare took the sandy bank in three lunging jumps, and Susan felt herself losing her seat. She grabbed at the animal's mane, clinging desperately.

"You danged hammerhead," she growled, subconsciously imitating Mitchell's talks with the dun. "Are you trying to break my neck?"

The mare strained against the reins as though the jump down the bank had fired her up to a run. Sensing the futility of trying to hold the animal back, Susan eased off the reins and grabbed for the saddle horn.

With the tension on the bit suddenly gone, the mare dug in hard and leaped forward. Susan clawed at the big snubbing horn as the animal galloped down the shoreline, hooves gouging the soft sediments for a hundred yards, before the shore was suddenly gone, blending into the steep bank once again. The mare crow-hopped to a stop and shook her head, rattling the bit.

Heart pounding with the rush of the gallop, Susan stroked the mare's neck, wondering what had gotten into the animal. She searched the opposite bank of the river, but she saw nothing that would account for the mare's skittishness and the sudden run down the river bank.

"We could stop and rest here for awhile," she told the mare. "There's a bit of shade here. That old cottonwood makes a fine shade tree and the breeze coming off the water is awfully nice." After a moment, she dismounted and led the mare to the water's edge where the animal dipped its big head and drank greedily.

Cautiously, Susan moved a pace upstream from the animal and hunkered down to fill her stolen canteen. She poured out the tepid, evil tasting remnants and sank the big jug into the cold freshness of the river. The wide mouth of the jug chugged at the river and spat mist like a geyser, but she paid little attention to the canteen, for the mare had suddenly pricked up her ears and now watched their back-trail expectantly.

Someone is on the bank above.

The thought was sudden and so strong that it made the hair on the back of her neck stand on end. Quickly, she dragged the canteen from the river, moved to the mare's side and yanked the Colt from Beazer's greasy holster. No sound came from the trail above, but the mare's ears still twitched, and Susan knew that the high, sandy bank would block much of the sound that might otherwise have reached her less sensitive ears. She felt her pulse rise in her throat.

Suddenly, a horseman appeared at the edge of the cut bank, following the tracks of the mare. The horseman hesitated for an instant then touched his spurs to his reluctant mount. The animal plunged down the bank and turned toward Susan.

The rider was less than forty yards away when she lifted the Colt and cocked the hammer. The rider reined his horse to a stop, waiting. Susan stared at the man over the notched tip of the Colt's hammer. The man looked vaguely familiar, yet unthreatening. Suddenly, her heart began to pound and her hands to shake.

"You don't need to kill him."

Susan looked over her shoulder to where Mort stood on the bank above her in the shade of a tall old cottonwood.

"My first thought was to kill him too, but the voice... he talked me out of it," the old man announced.

"Mort?"

"Lead your horse around those willows," he told her. "The bank gets lower just the other side and you can get up here on higher ground."

"I thought I'd have to cross the river," Susan answered.

"We probably will," the old man admitted," but we got six riders headed this way. We can't outrun them now, and I don't want to be swimming the river when they get here. We'd be sittin' ducks."

The old man watched as Susan led the mare around the willows and up the bank. The Pratt kid, obviously shaken by this near meeting with a bullet, followed silently until they were both at Mort's side beneath the cottonwood.

"Mitchell's a bit farther down river," Daniel reported solemnly.

"Get Susan behind the tree," Mort ordered grimly.

Still gripping Beazer's navy Colt, Susan edged the mare behind the wide trunk of the cottonwood and waited. Daniel nudged his horse up beside the tree, hemming Susan's mare between his own mount and the edge of the cut bank. The kid drew a short barreled .50 caliber Sharps from its scabbard, cocked the hammer back and rested the butt on his thigh.

"They might try talkin'," Mort growled, "but sooner or later they'll start shootin'. Shoot straight, kid, and don't stop 'til they're all on the ground. One of 'em's a skin walker an' he ain't gonna quit unless you put 'im down."

"What the blazes is a skin walker?" the kid yelped.

Moments later, the six riders plowed to a stop less than fifty yards away.

"That's my horse behind that tree, mister." The lead rider leaned forward a bit and stood in the stirrups. "That gal stole my horse an' I'll have 'er back."

"I reckon all you're gonna get is a chunk of lead, 'cause I ain't waitn' for no jury to hang you," Mort snarled.

Beazer's fat cheeks puffed out like the ruff on a grouse. Angrily, he grabbed at the pistol shoved behind his belt. The gun was barely clear when Mort's slug smashed his breastbone, flinging the kidnapper out of the saddle.

CHAPTER 14

Utah Territory
Ogden—September 1868

A hundred yards down river, Mitchell spurred the dun out of the river bottom and turned towards the cottonwoods just as the crack of Mort's pistol split the air. He spurred the dun into a gallop, heard the roar of the Pratt kid's Sharps and saw one of the horsemen dumped from his saddle. Fifty yards, and he was within range— twenty more and he was in the fray, the pistol in his fist belching smoke and lead. Suddenly, the afternoon thundered with the roar of gunfire and the angry buzz of flying lead.

The dun threw back its head and screamed, and Mitchell felt the stinging spray of flesh and the molten kiss of lead as a bullet sheared off the tip of the dun's left ear and gouged a trench in his gun belt. The dun slowed and came to a stop. Mitchell swayed in the saddle then dropped to the ground, yanked the long barreled Navy Colt from his belt and scooted behind a small cluster of Russian olive trees. He snapped off two shots, both of them wild and doing no harm, then scrambled for better cover as one of the horsemen charged toward him, firing his pistol as fast as he could thumb back the hammer.

At once, branches, leaves, and bark exploded in a swarm of lead as Mitchell became the closest stationary target. He dove to the ground and felt molten fire tug at his shirt sleeve even as the Colt in his hand roared, blasting out smoke and a forty-four caliber slug. The rider yelled and grabbed at his knee, and at the last moment, his charging mount veered, hooves gouging the ground, kicking a spray of dirt and fragmented sediments into Mitchell's face. The animal smashed through the spiked branches of the olive trees, crashed to its knees and plowed head-long into the trunk of a towering cottonwood. An instant later, the rider speared the solid mass of the tree like a long shafted dart. The dying horse struggled to rise then toppled over, blood covering its chest where Mitchell's bullet had punched through and into the rider's knee.

Abruptly, the shooting stopped. Gun smoke drifted, dispersing quickly as the breeze shredded plumes of sulfurous vapor into wispy tendrils. For a moment, all was quiet.

"That's the lot of 'em, Mitchell!"

Mort's bellow broke the silence, yet somehow infused the moment with a sense of rough justice and finality. The old man's tone seemed like a stamp of approval, and Mitchell felt a sudden release of all the anger he'd managed to gather up in the last two days. And with the anger, a far heavier burden seemed to dissipate, leaving him with a curious feeling of tranquility.

"Best come over here and take care of your gal," Mort added loudly as Mitchell dragged himself to his feet and collected the dun. "Blasted mare dumped her," the old man grumbled, taking the dun as Mitchell knelt at Susan's side. "I don't think she's hurt," he added. "Just bumped her head on a tree root or somethin'."

Mitchell knelt and scooped the woman into his arms just as her eyes opened.

"Collin?" Susan murmured.

"Yep. It's me," he answered quietly.

"My head hurts," She moaned softly.

"Your horse threw you, and you hit your head," he replied.

Mort knelt beside her, offering her water from his canteen. "Howdy ma'am," he said quietly.

"Hello, Mort," she said quietly. "It's good to see you again."

"I'm glad to see you too," the old man replied.

"Is it my time?" She asked.

"No, darlin', not 'til you're very old. 'Til then, you needn't worry about that."

"You goin' to hang me?" the boy asked suddenly.

"I might just shoot you," Mitchell growled. "Takes less time."

"I told 'em I didn't want nothin' to do with no kidnappin', but Dickson said you wouldn't care about that. Said you'd hang me anyway, 'cause I was in on it. Said I'd hang for sure if we was caught."

"Well, you're caught," Mitchell barked, "and much as I'd like to stretch that scrawny neck of yours, Mort won't let me."

The kid gave Mort a sidewise glance. "I'd rather hang than go to prison."

"Ah, shut up," Mitchell demanded. "You're makin' me tired. We ain't hangin' you, and we ain't sendin' you to prison. But you are going to help us figure out what the hell is going on." Mitchell lifted the girl in his arms. The kid took the canvas from Susan's saddle, folded it, and set it under the cottonwood. Gently, Mitchell set his wife on the tarp.

"Start off by telling me who Dickson and Harlow were working for," he told the kid.

"I wish I knew," protested the boy, "but they never told me nothin'."

"Listen, Daniel," Mort advised. "Your pa will take the strap to you for sure if we tell 'im what you been up to."

"How'd you know my name?"

"I know everybody's name, boy," Mort answered.

"I'd tell if I knew," Daniel answered, giving the old man a narrow glare. "All I know is that Dickson met with someone in Ogden. Dickson said the man was payin' us to guard a package to Corinne and get a fellow away from Ogden for a week or so. Dickson never told me why, and when he grabbed your wife off the steps of the hotel, I was scared stupid. All I could think to do was follow him and try to keep them from hurtin' her."

"Who was the man you shot in the saloon?" Mitchell asked.

"Don't know his name," Daniel answered. "I just know he was talkin' real friendly with Harlow, and they were both talkin' about comin' back to see your wife soon as they killed you."

"His name was Crawford," Mort responded. "He spent some time in Arizona, but he's been in Utah Territory about six months."

"Did you ever see the man who hired Dickson?" Mitchell asked the boy.

"Once, but I was too far away to see his face. Looked like he dressed real good. I never seen a horse or buggy though. So, he must have walked to the meeting."

"Where was the meeting?"

"In front of the Fife and Douglas smithy, on Fifth and Main."

"Where were you?"

"They sent me over to Browning's place to wait. Guess they didn't trust me."

Mitchell glared at the boy. "How old are you?" he demanded

"Seventeen."

"Collin, please." Susan touched his arm, and Mitchell felt his anger dissipate.

"I'm goin' to watch you like a hawk, boy. If you ever do anything to make me regret lettin' you go, I'll hunt you down and shoot you on the spot. That clear?"

"Yes, sir."

Suddenly, Mort clutched his belly. "I'm starved," he protested.

"It's barely past noon," Mitchell retorted.

"An' I ain't had a bite since early this morning."

"You hungry?" Mitchell asked the girl.

"Famished," she replied.

"I saw an eatin' place back in town," Mort confided.

Mitchell looked back toward Corinne. "That's twelve or fifteen miles back the wrong way. I'd rather not go back to Corinne just now."

"I reckon some folks back there ain't too fond of *us* right now," the old man agreed. "Maybe we ought to catch us a fat jackrabbit an' cook 'im up?"

CHAPTER 15

Utah Territory
Ogden—September 1868

*S*arah's walk back to the hotel was quiet and uneventful. It was early September. The days were still hot, but a few unseasonably cold nights, a number of them blowing cold rains, had taken their toll on the trees. The leaves were beginning to change colors and littered the ground in a carpet that shifted with every touch of the morning breeze.

Even the Lady-dog seemed to sense the change, turning herself into a multi-colored streak that barked at every stray cat and chased through backyards in a joyful, dirt tossing frenzy, and by the time Sarah climbed the steps of the hotel veranda, it was a dust covered dog that panted happily at her side.

"Mrs. Mitchell?"

The voice behind her was familiar, but one she had hoped to avoid. She turned, looking down from the veranda of the hotel. The handsome woman striding purposefully across Main Street was Mrs. Richards of the suffrage movement.

"Good morning, Mrs. Richards."

"These streets are a disgrace," panted the woman. She shook her skirts and stomped the mud from her shoes before lowering her skirt to the proper position. "It's like living in India, or some other backward and uncivilized village."

Sarah watched as Mrs. Richards mounted the hotel veranda and shuffled her feet in an attempt to rid herself of the vulgar touch of the unrefined. The affectation irritated

Sarah. She doubted the woman had ever been to India, and she resented the backhanded slur against the people of the Territory. Utah was part of a growing and changing western culture. No one had a right to denigrate the hard work of the people who had built this place, especially an outsider who saw herself as superior to the barbarians of the Territory.

"I understand they've been discussing ways of paving the streets," Sarah answered.

"And they will discuss it until we are all drowning in mud," the woman countered. "You know as well as I do that the Mormons control everything here. They will call meetings to plan meetings. In ten years, the streets will still be mud and horse droppings."

"That's entirely possible," Sarah acknowledged, "but I'm sure progress will be made."

"Only when the women of this territory are free from the perversions of this society," Mrs. Richards snapped.

Sarah waited, expecting the woman to work herself into a fiery tirade. But the woman fell silent as two bearded men passed on the street below.

"We are planning a large assembly next month," she said when the men were gone. "I've spoken with a few of the leading women in our movement, and we have agreed that you and your family could play an important role in helping lift the women of this territory out of their fiendish predicament."

"Mrs. Richards," Sarah protested, "I think I should explain something to you."

"My dear," the woman interrupted, "if you are trying to explain your sister's shameful attentions to Mr. Mitchell, you needn't. I saw the way she looked at him the other afternoon. I'm sure things will work out for you. I'm sure it's just an infatuation. When she meets the right young man, she will stop mooning over your husband."

The Richards woman planted herself in an empty chair then scooted up to a vacant table. "This assembly will make political history," she said, waving a hand at a nearby waitress.

"Two cups of tea," she called to the woman. "We would like you to speak at the assembly," she continued. "You have an eloquent manner about you Sarah…. May I call you Sarah?"

"I suppose…."

"Wonderful. Now, your speech should relate to the difficulties of women in a Society dominated by men. You grew up here, I understand."

"Yes…."

"Then you should have some marvelous insights into the way women are treated here, but you will need to be very adroit in presenting your information. There will be a number of Mormon women attending. They want the vote, but we could easily lose their support if we push too strongly against polygamy."

"Mrs. Richards, you don't understand."

"Now, don't be skittish. You will do fine."

Sarah watched in amazement as Mrs. Richards stood, adjusted her skirts and walked away. The woman had simply plowed straight ahead like a team fitted with blinders, ignoring everything that did not fit within her narrow view of the world.

"Your tea ma'am."

Sarah took a dime from her handbag, and when the waitress had gone, she sat quietly contemplating the empty chair and the cooling cup of tea.

"May I sit down?"

Startled, Sarah looked up at the owner of the soft, hesitant voice. The woman glanced furtively up the street then back to Sarah.

"Please, do sit down, Mrs. Miller."

"Please, don't call me that," the woman protested.

"Why ever not?"

"It was a mistake to marry that man. I want to be rid of the name and the man more than I ever wanted anything."

"I suppose you have your reasons," Sarah replied cautiously.

"I have reasons that would burn your ears, Sister Mitchell. But my word would mean little. Vernon holds a rather high position in the Church. I want a divorce, but Vernon will never allow it. He will never allow his reputation to be soiled by a divorce. He's like a man with two faces. In public, he is mild, considerate, and the picture of righteousness. In private...." Deborah Miller took a deep breath then forced herself to continue. "In private, he is a brute, and a wicked, perverted man."

"I don't understand. Why are you coming to me?"

"I want a divorce, so I can make a life somewhere else and perhaps marry someone decent."

"How does that concern me? Just leave the man."

"You know as well as I do that the law will not protect me."

Sarah knew. Probably every married woman in the country knew that in the United States and its territories, a married woman had few rights, if any. She simply became the property of her husband, and anything she owned became his as well. It was an impossible situation for a woman like Deborah Miller; for if she left Vernon Miller, he might simply send the Sheriff and have her dragged home. Under the law, she had no right to sue for divorce, and if she somehow convinced the man to grant her one, she might very well leave without a penny. Sarah was well aware of the woman's plight, and she was certain that Vernon Miller was unprincipled enough to take advantage of the situation.

"My father left me a large sum when he died last year," the girl confided, "but Vernon took the money and hid it away. Now, he acts as though it never existed. I could live on that inheritance, if I could lay my hands on it.

"I understand your situation Mrs. ... Deborah, but I don't understand what you think I can do about it."

"I'm prepared to let Vernon have the money, but I never told anyone about the property that Papa owned. Papa put that land in my name before he died. Papa said it was good land, and he was going to raise some cattle and farm the rest."

"So, you have some property," Sarah responded. "Could you live there?"

"As soon as Vernon found out, he would have me in court and do his best to take every square inch of that property."

"Quite possibly, but I fail to see what you think I can do about it."

"Not you, Sister Mitchell. Your husband."

"I don't understand."

"I know who you are, Sister Mitchell. You grew up here. But more importantly, I know who Brother Mitchell is."

"Something about that statement worries me."

Sarah searched the woman's face for a hint of what she knew.

"I know that your husband owns half of a silver mine in Colorado."

The information surprised Sarah and irritated her at the same time. Collin had said nothing to her about any mine in Colorado.

"I want to sell my property to your husband."

"I'm not sure he would be interested," Sarah protested.

"I think he will be," Deborah countered. "You see. There is a very nice vein of gold on the property. Papa took some of it and cashed it in before he died. That was the money Vernon took.

"I've had an offer for the property. Heaven only knows how they knew it was mine, but I don't trust them, and I think Vernon suspects something. That property is mine, not Vernon's. I won't let him take it from me."

Deborah glanced quickly about then turned back to Sarah. "I saw how you reacted to Vernon's attentions this morning. You must know how badly I want out, but I can't do it on my own. Vernon would never dare to do anything if your husband owned the land and the mineral rights. With the money from the land, and a share of the profits from any mine we develop, I could leave the Territory and start over."

"You would still need a divorce, and you said Mr. Miller would never agree," Sarah replied.

"That's true. But your husband knows President Young."

Sarah now understood what the woman knew. "Yes, he does."

"Don't worry. I won't tell anyone why Brother Mitchell is in Ogden."

"He's here to buy some land," Sarah advised.

"Definitely," Deborah agreed, "and I have just the land he is looking for."

"How did you know about his work?" Sarah asked.

"I was in Salt Lake last year when he arrested Aaron Sykes. And I remember hearing about how you met him ten years ago."

Sarah sat quietly, contemplating everything Deborah had said. "Where is your property?" she asked quietly.

"Northwest of Logan."

"How much land?"

"Ten sections."

"And how much do you want for it?"

"Ten dollars an acre."

"What!" For a moment, Sarah nearly choked. She calculated the amount in her head and took a swallow of lukewarm tea. Sixty-four thousand dollars was an outrageous price. "You can't be serious."

"That includes half interest in the mineral rights," Deborah protested.

"And what if the vein just disappears?" Sarah argued. "Gold often does that you know."

"I'm willing to work things out," Deborah retorted. "I just want to make an honest and fair deal."

"I'll tell you what," Sarah proposed. "You sell the land and half the mineral rights for two dollars an acre. If the vein is there, we will pay you one half of the profits plus one dollar per acre each year for eight years, unless the mine fails. After that, we'll pay you one-half of the profits from the mine."

Deborah Miller sat quietly for a moment then nodded. "I agree. If the vein disappears, I'll still get a fair price for the land."

"Now we just have to convince Collin," Sarah warned. "And the land had better be as good as you say, or he won't be interested."

"He will want to look at the property," Deborah concluded. "The boundaries are described in the deed. Your husband can copy those, and I'll draw a map so you can look at everything."

"I have to warn you, Deborah," Sarah confided. "This may not work. Collin has already looked at some property near trapper's loop. He's considering it very strongly."

"I understand, but I don't have any other choice. Vernon is well liked here, and he has all the right connections."

"I see."

"He lied when you asked him about the ear-cuff."

"They weren't buried with his first wife?"

"I don't know about that. All I know is that he lied about something. He has an odd little gesture with one hand when he lies."

"I had the feeling that he lied about the woman who asked about the ear-cuffs," Sarah admitted.

"I think the only person who ever asked about them was Vernon."

"Why did *he* ask? Surely he knew she had them made."

Deborah bit her lip and stood. "She never had them made," she said softly, "and he never discovered who gave them to her."

"She had a lover?"

"I don't know, but she wanted a divorce. Vernon refused. She finally lost heart and died of an unhealthy dose of rat poison."

"Oh, dear."

"She didn't kill herself," Deborah said quietly. "She thought Vernon had poisoned her. Rat poison will not be my way out. Please talk with your husband." Deborah Miller turned and left without another word.

Sarah watched the woman hurry to the corner of Sixth and Main where she turned east and disappeared from sight. She pondered what she had just learned from Miller's young and unhappy wife. Ruth Miller had been given the ear-cuffs, and Vernon Miller had tried, but had never discovered who had given them to his wife.

Why? She wondered suddenly. *Why would a man like Vernon Miller dress his wife's body with a gift from her lover?* It seemed more likely that Miller would have destroyed the ear-cuffs in a fit of rage. And that was only part of it. The man had acted as though he hardly remembered the ear-cuffs. Sarah couldn't believe that anything so threatening to Vernon Miller's pride would ever settle into the fog of forgetfulness. The man remembered every detail related to those ear-cuffs, and he had simply lied about it.

But did it matter? Miller's lies might have no bearing on Lester Reynald's death or the ear-cuff.... In Sarah's mind the ear-cuff was the key to the murder.

Back to Nephi Clarke, she thought. *That man didn't tell me everything*.

CHAPTER 16

Utah Territory
Ogden—September 1868

*I*t was late afternoon when Mitchell helped Susan into the saddle. The skies over the lake had grown ominously dark with the wraith like clouds of a fast moving thunder storm. Mort, now filled with jack-rabbit, ranged ahead, happily relating his escapades to a bewildered seventeen-year-old.

Mitchell and Susan followed close behind, taking an easy pace.

"I like your earrings," Mitchell confided.

Susan smiled brightly and touched her fingers to the back of one ear. "You should," she answered. "You picked them."

"Well, you make them look much better."

"You're a flirt," she protested. "But you needn't worry about me falling apart over a bad experience."

"I thought I might console you."

The girl grinned mischievously. "I'd like that. But I don't think we need an audience." She nodded toward their companions.

"Hmm."

"Did Nephi tell you about his earrings?" She asked.

"He told me he'd made only one pair of plain silver ear-cuffs," Mitchell responded.

"Did you show him the one you found?"

"I did, and he told me it was a mighty good likeness of the ones he made for an old woman a few years back."

"But it wasn't one of them?"

"He said the old woman died, and she was wearing the earrings when they buried her."

"Old woman? Why would he describe Ruth Miller as an old woman?" Susan protested. "And if he made only one pair, someone must have made copies," she concluded. "But who?"

"Doctor Wadman seemed convinced they were Indian jewelry," Mitchell replied.

"I suppose," she answered. "But, I've watched Nephi Clarke make silver jewelry since I was a little girl. It just looks so much like his work. That's why I went to see him."

"Would he lie?" Mitchell wondered.

"Never. Well…. I don't think he would."

"Then, Wadman may be right."

Susan frowned. "Maybe there's another silversmith in town," she suggested.

"You don't seem taken with Wadman's idea."

"I'm not."

"Tell me why," he prompted.

The girl shrugged and brushed at her skirts. "Because, we already know that Nephi made some exactly like them, and we have no evidence that Indians made anything like them."

"So, Nephi made a second pair then forgot all about it?"

"Maybe…." She hesitated. "I just don't know."

"All right," Mitchell conceded. "Let's just think about all the possibilities, and tomorrow, we'll sit down with Sarah and see what we come up with."

"That sounds fine," she answered. "Sarah was going to visit Sister Dalton. Maybe she learned something helpful."

It was evening when they finally stopped. Mitchell was saddle weary, and he could see that Susan was played out. She was as feminine and desirable as a woman could be, but he knew she would hang on until the last dog was hung. He caught her as she climbed down from the saddle. The dun stood patiently while he held the girl.

"I'd go out and shoot us a rabbit for dinner," Mort confided, "but this ain't a good place to be wanderin' around shootin' things."

"Why not?" asked Mitchell.

The old man pointed toward the lake. "Shoshoni camp just west of here and a bunch of Utes to the south. They might not take kindly to us."

Susan stared into the gathering darkness. "You think we should move on?" she asked quietly.

"I haven't heard of anyone havin' trouble with them up here," Mort answered. "But it won't hurt to be watchful."

Mitchell looked to the west where the sunset was casting an orange glow on the waters of the Great Salt Lake.

"It'll be dark soon. I think we've all had a long day."

"Just what I was figurin'," Mort replied. "I'll build a fire an' throw on some beans."

"It's gonna rain soon," the kid suggested halfheartedly. The boy's voice was hesitant, as though unsure of where he stood with Mitchell.

"It does," Mitchell agreed, looking out over the lake.

"What's your family name kid?" Mitchell asked. He was still watching the flash of lighting over the lake. The boy was silent.

"Name's Pratt," said Mort. "One of Orson's boys.... Least wise Orson adopted him when his real ma and pa died back in fifty-seven—Samuel and Mary Pratt. No relation to Orson, but Orson took him in, and Orson would kick his tail if he knew what Danny here has been up to."

Daniel Pratt stared at the old man. The look on his face was a combination of shock and terror similar to the look he might have after stepping on a rattler.

"Don't let Mort throw you," Mitchell cautioned. "He knows everyone's name. Him bein' the angel of death an' all."

"You know my pa?"

"Not personal like," Mort answered. "Kind of a demanding cuss though."

The boy frowned. "That's why I run off. Nothin' I did made him happy."

"Reckon you was wastin' your time on that," Mort advised. "Only Orson can make Orson happy. Kind of a state of mind. Your real pa, Samuel, was a good man, but he just never got the hang of bein' a farmer. Your folks was always poor, right up 'til the pneumonia finally got 'em."

The old man picked up a few pieces of kindling then moved off into the brush looking for more.

"Is he really the *angel of death*?" the boy asked Susan quietly.

Susan looked up from their supply packs. She had been looking for something more appetizing than the beans Mort had suggested. For a moment, she said nothing.

"He may need a bath and some clean clothes," she admitted finally, "but when my time comes, I don't think I'll mind if it's Mort who comes to take me home."

"Crazy old goat tried to shoot me one time," Mitchell complained, "but he sure knows a lot of folks who ain't got a notion who *he* is... gives me goose bumps sometimes."

"So, what are you goin' to do to me?" the boy asked.

"Reckon I ain't going to do anything to you," Mitchell replied. "You can go home to your folks if you want, or you can get some work and make a start for yourself. Just stay out of trouble."

"I'll stay outa trouble, but I ain't goin' home. I'm just one more mouth to feed."

"Then you'd better find work," Mitchell responded, "Because you're still going to have that mouth to feed."

"He could work for us," Susan suggested.

Mitchell looked at his wife. He thought he knew her reasons for making the suggestion, but he hoped she was using good judgment.

"You partial to that idea?" he asked, halfway hoping the boy would decline.

The boy nodded eagerly. "Yes sir."

Mitchell glared at the slate hard ground, trying to understand what Susan expected of him. "Fine," he said finally. "I'll work you hard most times, but I ain't a slave driver, and I'll pay you fair."

For a moment, Mitchell felt a twinge of gut wrenching fear and wondered if Susan was chafing a bit at the difficulties of a polygamous lifestyle.

"I understand," the Pratt kid answered.

"We'll work six days a week, unless I decide different," Mitchell continued, "and I'll pay you two dollars a day. That's about what they're payin' for labor at the lumber mills. When wages go up at the mills, I'll pay you more. If things don't work out, or you think the pay ain't enough, you come and talk with me. I don't want any hard feelings 'cause one of us thinks he's getting' the short end of the bargain. That sound fair to you?"

"Sounds fair, but I'll have to find a place to live."

"Where have you been living since you left home?"

"I stayed with some relatives in Salt Lake for about a week, but the last month or so I've just been campin' out and fendin' as best I could."

"Well, that'll have to end." Mitchell nodded toward Susan. "We've made plans to buy some land and raise a few head of cattle and some horses. I've found a place I'm thinking of buying. The owner has twelve sections. He's asking two dollars an acre. If I decide to buy the land, I'll sell forty acres to you at the same price. We can build you a place there. If we don't take that land, I'll make you the same offer wherever we settle."

"That's more than fair," the boy answered, "but I'll need at least a hundred-and-twenty acres. If you're willin' to sell 'em to me."

"A hundred and twenty?"

"If things don't work out, I'll need a place big enough to support a family."

"I reckon so," Mitchell answered. He paused for a moment, looking into the gathering darkness. "A hundred-and-twenty will be fine with me.

"Now," he said, nodding to the west, "keep your hand away from that pistol. We got company."

Mitchell moved to Susan's side, standing between her and the shadowy movement among the trees.

"Hello the camp!" Mort's call broke through the sound of wind whipping the trees.

"Who's that with you?" Mitchell demanded.

"Shoshoni," the old man replied. "Feller called Two Bears and some of his cronies. They've been watchin' for a bunch of Shoshoni from up north, an' saw us ride up. They want us to ride down to their camp."

The old man and the Shoshoni had stopped just outside the camp. Now, they stood waiting.

"They peaceable," demanded Mitchell, "or are they holdin' a knife to your throat?"

"They're peaceable," the old man replied. "They're just nervous about that storm a comin' in. Looks to be a bad one."

"Come ahead then," Mitchell responded, "but come careful."

The shadowy figures moved closer and finally coalesced into Mort and four Shoshoni braves. Mort raised a hand in greeting.

"How," he said. "We come in peace."

A large feather protruded from his battered hat. Susan clapped a hand over her mouth, nearly choking with laughter. One of the Shoshoni stepped forward.

"Mort makes a rather strange Shoshoni," he said, "but he has it right. We didn't come up here to cause trouble."

"That's right," Mort agreed.

"This storm looks pretty bad," the Shoshoni continued. "It didn't look as though you were very well prepared, and when we saw you had a woman with you.... Well—we thought you might fare better in our camp."

"Speaks good English, don't he," Mort observed happily.

"You speak very well," Susan told the Shoshoni.

"Thank you," the man replied. "I spent two years with a Mormon family in Salt Lake City. I had a knack for English."

Mitchell stepped forward and stuck out his hand. "I'm Collin Mitchell," he said, "and this is my wife, Susan. Mort you've already met, and Daniel here is a friend from down south."

"Pleased to meet you. I'm called Two Bears. My friends are Crazy Antelope, Little Elk, and Brother Joseph."

Each of the men stepped forward and solemnly shook hands. They were cleaner and more agreeable than Mitchell expected, and Susan was unexpectedly pleased at their greeting.

Two Bears shook her hand gently. "Brother Joseph is a baptized Mormon," he announced congenially. "He goes to church on Sundays, but he comes out here to live with his people."

"You're not a Mormon?" Susan asked.

"Never took with me," Two Bears replied. "I'm leaning that way, but I still value the beliefs of my people. So, I'm just undecided for now."

"How far is your camp?" Mitchell asked, pointing to the southwest and the storm clouds twisting the sky.

"Not far," the Shoshoni answered. "But the wind is getting worse. We should hurry."

They hadn't ridden far when Two Bears spoke quickly to his friends. A moment later, Crazy Antelope kicked his shaggy little mustang and rode hard to the west. Mitchell was puzzled, but soon decided that any prudent man would send word that he was bringing guests for dinner. An imprudent man would either change his ways quickly, or live a life of misery. Two Bears appeared to have learned his lesson. No doubt the woman of the house would be forewarned of their coming, as would the leader of the band.

They reached the Shoshoni camp less than half-an-hour later. By then, the wind had increased to gale force and Mitchell was ready to call it a day.

"I apologize for not bringing you into my home," Two Bears said as they dismounted before two large tents.

Militia tents by the look of them, Mitchell thought.

Two Bears pulled back the flap of one tent, ushering them inside. "My home is not large, and with four children…. I thought you might like some privacy; so I had Crazy Antelope round up some help and set these up for you.

"I traded with the Utes for the tents," he confided. "I'd be willing to trade them to you if you want them." He clapped Mitchell on the shoulder with a familiarity that surprised Mitchell more than the tents had. "I'll give you a few minutes to get settled then I'll be back with something for you to eat. It looks as though you'll need blankets too."

When the Shoshoni was gone, Mitchell settled Susan within the tent and began unloading their gear. He was barely finished when Two Bears returned.

"Am I disturbing you?" the Shoshoni asked as he peered inside the tent.

"No." Susan answered. "You're quite welcome."

Two Bears frowned. "I wanted to speak with you about something that is difficult for me. I'm not sure I can explain without saying something that might offend."

"Have your say," prompted Mitchell. "You've treated us well. I don't see any reason why you'd want to hurt us now."

"Then I'll try." Two Bears sat by the fire and folded his long legs. "Mort says that you'll soon meet with a man who is my enemy."

"Mort says a lot of things," Mitchell replied cautiously.

"When the angel of death speaks, you ought to listen," Two Bears suggested.

"Reckon so."

"This man has injured me three times," Two Bears said suddenly." He poked at the fire with a stick then continued. "My people have lived here for a long time. When they pass on to the next life, we bury them according to our traditions. When we do this, we place things with them—things that were their own and will be useful in the afterlife."

"We do similar things," admitted Mitchell, "although for different reasons."

"This man desecrated the graves of my family," said Two Bears. "I've studied your Mormon beliefs, Mitchell. I've read your Doctrine and Covenants, and now I want you to tell him that he has transgressed against me for the last time."

"I don't understand?" Mitchell replied.

"Your *law of retaliation*," Two Bears explained. "It says I must forgive the man every time he transgresses against me, *if he asks for forgiveness*. But he hasn't asked. Doesn't it say that I must forgive him three times, and after the third time God will place my enemy in my hand and I'll be justified in whatever action I take against him?"

"Seems like that's the way it reads," Mitchell answered, "but I'm not sure what you're getting' at."

"This man desecrated and robbed a burial of my ancestors," Two Bears continued. "I wanted to kill him then, but Brother Joseph read this law to me and explained that I should forgive the man. I find this hard to do. This man stripped the dead of their possessions. I tried to catch him in the act, but he is very slippery. When there was nothing left, he moved on. I hoped we had seen the last of him, but I was wrong.

"He found another place; one that I thought would be safe. But he found it. He opened the grave and took everything. He even took the body."

"That's horrible," Susan whispered.

"She was my wife," Two Bears muttered. "She died two years after our son was born. That was twenty years ago, before Mormons came to this part of the valley."

Two Bears poked the stick into the fire again, raising a cloud of sparks with the hot smoky air. "I want her body back where it belongs." His voice was as hot as the fire he stabbed. "When he took her possessions, Brother Joseph calmed me and read from the book. But he came back. Now he's in my hand. When you talk with him, Mitchell, tell him I will come for him."

"You plan to kill him?"

"In a heartbeat."

"Maybe you should wait until you find her body," suggested Mitchell. "If you kill him, you may never know what he did with it."

"I understand that," Two Bears admitted. "That's why I'm talking to you now. Mort says that you're looking for a murderer, and that you suspect a woman's body is somehow part of it all."

"Mort seems to know more about this than I do," grumbled Mitchell.

Minutes passed. Two Bears waited. Susan sat watching him, but Mitchell said nothing. If Two Bears was right, the ear-cuff and the dried piece of ear were part of his wife's remains. That would solve the question of the contents of the missing canvas-wrapped bundle, but it raised new possibilities and new motives for killing Reynald. Two Bears might easily have killed Reynald, but it seemed ludicrous to demand the return of his wife's remains, if he had already taken them from Reynald's store.

"Did you kill Reynald?" Mitchell asked finally.

"I assume that Reynald is the man who was murdered in Ogden. No, I had nothing to do with that. Why do you ask?"

Mitchell fished around in his pockets and hauled out the ear-cuff. "Does this look familiar?" he asked.

Two Bears took the silver cuff in the palm of his hand and studied it. He turned it over slowly several times then handed it back.

"I've never seen it before. White woman's jewelry."

"It's not made by Shoshoni or Navajo?" Susan asked.

"It might have been."

"Then, how can you say it's white woman's jewelry?" demanded Mitchell.

"Because she scratched her initials on the inside," Two Bears replied calmly.

"What!" Mitchell held the silver cuff to the firelight. "I don't see anything."

"It's faint," Two Bears admitted, "but it's there all the same."

Mitchell handed the cuff to Susan.

"He's right," she said after a moment, "but it is very faint."

"Looks like the letters *A* and *V*," offered Two Bears.

"No," Susan said, handing the silver cuff back to Mitchell. "It's an *R* and an *M*."

"*R* and *M*?"

"Yes," she said quietly. "Ruth Miller."

Mitchell pondered the possibilities. If the canvas covered bundle was the body Ruth Miller then perhaps Reynald had recognized the woman's remains—and the ear-cuffs.

"Wadman must have been wrong," he muttered, wondering why Ruth Miller's body would have been anywhere near Reynald's store. More than one person had seen her decently buried.

"Who is Wadman?" Two Bears asked.

"He's a doctor in Ogden," Susan answered, explaining everything they had experienced since arriving in Ogden.

When she finished, Two Bears frowned thoughtfully. "You thought the missing body was an Indian woman," he surmised.

"It seemed possible," Mitchell admitted. "Wadman said it would take a very dry burial place to mummify a body. It just seemed more probable, but now I need to reconsider."

"Are you certain this ear-cuff came from this missing body?"

"I'm not certain, but it seems likely."

"Then, it was not my woman. She was not wearing those things." Two Bears stood suddenly. "It's late. I'll speak with you again tomorrow."

When he had gone, Susan stood and stretched coquettishly. "I was right," she whispered. She shook her hair loose, letting it fall over her shoulders in waves of red-brown.

"You're an intelligent and perceptive woman, Susan Mitchell," Mitchell responded.

"I should be rewarded."

"Do you have something in mind?" he asked.

"After everything that's happened in the last two days," she said, letting her petticoats fall at her feet, "I need to be comforted. We can discuss my reward afterward—if you're able."

CHAPTER 17

Utah Territory
Ogden—September 1868

*H*ours later, Mitchell woke suddenly in the darkness. He grabbed for his Colt in a near panic, but found Susan's hand on his arm instead.

"You were having a nightmare," she said quietly. "You've had them quite often since you've come home from the Legion.

Mitchell stared into the darkness. "They make me nervous," he said quietly.

"Whatever for?" Susan asked brightly. "They seem kindly enough."

Finally, when he had said nothing, she asked quietly. "What happened, Collin?"

For a moment, Mitchell was silent, wondering just how much of that day he should reveal to the woman who held his heart. Suddenly, he realized that Nine-mile Canyon was a festering wound that needed a good cleaning, and there was no one better than Susan or perhaps Sarah for fixing what ailed him.

"Nine-mile Canyon," he said finally. "It was a trap.... They led us on then they just cut loose on us." He took a moment to collect his thoughts then he told her about Nine-mile Canyon.

"We chased Black Hawk for nearly three weeks. William Pace was a Lieutenant General in the Nauvoo Legion by then, and he led us up Nine-mile trying to retrieve some stolen cattle. It must have been a hundred degrees in the shade by ten o'clock that morning, and I wasn't a bit anxious to go chasing up that canyon. They were out there waiting," he told her quietly. "I could feel it."

In the darkness, memories flooded into his consciousness.

Pace looked up the canyon, considering the red-rock and steep cliffs of the mountains surrounding them. "Take five men, Captain," he said finally. "Scout five miles up the main canyon and a quarter mile up any side canyon. Locate the Utes, if they're out there. When you find them, send a rider back and we'll come on the run. Don't engage the Utes unless you can't avoid it."

"Yes, Sir," Mitchell replied.

"Mind you, Captain," Pace added, "I think they've high-tailed it out of here. I think we've seen the last of them."

"Yes sir," Mitchell answered.

"You sound unconvinced, Captain."

"Yes Sir. It just doesn't fit their past behavior. Seems like they set up an ambush every time they're being chased."

Pace frowned and stared at the towering walls of the canyon. "Maybe…maybe not," he muttered reluctantly. "Maybe we made things too hot for them, and they decided to run while they could. We were only half a day behind them when we left Spanish Fork, and we would have caught them by now if they hadn't abandoned those stolen cattle."

"Yes Sir."

"However, I don't think we have anything to gain by running blindly up this canyon," Pace admitted finally.

"We'll need to go easy, if we're going to make sure of those side canyons," Mitchell advised.

"You have an hour before I move the regiment, Captain. Leave a marker at every side canyon when you're satisfied it's clear. We'll advance until we overtake you."

Mitchell frowned into the darkness of the tent.

"I took three boys from Salt Lake and two older fellows from the Sanpete District," he said. "We were danged fools," he said finally. "We were cautious enough, but sometimes that ain't enough. Once we left the regiment behind, there was no way they could help us if things went sour. And I knew it. Two miles can seem like a hundred when there's lead tearin' everything around you to pieces.

"We were as far from the regiment as our orders allowed," he said, remembering the heat and the red-rock dust of the canyon, "about two miles up the main canyon and a quarter- mile into a side canyon leading off to the north. We'd seen the tracks of the main bunch head on up the canyon, but two ponies had cut away from the party and had gone up the side canyon.

"There was a dry riverbed forty feet wide and ten feet deep right down the middle of the canyon. The bottom was flat and full of sandy gravel and the tracks of those two ponies were easy to follow. Joe Clayton and Ezra Kelly were both privates from the Sanpete District. They were trouble from the start 'cause they both wanted some Ute hair to decorate their saddles, and they bragged about how they might even take a head or two if they got the chance.

"I didn't want either of them along, but Pace forced 'em on me 'cause he thought they were good trackers. The three boys from Salt Lake weren't much more than kids. Tom Williams had just turned twenty-one. He was going back to Salt Lake in a couple of months to get married. He'd been saving every dime of his pay and had a job lined up at one of the lumber mills.

"Will Jacobs and Andrew Larsen were both seventeen. I think both of 'em joined up 'cause they were an extra mouth to feed at home, and there wasn't enough to go around. But they were both good shots and could ride as good, or better than most of the men in the regiment. I figured on using both of 'em to run messages between us and the regiment. I never had a chance to send either of them."

In the darkness, Mitchell remembered the canyon, the smell of sagebrush and the taste of the red-rock dust heavy in the air and on his tongue as their horses plowed through the tall brush blocking the mouth of the side canyon.

Mitchell called a halt and for a good ten minutes, searched for movement. But in all the canyon the only movement was an occasional bird or an ironclad cutting from one growth of brush to the next—and not a sound, save those made by their own horses.

"Kind of creepy, ain't it?" Jacobs muttered softly. "Don't seem natural—no sounds and all."

"Could be fifty of 'em hiding in this brush," Mitchell agreed.

"Let us follow them tracks a bit, Captain," Clayton offered. "Kelly and me can go as far as that big rock. If we don't flush the devils out by then, we'll come back."

"I don't like it, Captain," Williams offered, sounding almost apologetic.

"I don't like it either" Mitchell answered," but we have to check it out. Williams, take that Sharps of yours and find someplace up in those rocks." He pointed to the cliffs on the western side of the canyon mouth. "Can you shoot good enough to cover them at four-hundred yards?"

"I can," Williams admitted, "but I ain't guaranteein' anything."

"Go ahead Clayton," Mitchell agreed." But don't start anything. Just make sure those two ponies went right up that canyon and didn't turn back."

"Sure, Captain."

Minutes later, with Williams standing watch in the rocks above, the two men made their way slowly up the dry wash. Jacobs and Larsen dismounted and took up positions in the rocks directly below Williams, guarding his horse and watching the main canyon for any sign that the main band had turned back.

Mitchell watched as the two legionnaires disappeared in the depths of the wash then reappeared minutes later as their mounts lunged up the gravely slopes of the wash and onto the floor of the canyon.

"See anything?" he called out to Williams.

"Nothing, Captain."

Suddenly, Mitchell felt a nervousness in his mount. It was nothing more than a slight tilting of the ears and a lifting of the head, but the gelding sensed something and was paying attention. He drew the long barreled navy Colt from his belt, cocked the hammer and watched the tall brush filling the canyon mouth.

"Watch close," he told the two boys at the base of the cliffs. "Something is out there."

Slowly, like a deer mesmerized by the light of campfire at night, Larsen stood and raised his rifle to his shoulder. Instantly, the sullen boom of a rifle filled the canyon and echoed into the distance. Larsen staggered back a step, stared at the blood on his shirt then dropped to his knees. A moment later, the boy toppled forward, sliding head first down the rocky slope. His body slammed to a stop among the larger rocks and lay half-buried in the talus that followed.

"Stay down!" Mitchell bellowed, but his words were lost in the sudden thunder of gunfire that shook the canyon. Wildly, he fired twice into the brush, but neither shot found a target.

Jacobs fought his way into the saddle while his mount spun in a wild circle. The boy brought the animal under control only to be flung from the saddle when a rifle ball punched a hole in his forehead.

Williams fired the sharps, sending a .45 caliber ball into the brush. Barely controlling his own frantic mount, Mitchell leaned out and snagged the reins of Jacob's horse, before the animal could bolt. Williams scrambled down the slope and into the saddle.

"Up the canyon!" Mitchell yelled, spurring the gelding to the north.

Williams Kicked his mount hard, and seconds later both animals galloped madly away from the thundering gunfire and the angry buzz of lead and arrows. A quarter of a mile into the canyon, near the edge of the wash, they passed the bodies of Clayton and Kelly. A hundred yards later, Williams slumped in the saddle and fell to the ground. He lay in the dust, unmoving, as Mitchell turned and walked the gelding back.

Cautiously, he dismounted and reloaded the empty chambers of the navy Colt.

"I didn't know if the boy was dead or alive, "Mitchell said quietly. "I barely had that Colt reloaded when three Utes came charging up the trail on foot. They started shooting as soon as they saw me standing there; then something hit me in the shoulder and all I could do was empty the Colt. I must have passed out, 'cause the next thing I remember, I was looking up at the sky and it was near twilight. There wasn't a sound in the canyon.

"I reached over and gave Williams a shove, but he was dead as a doornail. The three Utes were dead too, and I had a bullet hole right through my left shoulder.

"Williams' horse was gone. Mine was laying there dead and there were flies everywhere. I could hear the regiment firing away like every Ute in the territory was after them, but all I could do was strip my gear off the horse and hole up for the night. Next morning, I hiked out of that canyon and right into General Pace's camp."

For a moment, Susan was quiet in the darkness. "You didn't kill those boys, Collin," she said softly. "You couldn't have known it was a trap."

"I should have seen it coming," Mitchell muttered.

"Sounds to me like you did as much as anyone could expect," she argued. "We always look back on things and think we could have done better somehow."

"If I'd done things differently, those boys might still be alive," Mitchell replied.

"Maybe... maybe not," she answered. "Either way, they were there because they chose to be there. And they were old enough to know what they were getting into."

Mitchell fell silent as Susan wrapped her arms around him. Finally, he found peace of mind in the sound of the wind on the canvas walls of the tent, and he slept.

CHAPTER 18

Utah Territory
Ogden—September 1868

Startled, Sarah opened her eyes to darkness and the deep shadows of her bedroom. The wind rattled the windowpanes, blasting the glass with a hissing kiss of wind-borne sand. Her eyes searched the room. There *had* been a sound—something that had touched the quiet fringe of her dreams and brought her instantly to wakefulness. Yet the room was still, and she could sense nothing out of the ordinary. Nevertheless, without conscious thought, her hand had snatched the navy Colt from the table beside her bed. Obviously, her *hand* sensed something wrong.

There had been a sound, something not of the wind. She knew it as well as she knew anything, though her senses told her nothing. Still, she waited quietly, listening and straining for the softest hint of sound. She waited, imitating the motionless yet searching posture she had felt in Collin those times he had awakened beside her in the middle of the night.

In the darkness, time seemed to pass slowly, stretching infinitely, until she felt sleep drawing her downward, dulling her senses. Of course there were sounds, sand on the windows, the low moaning of the wind—sounds that brought a lulling rhythm to the darkness and drowsiness to her mind. She drifted, unable to fight the heaviness of her eyelids. The Colt lay heavy on the bedspread, heavy against her thigh. The darkness weighed on her senses.

Click....

Sarah opened her eyes. *That* sound she recognized. The sound of the metal latch of the outer door was faint, yet unmistakable. Quietly, she slipped from the bed, tossed the quilts over a pillow and crept to the corner of the room, beside the window. Silently, she settled into the space between the outer wall and a tall chest-of-drawers. She had left the shotgun there—loaded and ready.

She could hear them now, boots moving across the floor of the parlor—coming closer—two, perhaps three men. They moved carefully, but in the darkness of the parlor, they were blind, bumping tables, kicking a chair, cursing in whispers.

Sarah cocked the hammers of the scattergun and waited. Collin would never enter the room so stealthily after the events of the past few days. The men in the parlor were up to no good. She knew it without doubt, and when the bedroom door swung inward, she raised the muzzles of the side-by-side, feeling her hands begin to tremble. She could see nothing. The door blocked any view of the intruders.

Without warning, the room thundered with the flash of burned powder and the bellow of gunfire from the doorway. She had no target, yet she squeezed one trigger. The big ten-gauge roared, filling the room with a sulfurous cloud, and rattling the window panes. The stock of the shotgun slid between her arm and her side. The butt-plate slammed the wall behind her, and the door seemed to explode as buckshot tore through the thin wood. There was a cry of pain, and the gunfire ceased.

"I'm hit!" The complaint reeked of surprise.

"What the...," hissed a second voice.

"I'm shot in the butt, I tell you."

Sarah raised the Colt and fired two quick shots through the door. Someone fell. Cursing broke the silence that fell in the wake of her gunfire.

"Get me out of here," snarled an angry voice. "My danged knee is busted all to pieces."

"I'm full of shot, and you want me to drag your fat butt out of here?"

"Gutless slob," growled the first voice. "I thought we was friends."

Trembling, Sarah listened to the sound of a boot dragging across the parlor floor.

A trick

Something hard bumped the ruined door, and an instant later, the room lit up with a flash and a bellow. She felt the bullet pass her head and heard the angry smack of lead punching a hole through the wall behind her then the muzzle of her shotgun roared, illuminating the room in a flash of orange and red.

Someone yelled and fell thrashing and kicking the floor. Growled threats rolled out of the parlor followed by the sound of cursing and dragging boot heels.

"What the blazes is going on!"

The voice was barely discernable above the wind, sounding as though it came from the veranda below her window. Sarah heard a muffled reply and the sound of boots on the stairway. She waited. The boots stopped in the parlor. Quietly, she cocked the pistol.

"Light a lamp," said a voice she'd never heard before.

"Good Lord!" gasped a voice that could only be Goodwin. "There's blood everywhere."

Sarah heard the sound of the boots moving toward the bedroom door. She raised the pistol.

"Hold on, Goodwin." The boots stopped again. "Sister Mitchell?"

Sarah waited, listening.

"Sister Mitchell, it's Deputy Parker. I'm with Mr. Goodwin."

Silence held the room for a moment.

"They're gone, Sister Mitchell," said Parker's voice. "We came to help, if we can."

"I don't know you, Deputy," Sarah answered cautiously.

"I'll wait here and send Mr. Goodwin to you," Parker offered. "Will you trust him?"

"How do I know you're not holding a gun on him?"

"I'll send him in, Sister Mitchell. You talk with him. When you feel comfortable, we'll talk."

When there was no reply, Parker called out again. "I have two deputies searching the area around the hotel," he advised.

"Send in Mr. Goodwin," she agreed finally. "I'll talk with him."

Goodwin entered the room slowly, arm stretched out, the lamp held high.

"Mrs. Mitchell?" He asked, squinting past the glare of the lamp.

"Step away from the door, Mr. Goodwin."

Goodwin hesitated then stepped away. Sarah looked past the lamplight to the angry tightness of the man's mouth then to the blood on his shirt. She sensed a movement behind the door.

"Mrs. Mitch...."

The room shook with the angry roar of Sarah's Colt. Goodwin flinched, knowing that death shattered the door beside him and smashed the life from the man hidden behind it.

"Is he dead?" Sarah asked.

Goodwin glanced toward the twitching body. "Dang near," he answered. "How'd you know he wasn't a deputy."

"I didn't," she answered. "Not until I saw your shirt."

"My shirt?"

"You've got blood on your shoulder where someone grabbed you," she replied. "Besides, he was too cautious about coming in here. He shouldn't have had any idea that I was in here and ready to shoot. And he lied about waiting in the parlor. A gentleman doesn't enter a lady's bedroom without an invitation."

"Glad you asked me in," Goodwin said quietly.

"Is he the last of them?" Sarah asked.

"He's the only one I saw," Goodwin answered. "Anyone else must have gone out the back way. I ran into this fellow near the desk downstairs.

"I'd appreciate it if you'd send for a real deputy," Sarah suggested.

"I think they're already coming up the stairs," Goodwin answered.

Lamplight flooded the parlor, spilling through the shattered doorway and into the bedroom. Sarah moved to the bed. She seated herself on the mattress and laid the Colt on the night table.

"What in the world is going on, Goodwin?"

Sarah recognized Becker's voice even before he reached the bedroom doorway and the corpse lying on the floor.

"I wish I knew," Goodwin snapped. "I heard gunshots and threw on some trousers. When I came out my door downstairs, this no good skunk stuck a gun in my back and forced me to come up here to Sister Mitchell's room.

"He was ranting the whole time about how he was going to kill the witch... Pardon my language ma'am," Goodwin said, glancing at Sarah. "Then he shoved me up here to the door. I could see there was blood everywhere, and this fellow had blood all over him.

"He calls out to Sister Mitchell and says he's a deputy and pokes me in the back with that pistol to keep me quiet."

"So, how come he's layin' here with a bullet hole smack in the middle of his chest?" Becker demanded.

"Sister Mitchell didn't know him and wouldn't let him come in. He knew she would shoot, 'cause he'd already been up here when the shooting started. Sister Mitchell knew me, so this fellow shoved me on ahead. Then he sneaks up like he's going to try and shoot her while she's talking with me."

"I saw the blood on Mr. Goodwin's shirt," Sarah said quietly. "I knew something was wrong. I sensed someone moving behind the door. I knew then that the man had lied. So, I shot through the door."

"Well, I don't like it one bit," Becker snarled. "That's the second shootin' you've been in since you folks come to town."

"Those men broke in here and tried to kill me, Deputy Becker," Sarah replied angrily. "If I had stayed in that bed another minute, they would have succeeded."

"What in the world is the matter with you, Becker," Goodwin exploded. "Those fellows come in here shootin' my place up and tryin' to kill one of my guests, and you stand there talking like it's *her* fault. Why don't you take your sorry ass out of here, and drag that fellow with you!"

"I think you better watch your mouth, Goodwin," Becker growled.

"You're only getting what you deserve, Becker."

"I'm just doin' my job," Becker snapped.

"You ain't doin' it very well," Goodwin answered angrily.

"Gentlemen!" Sarah exclaimed.

The two men grew quiet at her outburst.

"I'm not in the mood for this," she informed them. "I'm tired. I want a different room. And I want this nightmare to end."

She took the Colt from the night table and laid it on the bed beside her. She pulled her dressing gown tight at the throat. She couldn't even remember putting on the dressing gown.

As though it matters, she thought. Yet suddenly and irrationally it did matter. She never slept in it and there had been no time to retrieve the garment from the chair beside the bed. Things had happened too quickly.

"I have another room downstairs," Goodwin offered, interrupting her rambling thoughts.

Sarah reached over and raised the hood of the lamp. She motioned Goodwin to her side. "I need a flame," she said quietly.

Goodwin lowered his lamp, letting her slide a long taper downward into the flame.

"I need another room temporarily," she told him. "Actually, I would prefer another suite altogether."

"I have three connecting rooms across the hallway," Goodwin replied. "If you want them...."

"I want them," she replied, "at least until I can discuss the situation with my husband."

"I understand," Goodwin answered.

"I don't think you do, Mr. Goodwin," Sarah replied. "I'm not staying in those rooms," she said quietly so the deputy couldn't hear. "I want you to rent them to me, and I'll keep most of our things here, but I want you to send someone you trust with a message for my father. I'll write a note asking him to come for me."

"You'll be staying there?"

"Only for a day or two," she answered. "When Collin and Susan return, I'll come back. But right now, I don't think I could stand to be here alone."

"I understand, Sister Mitchell, and I don't blame you a bit," Goodwin reassured her.

"This fellow ain't dead," Becker said in surprise.

"Good," Goodwin snapped. "We can try him for attempted murder and send him down to the point of the mountain for life. Now, drag his sorry ass out of here!"

Sarah glared at Becker as the big man dragged the limp body into the parlor and out of the suite. Moments later, she heard boot heels thumping down the stairway.

Sarah looked pointedly at Goodwin. "You make sure that no one knows we've changed rooms or that I've gone to my father's house," she advised him. "If I'm not here when Collin returns, you can tell him where to find me. But you will tell no one else."

"I won't tell anyone, ma'am," Goodwin promised. "And I'll make sure your things are moved into the new rooms."

When Goodwin had gone, Sarah dressed quickly. She tried her best to ignore the shattered door and the blood now smeared across the pine floors. She had never approved of violence, though she seemed caught in it often enough. The thought of harming another person twisted her insides and made her ill. She knew the world was a violent place, teeming with people who would stoop to anything—some for money—some for the pure pleasure they seemed to find in causing trouble.

Still, her view of life conjured up visions of a peaceful ranch where she and Collin could raise their children in an environment relatively free of the day-to-day madness of city life. Ten years of living near the Avenues of Salt Lake City had pretty much purged her of any desire to live in town. But those same ten years had taught her that some changes came harder than others, and uprooting a family was no walk in the park.

More like trudging through mud, she thought, remembering Susan's sudden change of heart and her arguments against leaving Salt Lake.

By the time her father arrived, Sarah was more than ready to leave the hotel. She heard him on the stairway first. Then he was standing in the doorway, shaking his head at the blood on the floor and the shotgun-blasted door.

George Flitton was a tall, heavyset, gray-haired man. She'd seen him less than six days ago, but now she realized how much older and grayer he looked. He stood in the doorway, clad in his homespun shirt, faded overalls, and a brown woolen coat, worrying the life out of an old hat.

"Goodwin says you need a ride home," he said quietly.

Sarah ran into his strong, comforting embrace. "I do, Papa," she answered. She stood, buried in his bearish hug for a long moment, remembering and relishing the comfort and safety she'd always found in his presence.

"This place looks awful," he muttered when she finally stepped back.

"It's been miserable since the day we got here," she replied, handing him the shotgun and a small travel bag. Briefly, she told him everything that had been happening.

"Those dogs deserve everything you gave 'em," he reassured her. "And I don't envy the fellows that took your sister. Mitchell ain't one to put up with anyone meddlin' with his kin, and I don't know anyone meaner than your sister when she gets angry."

"I'd like to stay with you and Mama until Collin and Susan return," Sarah said quietly, "but I don't want anyone to know I'm there...."

"Don't worry about that," her father advised." Goodwin told me a little of what happened, and we've got that all figured out. We'll get you home without anyone knowing where you've gone, and you can stay as long as you need to."

"I knew you'd understand, Papa," she responded. "I don't want to put you or Mama or the children in danger, but I just can't stay here alone."

"You just come home, and quit frettin' about it. When Mitchell gets back with your sister, we'll see about settling up with these fellows."

It was late afternoon when she awoke in her father's house. The smell of baking bread hung faintly in the air, and she knew that her mother was doing the work of three women, trying to make her oldest daughter feel welcome.

"Don't complain," her mother cautioned when Sarah entered the kitchen. "You and Susan never come up to visit, so you can't blame me for trying to make things nice when you're here."

"It's a two day trip Mama, and you know it," Sarah replied sweetly. "The children have been too small or ill when we thought about visiting."

Kathryn Flitton was silent, refusing to answer.

"The road runs both ways, Mama," Sarah said defensively.

The older woman stopped kneading the second batch of bread dough and looked up at her tall, red-haired daughter.

"I know that," she admitted reluctantly. "It's just easier to blame someone else."

"Oh."

"Mama!"

"Jacob!" Sarah scooped up the nine-year old, squeezing him tightly to her.

"Mama, you're suffocatin' me," he protested.

"I'm just glad to see you Jacob."

"My name is Jake, Mama. Papa calls me Jake."

"Yes, Jake," she conceded quietly, her face buried against the side of his neck.

"You're getting' my neck all wet, Mama."

"I know dear."

"Where's Papa? Did you bring rock candy?"

"Papa is with Aunt Susan," she answered.

"Is Mama here?" asked a voice from the kitchen doorway.

Sarah knelt and took the little girl in her arms, hugging both children tightly.

"No, Sarah. Mama isn't here," she answered. "She's with Papa and they will be home soon."

Tears filled the eight-year-old's eyes.

"I want Mama...."

"I know, dear.... Papa will bring her home soon."

"Did you bring rock candy, Mama?" Jake demanded.

"I'm sorry, dear. I didn't," Sarah answered.

She held both children for a long while, finally letting them go when they began squirming in her arms.

"You children go out back and play," their grandmother ordered.

Sarah gave the children one last squeeze and let them go.

"Stay in the yard," Mrs. Flitton admonished as the two went out the back door. "Play will do them good," she told her daughter. "Keeps them busy instead of getting homesick for their Mama and Papa."

"I know how they feel," Sarah replied quietly. She glanced around the room, looking for her youngest.

"She's napping," her mother said quietly. "You can look in, but don't wake her."

When Sarah returned, her mother looked at her sternly. "Tell me what's going on," she demanded. She gave the bread dough one last slap and covered the rounded lump with a damp flour sack.

"I really don't know," Sarah admitted, "but we've had people shooting at us since the day we got into town."

Her mother sat in one of the kitchen chairs, so Sarah took a chair on the opposite side of the table.

"If I didn't know better, I would think it had something to do with Deputy Becker asking Collin to investigate Lester Reynald's murder," she said quietly. "But there were men following us before Deputy Becker ever talked with Collin."

"Then, it must not have anything to do with Lester Reynald," her mother suggested grimly.

"Probably not, but I just can't think of a reason for anyone to shoot at us," she groaned. "And now they've taken Susan, and Collin has gone after her."

"My dear, you seem to forget that you've married a man that some folks would call a reformed gunman. When a man has a back-trail lined with headstones, you'd better expect some kind of retaliation."

"I did expect it," Sarah answered defensively, "but it's been ten years, and everything's been quiet for a long time."

"Calm before a storm," muttered the older woman. "Maybe they've been waiting for you to let down your guard?"

"Maybe," Sarah answered reluctantly. "And maybe it has nothing to do with our past. Maybe someone just doesn't want us finding out why Mr. Reynald was killed."

Mrs. Flitton frowned unhappily. "Either way, I think you should take the children and quietly leave town. I'm worried sick about your sister."

"I'm worried too, Mama. But Collin will bring her home safely."

Sarah looked up as her father entered the kitchen. For a moment, George Flitton stood silently, looking at his eldest daughter.

"I made some inquiries about that fellow who was following you the other day," he said finally.

"Good," Sarah responded. "What did you find out?"

"Nothing of any value," her father replied. "His name may be Jensen. Jason Jensen. But that's all I know. No one seems to know who he is or where he's from. I asked around to see if he'd been seen with either of the men who came after you at Browning's, but no one I talked to had ever seen them together."

"That's all?" Sarah asked, frowning.

"For now," he replied. "I'll see what else I can find out."

CHAPTER 19

Utah Territory
Ogden—September 1868

*I*t was mid-morning when Mitchell and Susan emerged into the brightness of a cool, yet sunny September morning. Small pools of rainwater dotted the camp, but already, the ground was drying, and the air was fresh and filled with the scent of sage. To the west, the lake was a flat, blue plate broken only by the up-thrust of the Promontory Mountains and two other mountainous islands. To the east, the ragged cliffs of the Wasatch Range rose to the heights of Willard Peak and beyond to Ben Lomond.

Mort strolled up beside them and stood watching the sky. "Nice mornin', ain't it."

"It's a beautiful morning," Susan answered.

"Where's Daniel?" asked Mitchell.

"Saddlin' up," Mort replied.

"He's leaving?" Susan asked in surprise.

"He's just goin' down to Ogden," Mort answered. "I figured the two of you would want to let Sarah know things was goin' well."

Mitchell took a folded sheet of paper from his pocket and handed it to the old man. "We wrote this last night."

"Figured you'd want to send word. I'll see that the boy knows how to find her."

Mort led the way through the Shoshoni camp. The camp was larger than Mitchell had expected. Scattered near the Bear River, nearly a hundred dwellings squatted on the sage dotted landscape. The camp was semi-permanent and seasonal, but had been in use for more than twenty years.

"Not many white folks come out here," Mort offered. "Leastwise, not since Urban Stewart shot Chief Terikee."

"I heard about Terikee," Mitchell replied, "but I never figured there would be trouble after seventeen years."

"Little Soldier never felt like the Shoshoni got a square deal," Mort replied. "They stole a few horses, but then the militia showed up. After that—well, mostly the Shoshoni got nothin' after that."

"Little Soldier wanted Stewart?" asked Mitchell.

"Yes, sir. Probably wanted to roast him real slow. But Lorin Farr told Stewart it was a dang fool thing he done, and he'd better run for it if he didn't want Little Soldier takin' him. So, Stewart run off."

"Seems like a long time," Mitchell argued.

"Maybe so, but things don't heal when folks keep pickin' at 'em."

"Two Bears is friendly," Susan protested.

"Don't count on that too much," Mort replied.

"Two Bears wanted your help. Otherwise, he and his friends might have played some mischief last night, instead of bringin' you down here to a nice dry teepee."

"Things could have been worse," Mitchell admitted.

"Things might get right nasty anyways," Mort confided.

Susan grabbed the old man by the arm and dragged him to a stop. "What do you mean?" she demanded.

"Today's a big day," he answered, waving his free arm at the camp. "Big medicine. Ball game," he squawked when Susan yanked on his arm again.

"Ball game?" Mitchell repeated.

"Yep. Big deal out here. They send out the invite then fellers start showin' up from every tribe in the Basin. Pretty soon, there's hundreds of 'em."

"What kind of ball game is this?" Susan asked.

"It's a mean one," Mort replied. "They get a bunch of fellers out in an open field, an' every one of 'em has a long pole with one end bent 'round in a loop. They got a little net in the loop, an' they run around the field usin' this thing to catch a leather ball an' fling it back an' forth 'til somebody manages to throw the ball between a couple of poles at either end of the field.

"I seen 'em play all day long. I seen busted arms, an' legs… teeth knocked out. I seen one big brave drop like a sack of beans when that leather ball hit him 'tween the legs. Knocked him cold. They like to trompled 'im before somebody dragged 'im off to one side."

Susan shook her head in wonder. "How does that affect us?" she asked.

"It's a man thing," Mort answered.

"It is a man thing." Two Bears said as he walked up behind them. "Prestige, power, big medicine, and of course there is the horse."

"Horse?" Susan wondered.

"The prize," he answered. "The horse will go to the winners as a symbol, but a very nice prize for the best player. Of course everyone on the winning side will expect to share in the prize. He is a fine stallion. I suppose I will have to give some of his foals as gifts, after he is mine."

"You're going to win him?" she asked.

"Of course. I am the best player. Brother Joseph is a good player, but now he's got religion, he tends to hold back a little. This is not a game for the meek or the faint hearted. Cautious players are often damaged."

"It'll be interesting to see," Mitchell admitted.

"Don't expect to sit with the women and the old men, Mitchell. Fifty Utes arrived yesterday morning. They are, as you whites say, 'meaner-n-hell'. Little Soldier is old and unwell. You will take his place. A man who rides with the angel of death should do well in the game."

Two Bears turned and walked quickly away, leaving Mitchell, Susan, and the old man staring at his retreating form.

"I seen that horse," Mort said suddenly. "You win him, an' I'd sure like to borrow him now an' again."

"Don't reckon I'll win anything," Mitchell replied, "seein' as how I never played this game."

"Ain't nothin' to it," countered Mort. "It's just pandemonium an' puredee meanness—like bein' in the middle of a stampede. You try an' catch the ball in your net then fling it between them poles, or to some other feller who's got a better chance of throwin' it in. That's it, except for trying not to get your nose busted or an eye poked out."

"That's encouraging."

"Ain't it."

They were standing in the same spot when Two Bears suddenly returned. "Have you ever played shinny with an Indian?" he asked, pointing toward a small group of men who had collected near the southern edge of the encampment.

"Never have," Mitchell admitted.

"New experience for you. Good."

Two Bears thrust a long stick in Mitchell's direction. "Take it. I've asked these men to allow you to play. They've agreed. It will be a new experience for them also."

Mitchell took the stick, prompted by Susan's elbow in his ribs. "Sure, I'll play, but you'll have to explain things."

"You strike the ball with the stick," Two Bears explained.

"That's it?" Mitchell looked at the stick, noting that it was about three feet long with the first six inches bent at nearly a right angle. It looked old and well used, and someone had taken a great deal of time to clean it, strip it of bark, and hand-carve the length of it with a knife. "This looks like someone's favorite stick," he suggested.

"It's mine," Two Bears answered. "I've had it quite a long while."

"Sure you want me using it? Clumsy fellow like me might break it."

"Don't worry about that," Two Bears replied. "If it breaks, it breaks. I haven't played for a long time anyway, and I can always make another." He took the stick and held it by the smaller end, stooped slightly, and swept the six inch bend across the dusty surface of the ground. Twigs, leaves, and dust scattered in its path. "This is not just a matter of striking the ball," he said. "It's a race. You hit the ball as you run the course. It's best to hit the ball hard and straight. Then you can sprint to the ball and strike it again. If you don't hit it along a straight path, you could run all over the valley and never finish the race. If you lose the ball and can't find it, drop another and continue the course. You'll have only three, so don't lose them all."

"That's all?" Mitchell asked.

"What other rules are there?" Susan asked.

"Rules?"

"Yes. Rules."

"Oh...." Two Bears smiled mischievously. "Don't fall down too often. It's also not polite to strike an opponent hard enough to break bones or do major damage." Two Bears leaned close and lowered his voice to a conspiratorial whisper.

Susan looked at the ground, pretending she hadn't heard, but her face was suddenly flushed, and both men could see her struggling to hold back her laughter.

"Most opponents wouldn't do such a thing," Two Bears added, "but given a chance, they will try to knock your balls off the course."

Susan clapped one hand over her mouth, but failed to stifle an explosion of laughter.

"The wooden ball!" Two Bears squawked defensively. "Take it!" The Shoshoni shoved the stick and three fist–sized wooden balls at Mitchell and stalked away.

"I think he's embarrassed," Susan gasped from behind her hand.

"His sensibilities *have* been strained," Mitchell replied as they walked toward the small group of ball players.

"You seemed anxious for me to play this game," he said quietly. "Why?"

"Two Bears is a good man," Susan replied. "I just think it's a good idea to make friends whenever you have a chance. When men get involved in competitions, they seem to develop a kind of respect for one another. Any kind of good relations with these people could mean a lot to us some day. I think they respect strength, ability, and honesty. Playing this game can give them a chance to know you for something more than just another white man who wants to raise a bunch of cattle on their land."

"You know I ain't a real friendly sort," Mitchell complained.

"That's why this is so perfect," Susan answered sweetly. "You can get in there and do the manly thing and knock each other around like a bunch of hairy apes. You'll enjoy it, and they will love you like a brother. It's perfect."

"I'm sure there's something wrong with your reasoning," Mitchell muttered.

Susan smiled brightly. "My reasoning is flawless. Just be yourself, and everything will be fine."

By the time Mitchell and Susan crossed to the southern edge of the camp, Two Bears was already speaking with the thirteen young men who had gathered there. "They are ready when you are, Mitchell, but Brother Joseph pointed out that you will run better in a pair of moccasins. Those riding boots are not made for running."

"These boots are all I have with me," Mitchell answered as he watched the half-naked warriors take practice swings with their sticks.

"Try those," Two bears said, pointing to a young boy running swiftly across the camp with a pair of moccasins hanging about his neck.

"Try to keep a steady pace," Two Bears advised while Mitchell laced up the soft buckskin. "Don't try to outrun them. Just keep up with them until you reach the marker at the hot springs. When you turn back and the camp is in sight, that would be a good time to fly like the wind if you want to win."

Mitchell shaded his eyes and looked south. "I don't see any marker," he observed grimly. "How far to the hot springs?"

"About three miles."

"Three miles!"

"Any farther and you would all be too tired for the racquet game this afternoon," Two Bears objected defensively. "They wanted to make it longer, but some of the Ute's have come a long way and Washakie wants very badly for us to win the racquet game and take their horses."

"What bands of the Ute are here?" Mitchell asked grimly.

"Several," Two Bears answered. "Weber, Shiberech, Timpanogos, even a few Elk Mountain."

"Will they cause trouble?" Susan asked, frowning.

"I don't know," Mitchell answered. He looked east toward the steep slopes and cliffs rising up to the heights of Willard Peak.

"They know who you are," Two Bears assured. "They're not sure what to think of you, but I've heard them talk among themselves. Some of them believe you are a demon spirit sent by the Shinob to punish those who rode with Black Hawk. Others say you are *Shenabavegan*, saved by God's power, because you alone survived the hailstorm of bullets at the canyon of the ancient ones.

"Some of them think you are just a very lucky man, and if they get the chance, they will try to take your hair. They are still angry and believe that Antonga Black Hawk will again lead them to war against the Mormons when he realizes they cannot be trusted any more than other whites."

"They won't be taking my hair without one heck of a fight," Mitchell growled as he finished lacing the moccasins.

"That's what they hope for," Two Bears asserted. He slapped Mitchell on the shoulder. "When the time comes for that particular game," he growled vehemently, "the rules will change. Then you must break their bones, remove their hands and feet, and take their hair."

Mitchell looked toward the Ute camp. He knew the Utes had not yet left their small encampment a half mile to the south east. But the image of twenty or thirty hostiles so near raised the hair on the back of his neck and stirred the memory of running gun battles and a hailstorm of lead at Nine-mile Canyon.

He'd never hated the Utes like some of the Saints down in the Sanpete District, but he knew how powerful the animosity had grown between the Mormons, the Utes, and even the Navajos in the central regions of the territory. As a captain in the Nauvoo Legion, he'd known there were good reasons for hunting down Antonga Black Hawk and his band of cattle stealing renegades.

The cattle thefts alone had been enough to guarantee the ire of Mormon settlers, but the killing of innocent men, women, and children by Black Hawk's raiders and Legionnaires alike had done nothing to quell the growing distrust and hatred on both sides. Luckily, he'd entered the war late and had never been involved in any attack on innocent Utes nor had he condoned the use of chain shot or the taking of trophy heads. In fact, his transfer to the Sanpete District had come late in the war and he had almost avoided the fighting entirely. He felt no hatred for the Utes, but he was keenly aware of their tenacity and prowess in war and knew that they made formidable enemies.

"Time to start," Two Bears urged. "They're getting anxious."

"I'm ready," Mitchell answered.

"Knock yourself out," Susan laughed. She threw her arms around his neck, kissing him hard. "Go make lots of friends!"

The warriors laughed and pounded their sticks on the ground. Reluctantly, Mitchell disengaged himself from Susan's attentions and lined up among the warriors. Laughing, one of the men slapped Mitchell on the back then puckered his lips and made kissing noises. Mitchell smiled, puckered his own lips and mimicked the young brave. The young warrior frowned suddenly then smiled as his friends roared and pounded their sticks on the ground.

Someone shouted, and the men on the line made ready. With a second shout, the race was on. Half the men were gone before Mitchell realized what was happening. Belatedly, he dropped a ball on the ground, lunged forward, and fell flat on his face, his legs entangled with the kissing warrior's stick. The warrior whooped and danced around then stopped and helped Mitchell to his feet.

"Real funny," Mitchell grumbled.

CHAPTER 20

Utah Territory
Ogden—September 1868

*T*wo hours later, Mitchell stood at the center of a writhing mob in a different game. Stripped to the waist, half-naked Shoshoni and Ute warriors milled about him in a tightly packed horde.

Suddenly, the buckskin ball was in the air. The field erupted, and Mitchell scrambled toward the ball. He moved like a stick caught in the dark waters of a spring runoff. The buckskin was caught and thrown. The mob surged northward. Poles and nets waved above dark heads like the lances of a Roman legion. Shoulders, elbows, and knees battered Mitchell as he fought through the pack. A shout rolled through the mob. Movement slowed.

Mitchell knew that someone had thrown the buckskin ball between the tall poles that stood at the northern end of the field, but he had seen nothing.

Suddenly, the warriors were moving again. The ball sailed high into the air, was caught, flew again. Eighty men shifted almost as one, following the path of the ball. Mitchell winced as an elbow hammered his ribs. For a moment, he struggled for air then surged forward, battering his way through the shifting mob of men.

The playing field was total chaos. Overhead, racquets waved, darted, and snatched at the deerskin covered ball. On the ground, moccasin covered feet shuffled, kicked, and tread upon anything that failed to move fast enough to escape the trampling of the milling herd.

Like everyone else, Mitchell took a beating. A fist in the back, the long shaft of a racquet to the back of his head, trampled toes and kicked shins, all combined to make him feel as though he'd been in a brawl and lost. The ball sailed up and down the field half a hundred times. Mitchell watched its every movement, but the buckskin evaded him at every pass.

An hour passed with no break in the murderous fight for the buckskin, and Mitchell was beginning to feel more than a little ragged when he felt Susan tug at his shirt sleeve.

"Water," she said, dragging him another foot from the edge of the field. Mitchell took the proffered water-skin and drank deeply.

"Be careful," Susan warned. "Those Utes are up to no good."

"How do you know?"

"Just a feeling," she admitted defensively. "Two Bears doesn't think they would do anything beyond the usual brutality of the game, but I'm concerned. The normal roughness of the game seems haphazard and unfocused. But what happens when fifteen or twenty Utes decide you are their target for retribution?"

Mitchell felt the hair rise on the back of his neck. He knew exactly how it felt to be the target of a Ute war party. He clenched his teeth. He seldom spoke of Nine Mile Canyon—the canyon of the ancient ones, Two Bears had called it—it was a bad memory, a memory haunted by the ghosts of five Nauvoo Legionaires and seventeen Ute warriors and a running gun battle in a narrow desert canyon.

"Shenabavegan," he muttered, remembering the pain of a rifle ball punching a hole just below his collar bone.

"Saved by God's power," Susan said quietly. "The war is over," she insisted. "Black Hawk and his raiders have made peace."

"Most of them," Mitchell agreed. "But not all," he added.

Susan kept watch as Collin rejoined the melee of the racquet game. From her point of view, the game was nothing more than the synchronized movements of a mob of half naked men. The mob thundered to the right only to stampede to the left a moment later.

There was no finesse to the game, no delicacy of play, no sharp interaction of intellect—nothing to attract a woman's interest—nothing except the shock of a primordial brute force that emanated from the mob like a tangible wall of emotion. The nature of that force was so primeval, so unnerving that her breath caught in her throat, and her heart pounded as an overpowering aura of maleness engulfed the camp.

As a female, she wanted to flee from the experience, but the sensation of raw, male virility seemed to charge the air and literally pinned her where she stood. And like a fox intent on her prey, her eyes captured and followed the ebb and flow of the pack and the dire-wolf who was her mate.

Intently, she kept watch, noting every vengefully malignant assault of three renegade Utes. Suddenly, an idea invaded her thoughts. She turned to Little Soldier. "May I borrow your knife for a moment?"

Little Soldier glanced at her in surprise, but unsheathed his knife and handed it over without comment.

Quickly, Susan went to a campfire and recovered a half-burned twig. Raising her skirt, she sliced off a large square of white petticoat.

Little Soldier smiled indulgently as she returned the hunting knife. "I do have paper and pencil," he offered.

Susan knelt and spread the swatch of petticoat on the ground. "Thank you, but this looks more ritualistic."

Little Soldier frowned suddenly. "You're not a witch, I hope."

Susan laughed. "Heavens no.... But they don't know that. Tell me their names."

The Shoshoni glanced at the players and shook his head.
I shouldn't, but Brother Joseph tells me they plan to do
Mitchell a great harm." He frowned at the mob of ball
players. "Anoosh," he said finally. "Kanosh and Toquana,"
he added.

"I don't intend to alter the game," Susan assured him.

"Anoosh!" she called loudly as the players swarmed by.
"Anoosh!" She called again. When the Ute stood before
her, she pressed the burned end of the twig to the white
cloth and wrote *Anoosh* in bold letters across the top. Below
that, she wrote *Kanosh* and *Toquana*.

"Tell him I've written his name and the names of his
friends," she told Little Soldier. "If they do any harm to my
husband, or play unfairly, I will give their names to the
Shinob."

"You do not need to tell me anything," Anoosh growled.
"Are you a witch that you can give my name to the
Shinob?"

Susan wadded the cloth into a knot. "Mort!" she called
out.

When the old man had joined them, she stared into the
Ute's eyes. "If I ask it, Mort will take your names to the
Shinob."

For a moment, Anoosh was silent, first looking closely
at Mort then back to the girl.

"Destroy the writing," he said finally. "I will tell them.
We will not harm your man."

Mort shook his head as the Ute rejoined the game. "I
give it about a month," he said.

"Give what a month?" Susan demanded.

"In about a month, every Ute in the Territory will
believe you're a witch who can give their names to a demon
spirit. I reckon the Utes will be mighty careful in dealing
with the Mitchells for a while."

"Anoosh didn't believe I'm a witch," Susan protested.

Mort smiled. "He didn't want to believe it, but he didn't want to take a chance. So, he backed down. Now, he can't go around tellin' his friends that a little slip of a girl frightened him by writin' his name on her petticoats.

"By now, his friends are convinced. And you, my sweet young lady, are a bona fide witch who called up the angel of death to deliver their names to the Shinob."

"You tossed a small pebble into the water," Little Soldier observed quietly. "It will cause many ripples."

An hour later, the stampede ground to a halt, and Mitchell moved wearily to Susan's side.

"I never felt so beat up in my life," he gasped. "I've busted horses a time or two, but these fellows beat all.... I've been trompled, bashed, smacked up aside the head with somebody's racquet, elbowed, and pounded good. And I think that bullet hole is open and bleedin' again."

Susan glanced at his side and the blood on his shirt.

"It's not too bad," she concluded. "I'll bandage it again later."

Two Bears strode to the edge of the field and joined them. "It was an excellent game," he announced. "You did well for a white man."

"At least I didn't lose any teeth," Mitchell acknowledged gratefully. "Brother Joseph had one of his front teeth knocked out. You'd a thought it was his birthday the way he was dancin' around showin' off that tooth. Funny lookin' thing too, looked like a little shovel."

Susan smiled and took him by the arm. "At least you're in one piece," she concluded.

"And you have a new horse," Two Bears added as Brother Joseph came toward them, leading a wine colored horse and a dozen Shoshoni.

CHAPTER 21

Utah Territory
Ogden—September 1868

*F*ive miles north of Ogden, a thin, sinuous rope of gray smoke rose from within a small stand of cottonwoods and drifted eastward on the wind. Mitchell sat back in the saddle and eased the grulla to a stop. He blocked the glare of the sun with his hat and squinted toward the trees. "Someone's camped over there," he announced when Mort rode up beside him. "You wait here with Susan while I see if he's friendly."

Mort frowned and shook his head. "He ain't, but I'll keep watch whilst you have a talk with him. Just remember, he ain't near as dumb as he lets on, an' he's a mean 'un when he's cornered."

It was Mitchell's turn to frown as he squinted into the distance. "I ain't even goin' to ask how you can see that fellow's face a hundred yards away," he muttered.

Mort grinned, raised his hat to the sun and imitated Mitchell's squint. "Plain as the nose on your face," he replied slyly. "It's that Groesbeck fellow. Looks like he's cookin' 'imself a can of beans."

Mitchell shook his head and nudged the grulla toward the smoke.

"Don't let him pull a gun on you," Mort warned loudly.

Mitchell guided the grulla into the long grass and the softer ground at the edge of the road leading south into Ogden. The wagon-rutted trail was cut deep and packed hard with rocks and dried-out mud. The rains of the past few days had worsened the problem, and the ruts had only grown deeper and more rugged with every new wagon braving the rain and the mud. Only a foolish man would chance breaking a horse's leg on such treacherous footing, and Mitchell had no desire to lose the grulla.

Just west of the sun-baked rut, Groesbeck tended his small fire. Overhead, the wind rattled the cottonwood leaves, masking the sound of the grulla's approach until Groesbeck suddenly looked up from the fire and realized he was no longer alone. Deliberately, he reached out and grabbed up the rifle that lay across his piled saddle and gear.

Mitchell snatched the long barreled Navy Colt from its holster and pointed it across the forty yards separating him from Groesbeck. "Don't make me shoot you!" he called out. He closed the distance between them, tossed one leg over the grulla's neck and slid to the ground with the forty-four still trained on its target.

"Who the blazes do you think you are?" Groesbeck fumed. "And why are you ridin' in here shoving that gun in my face?"

Mitchell smiled and ground-hitched the grulla. "Name's Mitchell," he said congenially. "I just wanted to ask you a few questions about Lester Reynald."

Mitchell advanced, keeping the bore of the forty-four aimed at Groesbeck's belly.

Carefully, Groesbeck leaned the rifle back against his saddle. "They said you was goin' to kill me," he grumbled. "I just didn't figure you'd do it in cold blood."

"What are you talkin' about?"

"They said you thought I killed Reynald, and you wasn't takin' any chances. Said you'd put me down like you did them fellers up to Corinne."

Mitchell frowned. "I ain't here to kill you," he growled. "I just want to ask some questions about your business with Reynald."

"Why should I tell you anything?"

"If you don't, folks are going to wonder what you're hiding. After a while, they'll start remembering how shifty eyed you were. They'll remember how Reynald didn't trust you, or how you said you wished someone would shoot the crooked little bugger. 'Course some of it would be true, but if we don't catch the real killer, folks will most likely brand you as the one they think did it. Your life will be ruined around here."

Groesbeck shrugged. "You'd probably help spread the rumors," he muttered unhappily.

"I wouldn't do that, but when folks asked me what I thought about the whole business—I'd have to tell 'em it was mighty strange how you wouldn't say anything—and how it seems to me that only a man who had something to hide would refuse to talk."

"I got nothin' to hide."

"Then tell me what kind of deal you had with Reynald."

Groesbeck stared into the distance. "I found stuff for him," he said finally.

"What kind of *stuff* did you find?"

"Injun stuff."

"Where did you find the stuff?"

"In caves and mounds – places like that."

"Burials?"

"Some. Most times, I never touched any dead folks. I just took old pots, beads, and arrow points. Reynald never took a lot of the stuff—said he only had a small market for it back east."

"How long have you been selling this stuff to Reynald?

"Two years…. Keeps me in spendin' money. But the place where I was getting' the stuff sort of dried up. I ain't done much business since then."

"You delivered something Monday afternoon," prompted Mitchell.

"And I ain't seen him since."

"What did you deliver?"

"Some pots, beads...."

"What else?"

"Aw for cryin' out loud, I didn't want nothin' to do with it, but Reynald told me he had a buyer back east that wanted an Injun mummy real bad."

Mitchell nodded thoughtfully, wondering how long Groesbeck could stay in the territory and avoid the Shoshoni. "You delivered a body to Reynald?"

"It was real old—all dried out.... You see, when I got everything out of the old place, I had to find someplace new. I tried tradin' with the Shoshoni for pots and things, but after one shipment, Reynald got a letter. Them folks back east was mad. They wanted the old stuff, and they knew the difference. So, I had to find another place to get the old stuff.

"I heard some talk about a place just a couple of miles north of Bingham's fort. I guess some kids was out there playin' and found some arrowheads and broken pottery. So, I figured I might give 'er a try.

"I went out several times and never found it. Then, about three weeks ago I found this big mound. I looked all over the thing for about a week before I spotted some bones. They was human, but I didn't find nothin' with them—just the bones under a loose pile of rocks. That got me fired up. I figured them bones must have got washed down, out of the mound; so I went up the side of it and started diggin'.

"Right off, I started findin' some arrow points and bits of pottery. The mound was real sandy there, and I was diggin' like crazy when the whole side of the hill fell. Dang near buried me alive. Anyway, I got back up, and there was this big old ledge of rock with a natural holler in it. I poked around a bit with a shovel, and there she was."

"There who was?"

"Injun gal—back in that holler. I knew I had me a good find—pots, arrowheads, moccasins and a dried up Injun gal."

"So, you took it all to Reynald."

"Not at first. I didn't want to fiddle with no dead body; so, I took a few pots and told Reynald what I found."

"And he wanted it all," Mitchell suggested.

"Danged if he didn't. Wanted that mummy real bad. Said some museum wanted something American to show up that Egyptian stuff they been diggin' up. Said he'd pay me fifty dollars. So, I wrapped 'er in a tarp and hauled 'er in."

"When you got to Reynald's place what did you do?"

"We hauled everything inside and set it on that big table."

"Did Reynald pay you?"

"Hell no!"

Mitchell holstered the gun. Groesbeck's story was making him ill. "How did Reynald survive? He wasn't selling any antique furniture."

"Hell, I don't know," Groesbeck protested. "He made a trip to Salt Lake once a month. That's all I know. He never made much off the stuff I sold him, 'cause there wasn't that much of it."

"You think he did some business in Salt Lake?"

"He must have, but I never had anything to do with it."

"Did he ever mention what he did before he came here?"

"We didn't talk about much of anything."

Mitchell removed the ear-cuff from his pocket and held it for Groesbeck to see. "You ever see this before?"

Groesbeck stared at the silver cuff then nodded. "Yeah. I seen it on that injun gal's body. At least it looks like the ones I saw."

"You saw more than one?"

"Yeah. There was one on each ear."

"This burial mound—how hard is it to find?"

"Like I said, two or three miles north of Bingham's Fort. The ledge is on the south side."

"I'll tell you what," advised Mitchell. "I'm going back to town tonight. You be at the White House Hotel Monday morning at nine. You're taking me out there, and you're showing me everything."

"Hell. I don't want to go out there again. 'Specially in daytime."

"You'll do it, or I'll shoot your ass right now and drag you back there tonight."

"Danged if you wouldn't do it!"

"Try me."

"Danged if I will. I ain't no gunman." Groesbeck hunched his shoulders, and jammed his thumbs in his belt. "Anybody ever tell you what an ornery skunk you are?"

Mitchell smiled stiffly. "Once or twice."

"All right, dang it. I'll be there."

CHAPTER 22

Utah Territory
Ogden—September 1868

Sunlight filtered through the open pattern of the window curtains, flooding the room with a subdued brightness and lacy shadows. Sarah rushed from her bedroom, and before Mitchell could close the door, Susan was trapped in Sarah's embrace.

"I've been worried sick."

"I was a little worried myself," Susan admitted.

"Are you hurt?" Sarah demanded.

"My tailbone is bruised a bit. That Dickson fellow dumped me right on a tree root. I'm fine otherwise."

Sarah frowned and brushed a hand through Susan's hair. "That Pratt boy told me you were fine, but it didn't help much."

Susan frowned. "Well, you can stop worrying," she sighed. "Why are we in different rooms?"

Sarah took her younger sister by the arm and led her to the nearest chair. "We had a little trouble with the other suite. So, I had Mr. Goodwin move us into these rooms. I've been at Mother's house since early this morning, so things are a little disorganized." She tossed a cushion on the seat, placed her hands on Susan's shoulders, and pressed her downward.

Sarah turned back to Mitchell and thrust herself into his arms, relishing the strength she felt in him. "I've been quite miserable without you," she murmured quietly. She gave Mitchell a long look then smiled. "I *have* missed you."

Mitchell held her close for a long moment. "While you and Susan talk, I'll roust out that clerk in the lobby and tell him we want a bathing tub and hot water up here right away," he said quietly. "When I get back, I want to know what's been going on. Then I'm going to sleep for a week."

Late the next morning, a loud knocking rent the stillness of the suite. Sarah closed her book, and feeling slightly irritated at the interruption, she set the book aside and stepped to the door.

"Yes?"

"It's the desk man, Mrs. Mitchell. I have a telegram. It came yesterday. For some reason, no one delivered it. I'm sorry...."

Cautiously, Sarah opened the door. The desk man stood quietly in the hallway.

"Don't blame you for that," He said, nodding at the pistol in her hand.

"A reasonable precaution, in view of past circumstances," Sarah replied. When the desk man had gone, she returned to her chair and studied the message.

"Who is it from?" Susan asked, her voice dripping with curiosity.

"It's from Collin's Uncle, William, in Denver."

"Uncle William, the silver King?"

"Yes," Sarah replied.

"And what does Uncle William have to say?"

"He says he has sent a letter, but he's afraid it will arrive too late. The letter explains things more fully." Sarah read on for a moment, but stopped suddenly. "Listen to this:

> 'Collin Stop Married Ellen In April Stop Hired Canfield On Her Recommendation Stop Noticed Large Withdrawals From Bank Account Stop Bushwhacked In August Stop Left For Dead Stop Bank Account Empty Stop Ellen And Canfield Run Off Stop May Come Your Way Stop Be Careful Stop William'"

"Oh, no," Susan whispered. "Collin will be very upset."

"These may be the people who have been trying to kill us," Sarah replied, calmly. "They bushwhacked Uncle William and left him for dead; they may try to do the same with his partner."

"But killing Collin will do them no good. He's willed everything to us." Susan replied.

"Exactly," Sarah concluded.

"Oh, dear!" Susan exclaimed. "Those men...taking me to Corinne.... and the man at the stable."

"And the ones who shot my room to pieces," Sarah added angrily.

"What about the children?" Susan demanded suddenly.

"No one knows we left the children with Papa and Mama," Sarah answered calmly. "If we're careful, no one *will* now, and they will be fine. Papa wouldn't let anything happened to them."

"We should let Papa know." Susan argued. "We should send Daniel with a note. That way no one would see us near the house, and Papa could still be prepared."

"Perfect!" Sarah responded.

An hour later, Susan stood near the front window and watched as Daniel Pratt turned down Main Street and walked his new, chestnut mare toward the southern end of town. "What now?" She asked quietly.

"First, you stay away from the window," Sarah admonished. "Then we find your new revolver and make sure it's loaded."

"It's in my handbag," Susan replied, "and it's loaded."

"Then, keep your handbag with you until this business is settled."

"I don't like this," Susan said. "Having someone threaten our family, I mean."

"Neither do I," Sarah answered. "Yet, somehow, it makes it easier to understand Collin's fierceness. I feel as though my back is to a wall and some invisible creature is about to spring on me and tear me in pieces."

"I do feel hunted," Susan agreed.

"Well, I'm not going to take it lying down," Sarah muttered angrily.

"What do you intend?"

"I don't know."

"I don't like the idea of hiding in these rooms," Susan said.

"Neither do I," Sarah replied. "Collin wouldn't do it, but he will expect us to stay out of sight until he finds this woman and her accomplice."

Susan shook her head. "I won't do it," she muttered stubbornly.

"He'll insist, if he knows," Sarah predicted.

"We have to tell him," Susan insisted. "We can't let him wander around unaware that these people could be trying to kill him, but I'm not going to be locked up in these rooms like a prisoner."

Sarah looked out of the window at the gray, dust-filled sky. "We'll tell him everything," she concluded, "but we'll have to stand our ground. If we don't, we could be stuck in these rooms for weeks."

Susan shuddered. "Good Lord! I couldn't stand that. I've got cabin fever already."

"Then, we'd better have a good argument," Sarah suggested.

"How many do you suppose there are?" Susan asked.

"How many?"

"People... how many people have they hired to kill us?"

"I hadn't considered it," Sarah answered.

"There must be several," Susan argued. "Counting Daniel, there were four in Corinne....if we ignore Beazer and his bunch."

"And three in my room the following night," Sarah added.

"That's seven or eight counting Ellen and Canfield," Sarah suggested.

"Less three in Corinne... and the one you shot," Susan replied.

"Leaving four or five," Sarah maintained.

Susan shook her head. "Too many," she argued. "Why involve so many? The whole territory would know what was going on."

"Perhaps there were only seven to begin with," Sarah suggested.

"Four in Corinne...."

"And three here," Sarah finished.

"That sounds more reasonable," Susan conceded.

"Leaving three...maybe more" Sarah concluded.

"Ellen, Canfield, and one other," Susan acknowledged.

"Whom we know nothing about," Sarah responded.

"We know they have money," Susan offered.

"Probably quite a large amount," Sarah admitted.

"And they'll spend the stuff like water," Susan predicted cautiously.

"Possibly."

"A man and a woman.... Single, or pretending to be husband and wife?" Susan asked.

"Either," Sarah admitted," but most certainly still working together."

"With at least one hired skunk."

"Whom we know nothing about," Sarah repeated pointedly.

"So we concentrate on the pair and hope the skunk gives himself away," Susan concluded.

"Fine," Sarah agreed. "Where do we start?"

"Right here in the hotel," Susan suggested. "Of course...." She stood suddenly and began pacing the room. "They have to stay somewhere," she argued, "and there aren't many places that will be good enough for a couple of thieving gentiles trying to fit into high society."

"They may not be gentiles," Sarah suggested. "And they may rent, or buy a house," she added.

"Yes, but it shouldn't be all that hard to find out who's new in town and throwing a lot of money around."

"We should talk with the Relief Society Presidents," Sarah suggested. "I'm sure they would know who's new in their Wards."

Susan nodded absently, knowing that the local leaders of the Church's society of women watched over one another and would know of anyone new in town. "We should ask the men," she advised. "They're bigger gossips than the Sisters. They probably know every move that's made, before it happens."

"What about places outside of town?" Sarah asked.

Susan was quiet as she considered the outlying towns. She thought it unlikely that their adversaries would frequent the farming communities. "I think we can worry about that later," she responded. "We'll have enough to do right here in town."

Sarah watched her younger sister pace the room. Susan was a high-strung, active young woman, but it was unlike her to assume leadership and wade into such an undertaking. Generally, Susan hung back, contributing her opinion; yet seemingly content to allow Sarah to take charge. For Sarah, it was a refreshing and welcome change.

"You seem quite certain of how to handle this," Sarah said cautiously.

"Listen, dear," Susan replied, "I usually keep my mouth shut and let you take the lead."

"I know...."

"But that doesn't mean I'm incapable of rational thought."

"I know that."

"It only means that I recognize your talent for working with people and getting things done. You project those lady-like qualities that I'd sometimes like to chuck out the window. You can reason when you're angry, but when I'm irritated I'd rather poke someone in the eye and get rid of the frustration."

"I know."

"Say that again and I'll poke *you* in the eye."

"What do you want to do?" Sarah asked quietly.

"I want you to understand that this has gone beyond talk. These people are trying to kill us. I'll give them a boot to help them on their way to a hotter place, before I let that happen. You asked me about my revolver... well, I bought a second one, and I've been practicing every day—Daniel says it ain't safe to stand in front of me now."

Sarah waited, knowing her sister had not finished.

"From now on," Susan said finally, "*we* hunt *them*. And when we find them, they'll know they've been in one ugly fight."

"I agree," Sarah responded, "but how are you going to explain this to Collin?"

"I intend telling him everything—except the fact that you and I will be hunting these people."

"Very well."

"I have another concern," Susan said quietly.

"Which is?" Sarah responded.

"Uncle William," Susan answered. "If they emptied his bank account, he'll be broke."

"We'll just have to send him some money," Sarah replied.

"I haven't the foggiest idea how," Susan admitted.

"Neither do I," Sarah answered, "but Mr. Goodwin may know how to handle it."

"Then we should speak with Mr. Goodwin immediately."

CHAPTER 23

Utah Territory
Ogden—September 1868

Samuel Hillard was fifty-three years old and had six wives and thirty-two children. They were a bickering and discontented lot and gave Hillard no end of pain. Hillard was no jewel himself and probably deserved much of what he got; being more concerned with his own comfort and happiness than that of his growing family. To appease the women, Hillard built three houses, each identical in every respect, and each designed to accommodate two of his discontented women and their children. The houses were not mansions, even by the standards of the time, consisting simply of a common kitchen flanked by a single large bedroom on either side.

Hillard's wives were not content with a twenty by twenty foot private living space and a shared kitchen. Still, they found some relief in the fact that they had any privacy at all, and the competition for Brother Hillard's attention was reduced significantly. Hillard managed this feat by building one house in the Salt Lake Valley, near the Jordan River. He raised the second twenty miles north, near the mouth of Farmington canyon, and the third he placed in Ogden City on the northwest corner of Fifth and Monroe.

Removing his wives to three distant geographical areas immediately relieved Hillard of two-thirds of the bickering. The homes in Salt Lake and Farmington were acceptable enough to the six discontented women, since their previous homes had been barely livable soddies built side-by-side on the eastern foothills of the Oquirrh Mountains. But the house in Ogden was unacceptable. It was too far from the social life of Salt Lake and not one of the six women wanted to live there. In fact, each woman hated the place for her own reasons and made sure Brother Hillard never forgot it. Each of the women knew that there was no hope of convincing Brother Hillard to sell the despised property, so they swallowed the situation like a bitter decoction of lobelia tea and hunkered down for war. The bickering stopped almost entirely, except of course, when Brother Hillard came to the Ogden house. When that blessed event occurred every third month, hell seemed to open her mouth serve up the proverbial gnashing of teeth.

Hillard had built the Ogden house during the summer of 1860 using adobe bricks—bricks his children had made from mud and straw trodden in a pit behind the house. In later life, the Hillard children claimed that, like the children of Israel, they had made bricks for an Egyptian taskmaster.

The Hillard house was just one of the places Susan had decided to visit that day. Her visit with Sister Anderson, earlier in the day had convinced her that each of the families she planned to visit had something in common— new neighbors. And none of them seemed to know anything about the new families who had just moved in. The Hillards were no exception, and after an hour of visiting, Susan was ready to give up the idea that any of those unknown people were Uncle William's pair of thieves. She was tired of visiting and ready to call it a day when she noticed a scrunched-up face peering through the window. At first, she simply identified the searching eyes as those of one of the Hillard children, but one look at the shock on Sister Hillard's face left no doubt that none of the Hillard children would risk the offence.

As the faceless shadow at the window disappeared, Susan was already rushing for the door. She had no idea what prompted her, but she had the sudden feeling that it was imperative that she discover the identity of that shadowy figure. She yanked the door open and plunged into the sunlight. For a moment, she squinted into the brightness. She was only seconds behind the man, but the boardwalk west of the house was clear for more than a block and not a soul stood between her and the White House Hotel. Without thinking of what she would do or say, if she somehow overtook the man, she rushed toward the hotel stables.

He couldn't have gone anywhere else.

The heels of her black, high button shoes clattered loudly on the boardwalk and she knew there was no hope of coming upon the man by stealth. She had ruined that prospect with her thoughtless rush from the house. The man would surely hear her rackety approach and run like blazes if he wanted to remain anonymous.

Still, she reached the stables at a dead run, and clutching her skirts high, she leaped from the boardwalk to the dry, hard packed ground. No one was in sight. She sprinted to the back of the building and caught a glimpse of a dark shirt disappearing through a small door on the south wall of the stable. Again, she sprinted after the man. She reached the door of the stables breathing hard, feeling the heat of the sun and a trickle of perspiration between her shoulder blades.

Her hand had hardly touched the door latch when the door swung violently outward, smashing against her knuckles and slamming her to the ground. Dazed and feeling vaguely disoriented, she felt a strong hand grasp the collar of her dress at the back of her neck. She fought the grip and tried to rise to her feet. But the fist tightened, and a strong arm yanked her off balance, dragging her backward, into the dimness of the stable.

"Help!" she screamed into the dimness. She twisted, trying to face her assailant, hoping to find some way to fight, but the fist clamped to her collar yanked her violently, and an iron hard arm wrapped itself around her throat. The arm tensed with a crushing force, stifling her yells and cutting off her air.

Wildly, she clawed at the arm, but to no avail. And when she gouged at the man's eyes, he simply batted her hands away with strength and a disdain that stirred a disturbingly potent anger within her. She was terrified. It felt as though she was caught in the grasp of an evil so malevolent that her entire world hung in a precarious balance.

Suddenly she felt as though she could stab the man to the heart for his utter contempt for her life. Still, when her hands fell away from the man's face it was with a sense of failure and despair. Suddenly, she wished she had never left the safety of Goodwin's hotel. Franticly, she clawed at her assailant again. Again, her hands were thrust away, but this time her hands came away clutching a hat pin, and the silly hat she could never keep on her head went skittering across the stable floor.

Pins.

The thought came with the sickening feeling that she had only moments before the arm crushed the life from her. Without warning, she dropped one hand behind her and stabbed upward with every ounce of strength she had, driving the foot-long hat pin into the man's thigh. She heard a bellow, but her senses were reeling.

Suddenly, the arm was gone and she sagged to the straw covered floor of the stable. The world grew hazy and far away. Perched on a precipice, she felt evil and darkness pushing her toward the edge and a fall into unimaginable depths. She fought the darkness praying for help. Light poured into the barn through the big double doors.

CHAPTER 24

Utah Territory
Ogden—September 1868

"*F*irst those men at Browning's—then Corinne—and now this. I don't like it," Sarah muttered angrily ten minutes later.

"I'm fine," Susan protested, holding a damp cloth to her chafed throat. "He wasn't trying to break my neck; he was just choking me to death."

"Just choking you," Sarah growled angrily. "You make it sound as though having some brute choke the life out of you is nothing unusual. You're lucky Collin was restless and went to check on the horses."

"My throat is fine," Susan asserted hoarsely. "It's my pride that's feeling damaged. And I'm not sure I'll go near the stables alone for awhile."

"I don't think it's safe to go anywhere alone for awhile," Sarah protested. "What ever possessed you to go chasing through town like that?"

"I don't know," Susan admitted lamely. "I saw someone watching me through the window at Sister Hillard's house and had the most uncontrollable urge to discover who could be curious enough to be peeping in windows."

"And nearly got yourself killed in the process," Sarah grumbled stiffly. "I don't think Collin will be at all pleased when he hears more about this."

"I'm not pleased about it, either," Susan replied. She stood and brushed at the dust and straw covering her dress. "My hat's ruined," she said absently.

"We'll buy you a new one, tomorrow," Sarah promised. "For now, I think we should stay here until we can talk about this with Collin."

Grimly, Susan looked at the western sky and the gathering clouds. "Next time I go chasing about town, I'm taking Mr. Colt along. And I'll stay away from the stables."

The sun was just disappearing when Sarah and Mitchell entered Jake Farney's store. The thin man closed the door behind them and hurried to the alley door. A moment later he returned.

"It's clear."

Mitchell crossed the alley and opened the door of the dead man's shop. Sarah hurried in behind him. Red orange light, from the lowering sun, filled the shop. Mitchell went to the front window. The street was empty.

"The jewelry is under the back counter," he said.

Sarah was already there. She looked up, shaking her head. "There's nothing here."

"Nothing?"

"Completely empty—not even an empty box. The shelves are empty."

"Dang it!" Mitchell motioned her toward the alley door. "Someone's been here." He looked around the room, hoping for some explanation.

Glass shattered and the wood of the counter seemed to explode amid the thunder of a gunshot. For a moment, Sarah stood petrified.

Angrily, Mitchell grabbed her by the arm and nearly dragged her from her feet. "You hurt?" he demanded.

Sarah shook her head. She was trembling and close to tears. Away from the window, he pinned her against the wall and held her close. He waited, but the night was silent.

"Let's go."

Quickly, they left the dimness of Reynald's shop, crossed the alley and entered Farney's store.

"I heard a shot!" Farney exclaimed. "What the blazes happened!"

"Some one took a shot at us through the front window. Had to come from Tolson's loft." Mitchell yanked the colt from its holster and jerked open the door. "You keep an eye on Sarah. I'm going over there."

Mitchell was more than irritated when he entered Tolson's smithy. The shot that had torn through Reynald's shop had come from Tolson's. The angle of the bullet's path left no doubt about that fact, and Mitchell was mad enough to beat the ornery little blacksmith senseless. Still, he had no proof that Tolson had fired the shot. The shot had come from the loft of Tolson's barn—Mitchell was certain of that, and the damage to the back wall of Reynald's place was a likely fit for the forty-five caliber Sharps that Tolson kept standing in one corner of the smithy. But, anyone could have gotten into the smithy, taken the Sharps and fired the shot from the loft. Beating the snot out of Tolson might relieve Mitchell's anger, but only a fool would beat up an old man without solid proof.

Mitchell strode past the forge and snatched the Sharps from its corner. The sulfurous smell of freshly burned black powder was strong at the muzzle.

"Don't move."

Mitchell stood still, waiting.

"Just what are you doin' in here?"

"Someone just took a shot at my wife and me," Mitchell growled angrily.

"So, you busted in here? Where's your wife?"

"I left her at Farney's place."

"Best give me a good reason not to shoot you," Tolson demanded.

Mitchell turned and faced the old man. "That shot came from your loft, and that gun was just fired."

"I ain't used that gun for over a month."

"Somebody did."

"Maybe so. I heard a shot. Heard a horse run off out back too."

Mitchell frowned at the old man. "How did they get in?"

"Same way you did. I ain't locked up yet."

"First your knife, now your rifle," Mitchell snarled. "Either you're a danged liar, or someone wants you to look like you're up to your neck in Reynald's murder."

"I ain't no liar."

"Then who hates you bad enough to try makin' you look guilty?"

"I don't know."

"That's 'cause there ain't no one else." Becker's voice came from the half-open doorway. "Put the gun down, Tolson."

Tolson eased the hammers down and laid the shotgun on the edge of the forge.

"I didn't kill anybody," he protested.

"We got your knife," Becker responded.

"That don't mean nothin'."

"I figure it does." Becker moved into the smithy. Behind him trailed another man with a badge pinned to his shirt. Mitchell said nothing.

"Reynald owed you five hundred dollars," Becker continued. "I figure you got tired of waitin' and tried to collect. When he wouldn't pay, you stuck that knife between his ribs."

"That'd be a stupid trick," Tolson argued. "I'd never get any money that way."

"But you would if you took that jewelry he had in his store."

"What are you talkin' about."

"Reynald had a bunch of jewelry in his store. We just come from your house. It was all there."

"I don't know what you're talkin' about."

Becker's partner lifted a leather apron. Its lower half was stained with darkish brown smears. "I'll bet you don't know anything about this either."

"It's mine," Tolson admitted, "but that blood is from a horse I was shoeing."

"You can tell that to a court," Becker snapped. "I'm arresting you for murder. You coming peaceable, or do I need to shoot you and have you drug over to the jail?"

Tolson shook his head. "You never did have the sense the good lord gave a turnip. Always looking for the easy way."

Mitchell finally spoke. "Seems a bit stupid for a man to kill someone with a knife he's scratched his name on then throw the knife out where it can be found."

"Nobody's askin' you," Becker snarled. "I figured you was smart enough to handle this job, but it appears to me that you ain't much good at it. We got enough evidence here, and that's all that matters."

"I don't agree."

"What!" Becker strode toward Mitchell, stopping just inches from the taller man. Mitchell struggled to hold his temper. The muzzle of Becker's cocked pistol was pointed squarely at Mitchell's lower ribs. "You're fired, Mitchell."

"Suits me," Mitchell growled. "But you better point that pistol somewhere else, and do it fast or I'm gonna crack your skull with it!"

Becker's face flushed red with anger. Mitchell sensed some inner struggle, as though Becker wanted to pull the trigger. Becker hesitated then turned the pistol aside.

"Get out," he hissed.

Mitchell stepped around the angry deputy and left the smithy. His anger was quickly dissipating, and in its place was a growing curiosity. Becker had never gone to Salt Lake City, and he was almighty anxious to jail someone— too anxious in Mitchell's view. But why? Even Becker should have known that tracking down a murderer would not be easy. Yet for some reason, Becker seemed willing to put the blame on Tolson.

Farney opened the front door of his shop and poked his head out. "Find anything?"

"Just Becker and a little rooster taggin' around with him."

"That'd be Aaron Gilson," Farney replied, stepping out onto the boardwalk. "Becker's teachin' him the Sheriff business."

"Looked like he was more interested in shootin' someone."

"He's full up of himself alright. Claims he was in Springfield Missouri three years ago when Bill Hickock shot some fellow named Tutt. Thinks he knows all about bein' a gunman now. Becker don't seem to notice how ridiculous they look—traipsin' around with their thumbs hooked in their belts and their coats thrown back so folks can see they're wearin' a gun."

"Seems a bit childish," Mitchell admitted. He was keenly aware of the navy Colt weighing down his own belt and Sarah's desire to see him shuck the thing and live a little less dangerously. Yet, even Sarah knew that there was little he could do about it and that he might never be free of the thing. Still, things could change. In fact, he had high expectations for the near future.

He hadn't said anything to either woman, but his Uncle William had wired him from Denver, saying that he had struck a good vein and the mine was producing silver ore worth nearly a thousand dollars a ton. Uncle William had put Mitchell's share in a Denver bank and would continue to do so until Mitchell told him differently. William had always said that he had filed the claim in both their names. "One day, we'll both be rich men, Collin," he had said. "You can count on that, boy."

Uncle William had always been grateful that Mitchell had trusted him, grubstaked him and kept him going when no other member of the family seemed to care if the old man lived or died. To the rest of the family, William was a black sheep, and they had put him out of the flock. Mitchell had never agreed with the way William had been treated. His relationship with the old man had started as nothing more than an attempt to irritate and shame the family. It had ended with a lasting friendship between two men who found they were much alike.

"Wearin' a gun doesn't make a man," Mitchell said, dragging his thoughts back to the present.

"No, it don't," Farney replied.

"Sometimes a man is forced to use tools that are not to his liking," Sarah advised. She stepped past Farney and took Mitchell by the hand. "Sometimes even the kindest men are called on to do things they would never choose to do. Most women are intelligent enough to respect a man who can stand up and do what has to be done. I certainly couldn't care for a man who didn't have the courage or the strength to take care of those he loves."

"Reckon that's a fair way of lookin' at it," Farney acknowledged. "I hear your Brother Brigham is a hard man and wouldn't hesitate to shoot the folks that cross him."

"That's not true," Sarah protested.

"Brother Brigham says we should defend ourselves," Mitchell responded, "even if it means taking the lives of folks that try to kill us. I don't think he ever said anything about shootin' anyone 'cause they disagreed with us."

"Maybe so," Farney answered, "but the truth ain't always the thing folks want to hear, and even when they hear it, they tend to twist things around 'til you'd never recognize it."

"Speakin' of truth, Jake...." Mitchell looked the tall man in the eyes. "You told that Richards woman some kind of a whopper."

Farney swallowed, glancing at Sarah. "Look, Mitchell, I didn't mean any harm. It's just that the woman has been badgering my wife and me, wanting us to get involved in this suffrage thing. We both got enough to do, keepin' food on the table and raising our kids. Neither one of us has the time to run around talking to folks. We tried to tell her, but she's like a herd of runaways when she gets going. You can't get a word in."

"So you told her we were good, church going Methodists?" Sarah scolded.

Farney shrugged. "Some of the things she talks about are a little too sneaky for my taste."

"You figured they'd be more to our taste?" Sarah snapped.

"No. I didn't. But I thought you folks would understand what she's up to. I couldn't make sense of it. I can make furniture, but I got no head for politics."

"She's up to causing trouble," Sarah answered. "She wants women in the territory to have the right to vote then she wants them to use that vote to make plural marriage illegal."

"You see," Farney insisted. "You saw that right off. I never even noticed."

CHAPTER 25

Utah Territory
Ogden—September 1868

*B*y mid-morning the next day, Mitchell was following Groesbeck on a narrow trail headed north. They rode quietly. Mitchell was in no mood to talk with the surly grave robber, and Groesbeck was quiet and withdrawn. The sun was high in a cloudless blue sky when they finally reached the hill-like mound, and Groesbeck dismounted at the southern slope. A raw cut was still visible where Groesbeck had hacked into the face of the burial. Sand and debris had collapsed into a small opening three-quarters of the way to the top of the mound, leaving a cliff like face of rock with a sandy alluvial fan at its base. Broken, dried-out and crushed bits and pieces of sagebrush and tumbleweed littered the slope.

Groesbeck pointed toward the jagged outcrop of rock. "Looks like the slope has broke loose and covered the little cave, but you can still see the top of it."

"I can see it," Mitchell replied. He studied the mound, wondering why he had come here. It was not a good place to bring Groesbeck. Two Bears had been deadly serious about killing the man, and Mitchell knew that Two Bears would make it slow and painful for the grave robber.

"You took everything?" he asked, knowing the answer would reveal little he didn't already know.

"Everything, except the things that was broke."

"What things?"

"Pots and some other gee-gaws."

"What kind of gee-gaws?"

"Mostly beads. Looked like some kind of necklace. It was all busted up and scattered. Hundreds of 'em... beads and little shells with holes in 'em."

"You broke the necklace?"

"Hell no. I never broke nothin' I could get paid for."

"Show me."

"Good grief man, can't you just let me be. There ain't no law against what I done."

"Maybe not, but Reynald was up to something, and the things you took from this place are the only trail I have. So, get your carcass up there, and show me what you saw."

Cursing, Groesbeck fought his way through the sandy alluvium and was soon kicking at the soil blocking the opening. Mitchell followed more slowly.

The sand was loose, and Groesbeck had left a well-defined trail straight to the burial site. No other tracks marred the slope—except his own.

"There dang it!" Groesbeck snarled. "Just like I told you, shells and beads everywhere."

Mitchell hunkered down on his heels and studied the chamber. It was nothing more than a small pocket eroded from the open face of the outcropping. The floor had been filled with sand and leveled, leaving a surface large enough for the woman's remains and the possessions Two Bears had left with her. Shells and beads littered the floor. Mitchell pointed to the center of the floor. "The body was there?"

"Yep."

"Any of the beads or shells on the body?"

"No. Everything was scattered on the floor, just like now. The body was layin' on top of them gewgaws out in the middle."

Mitchell stood and backed away from the opening. He felt a tightness in his chest and an urge to get away from the place. He was disgusted with Groesbeck and wanted to be rid of the man. "What about earrings?" he asked.

"Just some little silver clamp-on things," Groesbeck growled.

Mitchell frowned and looked north toward the hot springs and the Shoshoni camp. "Climb on your horse and get out of here. You'd be smart to get out of the territory. The Shoshoni, are not happy about you lootin' this grave, and they're lookin' for you."

Groesbeck's face lost its color. "You brought me here knowin' that! They'll kill me!"

"I expect so, but if you go as far as Denver or Tucson you might last awhile."

Groesbeck cursed and rushed down the slope. Loose sand caught at his feet, dragging him to his knees, but the burly grave robber struggled to his feet, staggered the last ten yards to the bottom of the mound and dragged himself astride his horse. The mare fought the rein as the big man turned, spitting in Mitchell's general direction.

"I hope they gun you down," he bellowed. Yanking hard on the rein, he jammed his heels into the mare's quivering sides and headed south at a gallop.

Mitchell watched the man ride, dust swirling under the mare's hooves until both man and animal disappeared in the trees. He knew it was the last he would see of the grave robber, and he couldn't help feeling a sense of relief. He hunkered down, settling back on his heels and breaking a twig from a stray branch of dead sagebrush. Snapping a small piece from the twig, he flipped it down the hillside.

The September sun baked everything in its sight, but a light wind from the southwest cooled the air with fitful gusts and bowed the grass in waves of yellow-green. Mitchell watched, letting the mesmerizing motion of the grass draw his mind into a moment of unfocused solitude. Only the wind broke the silence, rustling leaves—tipping grass. He took a deep breath, feeling the heat draw the ache from his back.

Later, half-an-hour—an hour—he wasn't sure, but his knees were cramped and his hat was uncomfortably warm when his eyes focused on a flutter of red amid the waves of yellowed grass.

"Now that's odd," he muttered.

It was as though he had seen the colorful movement much earlier, yet somehow paid no attention. The color reminded him of one of Susan's dresses, a vibrant color meant to draw the eye.

Susan was a vibrant type herself—meant to draw the eye. But he was at a loss, not knowing how to handle their present dilemma. His search for land had been less than productive. Susan and Sarah were, in their own way, pressuring him to build what each considered the ideal home in the ideal location. Yet, neither woman wanted to be far from the other. Things had been simple enough at first. Both women had agreed to separate houses on property outside of town. That had been a good enough plan, but recently Susan had changed her mind, claiming that she now wanted a house in the city. Mitchell wasn't sure what had changed her mind, but he was having fits trying to find a way to give them both what they wanted. Now, he just felt enormously weary. Again, the breeze laid the grass low, exposing the red flutter.

Finally, Mitchell forced himself to stand. His knees complained; his legs cramped; his feet pulsed with pins and needles. For a moment, he stood still, waiting for the complaints to ease. He wasn't sure time would treat him as kindly as it did some people—folks who seemed to age gracefully then just leave the world in their sleep. Somehow, he couldn't imagine that God would let him out of this world without giving him the full treatment, and in a way, that was fair enough.

At the base of the mound, he took the dun by the rein and walked nearly a hundred feet to the fluttering bit of cloth. He had expected some tattered bit of rag snagged on a root or branch, but the fluttering piece was part of something larger—something shallowly buried—something partially torn loose by the gouging hoof of a running horse, a pigeon-toed horse.

Milo.

Mitchell glared at the hoof-prints and felt the hair stand up on the back of his neck. They were fresh, so fresh that grass bent by the passing horse was slowly rising back to its original position.

He knelt and tugged at the exposed bit of cloth. A larger piece came free of the soil, but it took several healthy tugs and some careful excavation to free the rotting remnants of a red gingham dress.

He took the dress by the shoulders and held it at arm's length, gauging the size and the height of the woman who had worn it.

Slender. Not even as tall as Susan.

The dress was in bad shape. Little of the original color remained, and in general, the entire dress had faded to a dull, rust colored brown.

Carefully, he folded and rolled the rotted fabric and stuffed it in his saddlebags. He wasn't sure why he did it. At first, he thought the dress was nothing more than household trash. But that thought was soon discarded. The mound was nearly three miles from any habitation, and it was unlikely that anyone from town would travel so far to dump the household garbage. In fact, most folks found places much closer to home. The idea had other flaws as well. First, no one with a lick of sense would come so far to get rid of a single dress. In this valley, every scrap of cloth was used and reused until nothing remained but little squares stitched together in a quilt. And second, no one would ever take the time to bury the thing. The whole idea was absurd.

Mitchell studied the hollow in the rock face of the mound. Something about the little crypt disturbed him. He couldn't pin it down, but there was *something* troubling about the shells and the way they lay scattered on the floor.

Dragging his attention from the mound, he searched the tall grass. Milo's hooves had cut a trail that was easy to follow. From where he stood, the trail simply turned south toward town. But it wasn't where Milo was going that interested Mitchell.

"What's he been up to?"

Taking up the dun's rein, he followed Milo's back-trail. Thirty yards to the east, Milo's tracks disappeared near a small cairn. Some of the stones had been knocked about; still, the pile was relatively undisturbed. Milo's hooves had torn the ground nearby, and there were earlier signs of a wagon's passing, but the elements had blotted out any earlier activity.

Mitchell stopped, and retrieved a stray rock. It was small, hardly bigger than his fist. In fact, the entire rock pile was smaller than he had imagined. Yet, Groesbeck had told the truth. Here and there among the piled stones, human bones were plainly visible. Resigned to the possibility that the dress and the bones were somehow connected, Mitchell knelt and began shifting the pile.

Within minutes, he had uncovered enough to satisfy his curiosity. The bones were a jumble—a disarticulated pile. The skeletal remains seemed complete, but nothing was where it should be. He'd seen a few burials, mostly flat out on their backs, or all curled up in a bundle, like a sleeping baby. But this looked as though someone had shuffled the bones like a deck of cards before dumping them in an unruly heap. And they were dry. Parts that had been exposed to the sun had been bleached white and cracked, while others were merely aged or bored with insect holes. But on the whole, it seemed a strange way for anyone to bury the dead.

Somewhat anxiously, now that he had uncovered the thing, Mitchell examined the bones. He didn't know much about human anatomy. He'd never had an interest in it. About all he'd learned in school was to read and write, a little arithmetic, and a few other less useful things. But he was an observant man.

Carefully, he rebuilt the skeleton. Piece by piece, he laid out the parts he knew—the skull, the backbone. The lower jaw had come loose—mandible he'd heard a doctor call it one time. He put the jaw where it belonged, noted a missing tooth and moved on to the arms and legs. When he had finished, the major bones were in place, but many were still jumbled in the pile.

"Not as easy as I thought," he told the dun. The animal stood calmly, ignoring him. "Looks kind of short," he observed.

The wind continued to buffet the grass, beating it to the ground time and again as Mitchell studied the bones. Finally, he stood and stretched then retrieved a bit of twine from his saddlebags. Using the twine as a measure, Mitchell gauged the length of the reconstructed skeleton. He tied a knot in the twine then stood and held it close to his body, letting the end dangle to the ground. The knot was barely as high as his chin.

"Yup," he said. "Kind of short for a man. And the bones are small. Bet it's a woman." The dun dipped its big head and nipped at the grass.

"Problem is," Mitchell muttered, "this ain't no mummy." Mitchell hunkered down beside the bones, carefully looking for anything that might help. After twenty minutes, he had found nothing. As far as he could tell, the bones could have lain there a hundred years.

"About tall enough for that dress though," he concluded.

Finally, convinced there was nothing more he could discover, he began the task of replacing the bones within the cairn. He disliked disturbing the place, but finding the dress and the cairn so close together made it hard to believe that the bones belonged to anyone but Melinda Tolson. Yet, even if he was right, he had no way of proving it. Even if Alfred Tolson could identify the dress as his daughter's, nothing really connected it to the bones.

Suddenly, he felt tired, like a weight had descended squarely on his shoulders, and he wondered how he would feel if his own daughter suddenly ran off and was never seen again. The thought didn't set well. In fact it made him downright ill just thinking about it.

"Tolson must be one unhappy man," he muttered. A man that unhappy might have finally lashed out at whomever he blamed for the girl's disappearance. Yet ornery as Tolson was, Mitchell found it hard to believe the blacksmith would stick a knife in a man six years after the fact. For all his blustering and waving of shotguns, Tolson seemed more likely to hole up like a wounded critter and let his wounds heal.

Bone followed bone into the hollow of the cairn. They didn't stack well, and when the skull finally topped the pile, it sat for a moment, eyeless sockets staring at the sky. Suddenly, something shifted, and the skull rolled to one side. Mitchell stared at the teeth.

"Now that's mighty strange," he muttered.

CHAPTER 26

Utah Territory
Ogden—September 1868

*T*he ride back to town was quiet and uneventful, except for a hard wind blowing in from across the lake. A southwest wind always brought the chance of a storm, yet the sky seemed clear enough for the moment.

Mitchell walked the dun slowly down Main Street. Ogden had started out as a forlorn little town, but it had grown fast. Main Street was now dotted with buildings and more cropped up every day. Things had toned down a bit since he had come through town ten years earlier. The city police kept an eye on things now, and the only excitement he'd seen lately had been a bunch of teenage boys out skylarking. They rode like blazes down Main Street, touched off a couple of rounds from the one pistol they had between them then rode straight out the north end of town. The city police had charged out of town in hot pursuit. Four hours later, tired, dusty, and cussing mad, the officers had returned empty handed.

When the dust had settled, Mitchell had leaned back in his chair, finished his coffee and blamed the whole incident on youthful exuberance and the influence of the dime novel.

Today, Main Street seemed quiet and lazy. The three-mile stretch of hard-packed dirt held an assortment of slow-moving horses, buggies and wagons. No one seemed in a hurry. Even the occasional dust devil turned at a snail's pace, disintegrated at the touch of a wagon wheel, or dissipated unenthusiastically in the middle of the road.

The dun caught the feeling, shifted to a slower pace and plodded south to the same sluggish tune. Mitchell settled himself in the saddle, and gave the dun his head. The animal plodded on, past Second Street and a Tabernacle that was still unfinished after thirteen years—past Third Street and Doc Wadman's office.

Mitchell reined the dun to a stop and with a sense of foreboding, dismounted in front of the doctor's little clapboard office.

"This conversation is at an end!" Wadman snarled, ten minutes later. He snatched Mitchell's hat from the credenza and hurled it at the outer door. The hat sailed perfectly, curved wildly at the last second, and slammed the corner coat rack, wedging itself between two coats. For a moment, both men stared at the hat, saying nothing.

"You seem a mite touchy about this," Mitchell accused.

"You'd be touchy too," snarled Wadman. "I got that stinking letter six months or a year after that girl took my horse. I never did anything but tell the truth about the whole miserable deal. And look what it got me! I'm darn near broke. The city police came in here and tore everything to pieces looking for evidence. They practically accused me of killing the girl. They even ripped my books to pieces. What did they expect to find there, dissected parts pressed like leaves between the pages of Byron's poetry?"

"Love letters?" Mitchell suggested.

"Good lord man, I'm fifty-six years old and homely enough my dog wouldn't kiss me! That girl never said more than 'hello' 'til the night she asked for my horse. And even then, she was in an almighty hurry."

"So how is it that she came to *you* for a horse?"

"I don't know."

"Had she ever borrowed a horse before?"

"No."

"Then why in the world was she here?" Mitchell demanded.

"She was looking for Reynald. She asked about Reynald, and I told her he had just left. I didn't want to let her take the animal. He was tired. I'd been out riding all day and just got back in town. She saw the horse and wanted to ride him over to Reynald's place."

"Why was Reynald here?"

"He came asking about something to help him sleep. He said he was having nightmares and hadn't slept for three nights. I tried to talk to him about his diet, but he was anxious to leave."

"Where was he going?"

"Back to his shop, I think."

"You don't know?"

"I'm not sure.... He hadn't been here five minutes when some kid came running up and gave him a message."

"Did you hear the message?"

"No. But he told the kid something and sent him running."

"I don't suppose you heard any of that either," muttered Mitchell.

"Yes I did," continued Wadman. "He said 'tell him I'll be at my place.'"

"That's it?"

"What more do you want!" Wadman snapped. "You're lucky I can remember that much after six years."

"Who was the boy? Maybe he would remember who sent him after Reynald."

"I really don't know," Wadman answered. His voice sounded tired, and his face suddenly looked haggard. "Someone ought to know him though. It was the kid Ruth Miller paid to feed and water their animals."

Mitchell frowned. "Ruth Miller was dead," he argued.

"Yes, she was," Wadman growled, "but Vernon Miller kept the boy on for a while."

"You think Miller sent the boy?"

"He could have."

Mitchell watched Wadman's eyes. "What if the girl never wrote that letter?"

"Of course she wrote it. Who else could have?"

"That's exactly what I'm wondering," Mitchell answered. "If she didn't write it, who did? And why?"

"I showed that letter to Al Tolson. He said it looked like her hand."

Mitchell shrugged. "I don't doubt it was written in a woman's hand. But what if Melinda Tolson never went to Denver?" he suggested.

"The letter was posted from Denver," Wadman objected sullenly.

"I'm sure it was, but someone else could have written it."

"Why would anyone else send money for that horse?"

Mitchell glanced around the office, noting the rundown look of the place. "The money could have been sent to convince you and everyone else that the girl was in Denver and doing well enough to pay you for the horse. Alfred Tolson never believed his daughter would run off and never contact him again. He told me she was headstrong, but they got along well enough."

"They did most of the time, but I saw her screaming mad at times."

"Tolson admits that, but he says she always cooled off and they worked things out."

Wadman shrugged. "I suppose that's true enough."

"The point is," Mitchell continued, "the girl didn't write her old man. She just took off. It doesn't make any sense."

Wadman looked out the front window and took a deep breath. He blew the air out between pursed lips. "You're right," he concluded. "If she wrote me, she would have written her father."

"When she left here, did she ride toward Reynald's place."

"Yes," she did."

"Anyone else see her?"

"Someone saw her ride down Fourth Street. And later, about dusk, someone saw her riding south through Riverdale."

"Who saw her in Riverdale?"

"I don't think I ever knew, but they should have a record of it, over at the Courthouse."

"How was she dressed?" Mitchell asked suddenly.

"She was wearing a dress—high collar—might have had some lace work on it, but I'm not sure."

"What color?"

"Red, I think.… Maybe it was brown.… I'm not sure."

"You know anything about teeth?"

"Some, but I don't do any dentistry. The fellow across the street can fix you up though."

"Thanks."

At the door, Mitchell reached out and snatched his hat from the coat rack. He opened the door then paused to look back at Wadman.

"I found a red dress and a woman's bones about two miles north of town. Sort of makes me wonder if there's a horse and saddle out there too."

Wadman's jaw tightened and his face flushed angrily.

"Thanks for the help," Mitchell muttered as the door closed firmly behind him.

CHAPTER 27

Utah Territory
Ogden—September 1868

At the rail, Mitchell unhitched the dun, climbed into the saddle and rode to the opposite side of the street. He felt a bit guilty that he hadn't crossed the street on foot, but he had no desire to run a gauntlet of horse manure just to see a dentist. The smell of a dentist's office was bad enough without adding the stink of horse dung to the mix.

"Clean-up crew is a little slow today," announced the dark haired man standing in the open doorway.

The man looked too young to be a dentist as far as Mitchell was concerned. "Looks like they left town," Mitchell replied when the dun was hitched once more.

"It ain't always this bad," the man replied, fanning himself with a worn looking hat.

"Sometimes it's worse," Mitchell answered, anticipating the dentist's reply.

"You got a tooth needs looking at?"

"You might say that," Mitchell answered.

"Well come on in, and let's take a look." He stepped aside, but stuck out a hand. "Name's King.... Nathan King."

"Collin Mitchell." Mitchell took the man's hand, glancing quickly around the office. It was a small, one-room office dominated by a tall, black chair bolted to the center of the floor.

"Have a seat."

Reluctantly, Mitchell leaned against the edge of the black chair. "Listen," he protested, "I'm not here because I've got a toothache."

"I'll have to write this in my journal tonight. Nobody comes in here just to pass the time of day."

Mitchell grinned. "I did come here to talk about teeth."

"Good lord, not so loud! You want to get us arrested?"

"Arrested?"

King laughed. "Just pulling your leg. Why, just this morning, I must have heard half-a-dozen people talking about tooth care. I guess it just took me by surprise. So few in one day, you know?"

"Business ain't so good?" Mitchell asked.

"Not a darn bit."

"What do you know about teeth?"

"Thirty-two per head—give or take."

"What can you tell me about this tooth?"

Mitchell fished the object out of his pocket and dropped it into King's hand.

"Human—upper incisor. Right side, maybe, judging by the wear.

"Anything else?"

You must have found it. It looks as though it's been exposed to the weather."

"What do you make of the shape?"

"Well, I've seen all kinds of shapes."

"So it's not unusual?"

"No, it's not unusual."

"Oh." Mitchell felt a sudden let down. Somehow, he had placed too much significance on the shape of the tooth.

"Sorry to bother you. I just...."

"Not unusual for an Indian," King finished.

"So it is different!" Mitchell exploded.

"Hell yes," King replied. "Had you snookered for a second though, didn't I?"

"Yes you did."

"See this dished out area in the back?"

"Makes it look like a little scoop shovel," Mitchell replied.

"Sure does," King replied. "I've seen that shape a few times. Never on any white folks though."

"Indians?"

"Always."

Mitchell shook his head, frowning. "Dang it!"

"Something wrong?"

"I guess so. I found some bones with that tooth. I thought maybe it belonged to a white girl who disappeared a while back."

Mitchell looked out the window just as the street crew appeared. The three men started shoveling, quickly tossing manure from the street into a wagon-bed.

King watched the crew through the front of the window. "They fling that stuff pretty good, don't they?"

"Downright professional," Mitchell responded.

"Well look at that," King squawked. "There's one of those Flitton girls. I haven't seen either one of 'em for quite a spell. Folks say they're both married now. One of 'em married a gunman...a real hard case they say."

"You don't say...."

"Yes, sir—still, a fine looking woman."

"Yes, she is," Mitchell agreed. He watched as Sarah stepped down from a new buggy and entered Wadman's office.

"That tooth didn't belong to Melinda Tolson," King confided a moment later. "I remember looking at her teeth a time or two. They were flat on the back—just like yours. Only thing I ever had to do to her teeth was smooth off a chipped cusp on one canine."

"Canine?"

"The eye tooth," King answered.

"It was just a possibility," Mitchell said. He dropped the tooth back in his pocket and nodded toward the window. "Looks like that Flitton gal is headed this way."

King smiled suddenly. "You don't say."

King wandered to the window and watched as Sarah crossed the street and stepped up to the door. King moved to the door, opening it just as Sarah's gloved hand touched the knob. Sarah flinched and drew back with a sharp breath.

"Sorry ma'am. Didn't mean to startle you."

"I've had recent problems with doors that open suddenly," Sarah replied. "I'm nervous as a cat."

"A cat with claws,' Mitchell cautioned.

"Hello, dear," Sarah responded. "Doctor Wadman said you were here."

"Mr. King," said Mitchell, "this is my wife, Sarah. Sarah, this is Mr. Nathan King."

"Pleased to meet you, Mrs. Mitchell."

"And I you Mr. King."

King fidgeted, as though embarrassed.

"Mr. King was just telling me how the Flitton girls had grown into fine looking women."

"That's kind of you, Mr. King. I'll let Susan know."

King swallowed, struggling for words.

"I think that Nathan would rather you didn't," Mitchell advised.

"Why in the world not?" Sarah protested. "I think Susan would be flattered."

Mitchell looked into her eyes and winked. "I think Nathan is concerned that Susan's husband might take things wrong."

"I see," Sarah gasped. "I hadn't thought of that—he is sometimes a bit touchy about things...."

"A real hard case," Mitchell prompted.

King seemed pale as he took a firm grip of the back of the black chair.

"He does seem overly fond of firearms," Sarah admitted.

"Didn't he just shoot a couple of fellows up in Corinne?" Mitchell asked.

"But that was different," Sarah responded. "They actually laid hands on her."

"That's true."

"Are you talking about me?" Susan asked as she stepped through the open doorway. King glanced out of the window and let himself lean against the black chair. The buggy was now parked outside his office with the Pratt kid leaning back in the seat, sunning himself.

"Hello, dear," Sarah replied." We were discussing your husband's ornery disposition."

"Your discussion appears to have made this gentleman ill," Susan observed.

"I believe it has," Sarah agreed.

"Perhaps you should introduce us, Collin."

"Of course," Mitchell agreed. "Mr. King this handsome young woman is my wife Susan Mitchell. Susan this gentleman is Mr. Nathan King."

"Pleased to meet you, Mr. King," Susan said sweetly.

"Nice to meet you, Mrs. Mitchell." King said, looking sidewise at Mitchell. "So, you're the gunman."

"Good heavens!" Susan exclaimed. "What have you two been up to?"

"We were just pulling his leg a little," Mitchell protested.

"They did a dang good job of it too," King admitted. He seemed to take a hold on his nerve and stood away from the black chair. "I guess I was overdue for a good leg-pullin'. I'm always fooling with folks, but it ain't often they get the best of me."

"Well," Mitchell confided, "I ain't much of a gunman."

"He's really just a big pussycat," Sarah offered.

"That ain't much consolation," King replied. "I've seen some old tomcats that were hard as nails and meaner than a wounded bear."

"Just a big pussycat," Susan agreed.

"Collin?" Sarah asked. "If you're finished here, we'd like you to come to dinner. Our new ranch foreman says he's hungry."

"I'm finished here. Mr. King was quite helpful."

"Glad I could help," King replied. Surreptitiously, he wiped the sweat from his forehead when the door finally closed behind his three new acquaintances.

"Nice outfit," Mitchell acknowledged as they stepped into the warmth of the afternoon sun.

"Mr. Pratt says that fine-looking women need a fine-looking buggy for traveling around town," Sarah answered brightly.

"I can certainly agree with that," Mitchell replied.

"We didn't have the heart to tell him we have two of them at home," Susan confided.

"Bought the horse too?" Mitchell asked, studying the lines of the well-built chestnut mare.

"I believe so," Susan answered.

"I'll have to make sure Mr. Pratt is aware of the household budget," Sarah admitted.

Mitchell looked at the shiny new buggy and shook his head. "No.... That money is for the household. I'll give Mr. Pratt a monthly budget for the ranch. The horses and buggy can come out of that."

Sarah smiled. "I was a little concerned about the expense."

"Do you need more for the household?" Mitchell asked.

"Well...."

"Yes we do," Susan admitted. "We've been trying to operate on our normal budget, but with the cost of the hotel and meals.... It's just a little expensive."

"How much do you have left?" He asked.

"About two hundred dollars," Sarah answered. "That will last a while, but we are spending much more than usual, and we don't know how long this trip is going to last. You really haven't told us much."

"We do need to talk about money," Mitchell replied. He looked at the cloud-covered September sky. "We can discuss that tonight. In the meantime, we have three thousand dollars in the hotel safe. Pay the hotel for the rest of the month. Each of you can take five hundred for spending money, and give that Pratt kid a hundred dollars for a bath and some new clothes. He's getting a little gamey."

Both women were silent for a moment, staring at him. He could almost hear the words before they spoke.

"No leg-pulling, Collin. This is serious," Susan scolded.

"Susan's right," Sarah added. "Normally, two hundred dollars would last a long while, but the hotel is charging us five dollars a day for that suite of rooms. Three more weeks will take half the money we have left."

"I'm not pulling your leg," Mitchell assured them. "The money is in the safe, and you can use half of it—but no more buggies. I've made a deal with Jake Farney. That will take a large part of what's left." Mitchell peered at the sky again then looked straight at the Pratt kid. "Daniel!"

The kid went ridged, as though someone had shoved a ramrod up his backbone. "What....?"

Mitchell took Sarah by the hand, helping her into the buggy. When Susan was seated, he looked at the Pratt kid again.

"The ladies are going over to the hotel to get some money." He handed the kid two silver dollars. "Stop someplace along the way and get two pillowcases and two sticks of dynamite."

Susan reached out and slapped him on the shoulder.

"Just make sure you wear those pillowcases," he told her. "I don't want anyone to recognize you when you blow that safe."

"I knew it," Susan accused. "That King fellow touched him off."

"Just when we thought we had him trained," Sarah added sweetly.

"You can train a horse or a monkey," Susan concluded. "Men are hopeless."

"It's the forehead," Sarah replied, ignoring Mitchell's attempt to speak. "The male forehead is a lot like those cowcatcher things on the front of a train. Everything just bounces off."

"All right," Mitchell muttered, "Just tell the clerk what you need, and Goodwin will take care of the money."

The Pratt kid smiled, and took up the reins. "You just keep smiling Daniel," Sarah advised. "You are headed for the nearest bath."

"But it ain't even Saturday," the kid complained.

"If that odor wasn't so firmly attached to your portion of the seat, you might have escaped until Saturday. But it's trailing you like a lost puppy. So you and Brother Mitchell are welcome to have dinner with us this evening—after you both have a closer relationship with some soap and water."

"Huh?"

"She says we both need a bath, Brother Pratt."

"And a shave," Susan suggested.

"Yes ma'am," Mitchell answered politely.

"Good," Sarah concluded, holding out her hand for the reins. "Daniel, you can ride double with Brother Mitchell while searching for soap and water. Susan and I will meet both of you later at the hotel."

The buggy was two blocks south before the puzzled seventeen-year old turned back to Mitchell. "You been up the canyon to watch them fellers layin' track for the railroad?" he asked suddenly.

"Rode past one time," Mitchell answered. "Never did more than look a little as I rode by."

"They got twenty-two cars full of Irish fellers layin' that track," Daniel replied. "They say one rail weighs seven-hundred pounds, and it takes five men to lift one off a flat car and set it down on the ties. Takes four-hundred rails to the mile," he concluded.

"Rough work," Mitchell answered.

"Put your women in charge," Daniel suggested. "They'd have track laid all the way to California in a month, and them Irish boys would be hatin' the woman that invented bath tubs and soap."

"Two months," Mitchell replied soberly. "They aren't always as tough as they act."

"Tough enough, I'd say," Daniel argued.

"People are not always what they seem, Brother Pratt," Mitchell replied.

"How so?"

"Ever see one of them Greek tragedies?"

"That's some kind of a play, ain't it?"

"Exactly."

"I don't get it," Daniel said, shaking his head.

"In a play, folks dress up and pretend to be someone else, don't they?"

"Yep."

"Sometimes they wear masks too, right?"

"I suppose."

"Well, old Shakespeare, or somebody, said 'all the world was a stage.' I figure he meant that everyone dresses up and puts on a mask; so other folks see what we want them to see, not what we really are."

"Why would people do that?" Daniel demanded.

"I think it's 'cause deep down inside we're all just scared little kids, and we're afraid to let folks see our real selves. We know that folks would see how vulnerable we are, pack up like a bunch of wolves and tear the shit out of us. So we put on these masks for protection."

"Sounds like a lot of work," Daniel protested.

"I figure we do it so much we don't even notice," Mitchell confided.

"Don't guess I ever done it," Daniel said quietly.

"Me neither," Mitchell agreed.

"Don't know about that," Daniel protested. "Folks around here think you're a hard case. You must have done something to make 'em think that, 'cause you ain't such a bad sort when a fellow gets to know you."

CHAPTER 28

Utah Territory
Ogden—September 1868

*T*he Sharpe place was a small log cabin of weathered brown logs chinked with four inches of mud and set on a foundation of rough-cut sandstone. The roof, covered with wooden shakes, had enough slope to allow the winter snows to slide down its surface and pile up at the base of the cabin walls. Sharpe had gone to Salt Lake City ten years earlier, and when he came home, he brought with him enough windowpanes to build four large windows. Now, the six-paned windows allowed in enough light to brighten the place substantially.

Inside, the place was cozy and comfortable. Sharpe had whitewashed the walls, sanded the pine floors, and trimmed the doorways and fireplace. He painted all the trim a soft, mustard color that was easy on the eye, but it was a color that Mitchell disliked from the moment he saw the place.

The place was small. Mitchell would never have been able fit his family into the place, as even one wife and one kid would have found the twelve by eighteen foot room small and constraining. It was obvious the Sharpe's five boys slept outside during the summer and in the wintertime, crowded around the pot-bellied stove and slept on the floor.

Outside, Mrs. Sharpe had planted a nice garden of yarrow near the back door, making it obvious that both she and Mr. Sharpe had a taste for yarrow tea. On the back wall, she had hung her tub and washboard and the wooden pail she used to fetch water from the well and milk from the goat.

Sharpe was obviously an industrious man. Twenty feet from the back door, he had built a single stall out house and a wood-box—a wood-box full of dry kindling. The cabin had an attic of sorts, a small crawl space reached by an outside ladder leading to a small door in one gable, or the trap door in the ceiling near the fireplace.

The *yard* consisted of the acre immediately surrounding the house, and Sharpe had secured that portion of the farm with a four-rail fence. The fence did a good job of keeping out the livestock, but did nothing to protect Mrs. Sharpe's small garden from the rodents, the jackrabbits and the hordes of ironclads. The rabbits fell prey to Mrs. Sharpe's ten-gauge side-by-side, but the ironclads were another matter altogether—a matter the Sharpe's left to God and his army of seagulls.

An hour after reaching the farm, Mitchell patiently cut a forked stick from a branch provided by the insistent owner of the farm.

"In town, they said you was a dowser," Sharpe said enthusiastically. "I never done any water-witchin' myself, but I heard folks talk about it. Pretty much comes down to veins of water runnin' all over underground like veins of silver or gold. So folks say. But I ain't got any idea where to start lookin'."

"I never seen it that way," Mitchell said quietly. "Veins and all that..." He pointed toward the mountains to the east. "See how those mountains have ridges and valleys and hard and soft ground? I think the roots of those mountains go down deep and keep spreadin' out, gettin' wider and deeper at the base. Way out here, I think the water sinks down into the soil 'til it hits the low spots and the hard rock then just sits there like big underground lakes.

"Maybe the water just saturates the ground in the low places," Mitchell suggested. "I really don't know. Maybe when you dig a well, you just open up a place for water to seep out of the saturated ground and fill up the hole."

"I don't see it makes much difference," Sharpe argued. "Either way you're gonna get a dry hole if you don't know where the water is."

"That's true," Mitchell answered. "And I can't figure how a fellow can tell where the low spots might be..."

"You're sayin' you don't trust what that forked stick is tellin' you," Sharpe acknowledged reluctantly.

The farmer stared out across his fields. His mouth tightened with a grimness Mitchell had seen often enough on the faces of Legionaires caught in the withering fire of Black Hawk's Ute warriors. His own face had taken on that hard, thin-lipped scowl when the angry buzz of rifle balls ripped the mountain air, tearing the bark from the pines and the life from the Legionaires trapped in the steep, dry canyons of the Wasatch Mountains.

"I really got no choice," Sharpe muttered. "I need that water. We can't keep runnin' three households on boiled crick water. We was managin' with just one well, but I shoulda had enough sense to dig a new well for each of the boys when we put up their homes. It woulda saved us a lot of trouble.

"You a religious man, Mitchell?" He asked suddenly.

"I guess so," Mitchell admitted.

"I hear tell that Oliver Cowdery was a rodsman, and Brother Joseph once told him it was a gift from God."

"I heard rumors, but nothin' certain," Mitchell replied.

"I never been much of a religious man," Sharpe confessed. "Not that I don't believe in God or anything like that. But with the farm and all, I just never felt like I had the time to get all involved in goin' to meetin' and spendin' hours listenin' to some other farmer tellin' me how he thinks God wants me to behave. 'Specially when that same feller can go home and beat on his wife and kids. Seems a bit hypocritical to me."

"Reckon so," Mitchell agreed.

"Heard tell you was a High Priest, though," Sharpe said suddenly. "I'm a prayin' sort of man, but most times, I ain't so sure I'm gettin' through. I figure someday I might get the hang of it. When I do, life might make a little more sense.

"But I was wonderin' if you'd pray with me, Brother Mitchell," Sharpe said quietly. "I need that water real bad, and I ain't on very good terms with some of the local church folks."

"I don't think you need them or me," Mitchell replied. "What counts is whether you're on good terms with God."

"I just figured he might pay a little more attention if *you* was to ask," Sharpe said defensively. "Seein' as how a High Priest ought to be the kind of feller that could do his talkin' face-to-face if the good Lord had a mind to visit with him."

Mitchell heard light footsteps behind him, and felt Sarah take his arm.

"Mort says Collin has God's ear," she said softly. "He says God whispers to Collin, and sends him where he needs him."

"I'd say, that's a sight better than most folks can claim," Sharpe admitted. "But who's this Mort feller, and how does he come to know such a thing?"

"Mort is the angel of death," Sarah announced sweetly.

"The what?"

"The angel of death," Sarah repeated. "He met Collin up on Trapper's loop one night about ten years ago and sent him to rescue me from four murderers. He's been coming around to visit off and on since then."

"He *says* he's the angel of death," Mitchell muttered grimly. "Mostly, he just seems like a crazy old coot."

"I'll admit he could bathe more often," Sarah conceded congenially. "But he's not crazy."

"Maybe not," Mitchell conceded, "but he sure makes you wonder at times."

"Well, if he's right, and God is listenin', then it ain't gonna hurt if you ask him to show us where to find that water," Sharpe concluded.

Sarah smiled sweetly. "Go ahead, Collin," she prompted. "You can do that much for the man."

Mitchell looked at his wife. She knew he hadn't prayed for a while. For more than a year, he had ridden the desert canyon lands, chasing Back Hawk and his renegade band over the southern half of the Territory. He'd prayed often enough when rifle balls and Ute arrows filled the air. He'd prayed mighty hard just fourteen months ago down in Nine-mile Canyon.

Mitchell looked to the northeast. There, Ben Lomond Peak thrust into the sky, burying itself in gray and white cotton-ball clouds. He took a deep breath, and looked down into the depths of Sarah's blue eyes.

"I'll pray with you, Brother Sharpe," he said finally. "Let's see if God wants to talk with either one of us."

CHAPTER 29

Utah Territory
Ogden—September 1868

"*W*hat's goin' on, Pop?" Andrew Sharpe called out from the back porch of his house, as more than two-dozen of his relatives and a half-dozen barking dogs invaded his yard, all of them trailing along behind a man with a forked stick in his hands.

"Come on out here, Andy," Sharpe rumbled loudly. "This here's Brother Mitchell, and he's gonna find us a place to dig that well I been promising you."

"Heard tell of folks that could do that sort of thing," Andy said when he joined the crowd of family now spilling into the small orchard next to his house.

"Brother Mitchell don't take much stock in it," Sharpe admitted. "Says the stick just moves 'cause his hands move. I'm figurin' God could give him a tweak at the right time and that old stick will point right where we need to dig."

"Sounds good to me," the younger man replied. "I'm getting' mighty tired of haulin' water from the crick."

"I hear you, son. My old bones don't like it none either."

Suddenly, the stick in Mitchell's hands twisted violently, tearing the bark from both ends.

"You see that, Pop?"

"Darned right," Sharpe admitted loudly. "I seen all of it, Mitchell, and I don't see how you done anything to make that stick move like that. So I'll just keep on believin' God pointed that stick to water, and we'll be diggin' a well right where your standin'; thank you very kindly."

Mitchell looked down at the ground. He still felt as though he had done something to cause the movement, but he wasn't even sure what he might have done. In any case, he would never convince Sharpe now—especially if Sharpe found water.

"Well," he said reluctantly. "Folks claim a strong reaction like that means the water's close to the surface and there's lots of it."

"Fine by me," Sharpe acknowledged congenially. "The less we dig the better. Right, son?"

"You bet, Pop."

With a swipe of his foot, Sharpe cleared a spot near Mitchell's feet then produced a hammer and a two-foot long stake. "We'll gather up the boys and any neighbors and family that can spare the time," he said as he pounded the stake into the ground. "We'll have a well here in no time at all."

Two hours later, the hole for Aaron Sharpe's well was six feet in diameter and ten feet deep. Five men and four boys took turns, two at a time, picking and shoveling like crazed gophers at the bottom of the pit. Those at the top raised and lowered buckets as quickly as the men below could fill them.

"Look at the way the soil changes as we get deeper," Mitchell told Sharpe as the two of them worked a shift with the pick and shovel.

"Changes color, don't it?" Sharpe replied, wiping the sweat from the back of his neck.

"It ain't just the color," Mitchell pointed out. "It's like layers in a fancy cake. And the texture's different too."

"You're makin' me hungry, talkin' about cake," Sharpe replied.

"It's all layered like the silt you get from a river at spring runoff," Mitchell suggested. He brushed one hand across the surface of one wall, noting the differing colors of each layer. "If you look real close, there's lots of even finer layers... like pages in a book."

"So, you're thinkin' we're diggin' in an old river bed?" Sharpe asked.

Mitchell shook his head. "No I'm thinkin' it's an old lake bed," he answered.

"I reckon it could be," Sharpe conceded. "Some of the ground around here is pretty marshy. I reckon the lake could of covered this area some time in the past. I suppose Noah's flood covered everything once."

"Some folks claim the lake covered the whole valley way back before Christ," Mitchell admitted.

Sharpe looked closely at the wall. "Reckon you could tell what year that there leaf was on the bottom of the lake if you could count all the layers," he said with an odd hint of curiosity in his voice.

Mitchell stared at the old man, suddenly remembering the broken shell necklace beneath the body Groesbeck had stolen. "I'll be switched," he muttered grimly.

CHAPTER 30

Utah Territory
Ogden—September 1868

*A*t the hotel that evening, Mitchell looked at the two women in his life and wondered how he was going to handle his confession. "I haven't been completely honest with either of you," he said carefully.

Neither of the women spoke, giving him the impression that those few words had ignited a flame that for the moment was contained, but might easily flare into a man-killing inferno.

Hastily, he continued, hoping to explain before either of them had time to conjure up their own illusions of the depths of his deceitfulness. "We didn't come here just to look for land," he said.

"Another woman," Susan muttered morosely.

"Good lord, no!" he protested. "Well.... You might say it's another woman."

"I knew it," Susan insisted.

Sarah's eyes seemed to harden, and her voice was like stone to Mitchell's ears. "At this point," she cautioned, "a wise man would choose his words very carefully."

"We are here, because Brother Brigham sent me to look for a woman."

"He's found plenty of them on his own," Susan observed stiffly. "Why does he need help now?"

"It's not for him," countered Mitchell. "Now, just let me tell this straight through then you can give me what for, if you like."

He took the box containing the red dress and placed it on the low table between them.

"President Young got a letter a few weeks before we left Salt Lake. The letter was from a man here in Ogden who complained that his daughter had been missing for six years, and the county sheriff had done nothing to find her in all that time. He wrote some things that irritated the President, but tweaked Brother Brigham's sense of fairness. So, President Young asked me to find her. He knew I was losin' my job with the Marshall's office. The Territorial Marshal argued that he didn't have enough deputies to be wastin' time on something that happened six years ago, but he finally gave in 'cause he was firing me anyway. So, I'm here to find her—dead or alive."

"Melinda Tolson," Sarah said suddenly. "You're looking for Alfred Tolson's daughter."

"I am."

"Sister Dalton mentioned her. She was seeing Lester Reynald. Her father didn't approve, and they quarreled the night she disappeared. I suppose you knew this already?"

"No, Tolson's letter wasn't very detailed," he admitted. "But I did learn some of it from Farney."

Sarah nodded. "Sister Dalton says that Melinda borrowed a horse from Dr. Wadman and left town. Six months later, she sent money to pay for the horse. The letter came from Denver."

"That's what Wadman and Farney both told me," Mitchell replied. "They seem to know quite a bit about the whole affair."

"Yes," Sarah agreed, "But she never wrote her father or anyone else, according to Sister Dalton."

Mitchell contemplated the package on the table. "I made Groesbeck take me to the burial mound this morning. Did Susan tell you anything about it?"

Sarah nodded. "She said that it was a Shoshoni burial—a woman who died fifteen or twenty years ago."

"That's true. Groesbeck looted the burial and took everything, including the body—a mummified body."

Sarah shuddered. "That's a ghoulish thing to do."

"I agree. I was tempted to shoot Groesbeck on the spot, but I decided that Two Bears had better reasons than I did. So, I told Groesbeck that the Shoshoni were hunting him and let him run for it."

"They'll find him," Susan announced.

"I'm sure they will," Mitchell replied. "But after he left, I looked around a bit." He paused, letting the thought dangle like a tantalizing tidbit.

"You found something," Susan prompted.

"I did." He laid a small envelope on top of the package and pushed both objects toward the younger sister. "Open it."

Susan opened the envelope and dumped its contents on top of the larger package.

"It's a tooth," she said quietly.

"Not just any tooth," he replied. "Do you remember the ball game at the Shoshoni camp?"

"That was the most violent game I've ever seen," she answered.

"You remember that Brother Joseph had one of his front teeth knocked out?"

"Yes."

"Well, something seemed odd about the shape of his tooth. And when I found this one among some rocks near the mound, I saw the similarities; so I picked it up."

"You think this is Brother Joseph's tooth?" she asked.

"No. I think it belonged to Two Bears' wife. And I think her bones are buried under that pile of rocks near the mound."

"How can you be sure?' Sarah asked.

"I'm not. But I took the tooth to Mr. King and asked him if he had ever seen anything like it. See the way it's scooped out on the back surface—like a little scoop shovel?"

"Yes."

"Well King told me that he's never seen that shape on any teeth except on the few Indians he's worked on. He says the back surface on white folk's front teeth are pretty much flat, nothing like this."

"So what does this have to do with Melinda Tolson?" Susan asked.

Mitchell pushed the box toward Sarah. "Open it."

Carefully, Sarah lifted the lid. "It's a dress," she concluded.

"Tell me what you think about it?" Mitchell asked.

Susan frowned. "It's very dirty," she answered.

"And faded," Sarah added. "It feels almost brittle, not moist like you'd think it would be, after being buried."

"And it's out of style," Susan observed, "so it's several years old."

"According to Tolson's letter, Melinda was wearing a red dress the night she ran off. She left everything she owned, borrowed a horse and hasn't been seen since. She took only the clothes she was wearing."

"Why would she borrow a horse and not even take a change of clothing?" Susan demanded.

"Susan's right," Sarah agreed. "If she intended to leave town, she would have come back for her things."

"Do you think this is her dress?" Susan asked.

Mitchell frowned thoughtfully. "I don't know, but I wonder why anyone would take that dress three miles north of town and bury it in the middle of nowhere."

"That makes even less sense," Susan protested.

"It does," Mitchell agreed.

"But what about the letter and the money she sent from Denver?" Sarah asked quietly.

"Good point," Mitchell admitted.

"You don't believe it." Sarah concluded. "You don't believe there was a letter."

"There may have been a letter," he answered, "but Melinda might not have written it."

"I'm getting confused," Susan complained.

"Me too," Sarah admitted.

"You are not alone," Mitchell agreed.

"I talked to Vernon Miller," Sarah confided suddenly.

"Ruth Miller's husband?" Susan asked.

"Yes," Sarah replied. "He's a very disagreeable man."

"What did he say?" Susan cajoled.

"He admitted that his wife, Ruth, had a pair of silver ear-cuffs, but he claimed they were buried with her."

"He's lying," Susan cried angrily. "We found her initials scratched on the inside of the one Collin found in Mr. Reynald's hand."

Sarah nodded. "That's what Deborah, Miller's new wife, said. She didn't know if the ear-cuffs were buried with Ruth Miller, but she knew that her husband lied about something while I was talking with him."

"Did you learn anything useful?" Susan asked."

"Only that Ruth wanted a divorce, and Mr. Miller refused. Nephi Clarke admitted that he and Ruth were close friends. He admitted giving her the ear-cuffs because Miller treated her badly. Deborah claims that Vernon knew that another man had given Ruth the ear-cuffs."

"Nephi told me that Ruth asked him to make the ear-cuffs," Susan complained unhappily.

"I don't think Nephi told any of us the whole story," Mitchell admitted.

"Reynald must have taken the ear-cuffs from Ruth's body," Susan argued.

"I don't know," Sarah answered. "Groesbeck told Collin that he delivered the mummified body of the Indian woman."

"An Indian woman wearing silver ear-cuffs," Mitchell added.

"Maybe Miller removed the ear-cuffs and sold them to Two Bears," Susan suggested.

"Two Bears said his wife died fifteen years ago, that's nine or ten years before Ruth Miller died," Mitchell responded.

"That's true," Susan agreed.

"So, how did Ruth's ear-cuffs end up on the body of a woman who had been dead and buried for nearly ten years?" Sarah demanded.

"I think we need to narrow things down a bit," Mitchell suggested. "I think we're all convinced that the ear-cuff belonged to Ruth Miller. And we know that it turned up six years later with a piece of human ear attached to it. But it couldn't have been buried with Two Bears' wife. The whole thing is confusing."

"All these things seem to be connected somehow," Sarah concluded.

"They must," Mitchell acknowledged. "I'm just not sure *how* they connect."

For a moment, they sat quietly, each of them considering the possibilities. Finally Sarah sighed. "Could we discuss something else for a moment?" she asked.

"Might as well," Mitchell replied thoughtfully.

"I told you that I talked with Deborah Miller," Sarah said at last.

"You mentioned her," Mitchell acknowledged.

"She has a business proposition. She asked me to discuss it with you."

"Is Mr. Miller involved?"

"No, he's not," she replied. "In fact, Deborah made it clear that this is strictly between you and her."

Carefully, Sarah recounted her visit with Deborah Miller and the one sided conversation with Eliza Richards. Susan listened intently then quietly went to the window and opened the curtain. The afternoon sun poured through the glass, filling the room.

"We need to set things straight with that Richards woman," Mitchell warned.

"She hears only what she wants to hear," Sarah replied.

"We did agree to remain as inconspicuous as possible," Susan cautioned.

"But I don't think we should become involved in this woman's schemes," Mitchell argued. I've heard rumors that Congress is discussing a bill to disenfranchise anyone who practices plural marriage in the Territory."

"Woman's suffrage will accomplish nothing for us, if that happens," Sarah admitted. She sat quietly after that, not wanting to broach the subject of Deborah Miller's land. She felt it was a good move for all of them, but with Susan's objections to rural life, it seemed wiser to let Collin pursue the issue.

"You're much too quiet," Mitchell observed, looking at Sarah. "Generally, I'm in hot water when that happens, but this time...."

"It's that business thing," Susan confided. "She always plays silent when she decides she likes something and wants you to go along with her decision. She waits for you to get curious enough to ask about it."

Sarah flashed a sharp look at her sister. Susan smiled sweetly and returned to her chair.

"Very well," Sarah acknowledged. "I am impressed with this offer."

"Tell us about it," Mitchell suggested.

"Yes, tell us about it," Susan echoed.

Sarah glanced at each of them then began explaining Deborah's situation. When she had finished, Susan's face was grim.

Mitchell leaned back in his chair. "You believe her story?" he asked.

"Yes."

Susan sighed and seemed to sink into her chair. She knew that this would change everything. Now, there would be little chance that Collin would settle them in town. "How could we ever begin to afford such a place," she objected. "Even if the mine produced, we don't have nearly enough money to buy the land."

Sarah looked closely at Collin. "Deborah suggested that we use some of the money from your silver mine," she responded.

Susan stared at her sister then turned suddenly on Mitchell. "What silver mine?"

"It's not really mine," Mitchell replied defensively. "Well... half mine. My Uncle is sort of a black sheep in the family. Always wanderin' around the mountains—never held a respectable job according to the family. He was always dreamin' of strikin' a rich vein of gold.

"About two years ago, I saw him in Denver. He was broke. He told me he had run into traces of silver just south of Leadville, but he had run out of just about everything. So he headed back down to Denver to find a stake. When I ran into him he had used up what little silver he had panned out, and no one would take his word about the strike.

"Anyway, he asked me for help. I had two hundred dollars. It was all I had. When I gave him half of it, he just looked at the money and said: 'That's half of everything you got, ain't it boy.' For a minute, he looked like he was going to cry. I could see him swallow hard and try to keep from breakin' down. When he could finally say something, he just looked at me and said 'You just bought yourself a partnership, son."

"I haven't seen him since then. But about a year ago, I got a letter from a bank in Denver. The letter said my Uncle had set up an account in my name, and he had given them instructions to contact me and see what I wanted to do with the money."

"At first, it wasn't much, only what William could bring down the mountain on a couple of mules. But the last three months have been good. I told the bank in Denver to send half of everything to our bank in Salt Lake and keep the rest in the Denver account."

"Collin?" Sarah asked quietly, her voice sounding strained.

"Yes?"

"You haven't told us if we can afford the land," she replied.

"How much do you have put away?" Susan interrupted.

"*We*," Mitchell answered. "*We* have nearly twenty-five thousand in Salt Lake."

"Oh my...."

"Between the two banks and what we have in the hotel safe—roughly fifty-four thousand dollars."

"Why didn't you tell us?" Sarah demanded.

Mitchell shrugged, feeling miserable. "It was such a small amount at first. I just forgot the whole thing until two weeks ago when some fellow in Salt Lake came to me askin' if I'd be interested in investing in another silver mine. After that, I marched right down to the bank."

"And your uncle, William?" Susan asked, glancing toward Sarah. Sarah shook her head slightly.

"Haven't heard from him," Mitchell answered. "I thought once the railroad comes through, we could leave the kids with your parents, and the three of us could go to Denver and then maybe Leadville."

"Children, Collin," Sarah corrected. "Kids are goats. We have children."

"Yes, ma'am."

"I'd like a trip to Denver," Susan admitted.

"The point is," Mitchell continued, "we can afford the land, but until two weeks ago I had no idea William had sent so much money."

"The question is whether you want to look at the property, or even consider the thing at all," Sarah said softly.

"I haven't made any other commitments yet," he answered. "It might be worth a trip up north."

Mitchell sat quietly for a moment, first looking at Sarah then turning his gaze on the younger woman. Sarah's eyes seemed brighter, as though news of the mine in Colorado, or the prospect of buying Deborah Miller's land excited her, like a hidden reservoir of energy striving for release. But Susan.... Mitchell took a deep breath. "You don't seem pleased," he told her.

"I'm not anxious to live that far from town," she replied.

"I know," he answered "I've been trying to find a way to work that out. I think having separate households is a good idea, but I was hoping to build them within a mile or two of each other, on the same property."

"I doubt you'll find anything that will meet all our requirements," Sarah said quietly.

"I am having some difficulty," Mitchell admitted.

"We should look at the land," Susan acknowledged. "It may be what God wants for us."

Mitchell looked at Susan for a moment before speaking. Finally, he turned to Sarah. "Tell Sister Miller we'll look at her land."

CHAPTER 31

Utah Territory
Ogden—September 1868

*T*he next morning Mitchell entered the county jail and made his way to Alfred Tolson's cell. Inside the cell, Mitchell sat on the straw mattress. Tolson paced the tiny room.

"I didn't do it, Mitchell."

"Appears you did," countered Mitchell.

"I don't give a hoot what it looks like."

"A jury will."

"I'm tellin' you—somebody stole that knife."

"Listen, you ornery old fart, Becker has enough to convince a jury. So, you ain't got a prayer of gettin' off, unless you can prove who really did it."

"How am I goin' to prove anything!"

"Tell me about the blood," Mitchell interrupted.

"I told you and Becker about that already."

"Tell me again."

Tolson frowned. "The horse was foundered," he began in an irritated growl. "I was trimmin' out that pulpy white ring that grows in behind the outer shell of the hoof."

For a moment, Tolson stood at the barred window, looking to the northwest. Nearly two blocks away, the scene of the murder was discernible as nothing more than a dark line separating the backs of the two shops.

"I've trimmed a few of 'em that way before," Tolson continued. "Seems to fix 'em up."

"You cut out the white pulp?" asked Mitchell.

"You bet. It's like havin' putty jammed under your fingernails—makes 'em hurt. The horse gets foundered, and that white stuff starts buildin' up. There's a white ring there anyway, but founder seems to make it grow. Makes their feet hurt havin' all that pressure pushin' out on the shell of the hoof. I trim out the white pulp every three months or so, and pretty soon it gets back to normal. Cures the founder."

Tolson turned and looked at Mitchell.

"Anyway, I cut that one a little too deep, and she bled on the leg of my apron."

"Becker says Reynald owed you money,"

"Five-hundred dollars."

"Let's say I believe you," suggested Mitchell. "Who could have taken the knife?"

"Hell, anybody could've walked in there and took the thing."

"No," countered Mitchell. "Not anyone. You told me someone took the knife the day before the murder."

"That's right."

"So, the knife was hanging on the wall last Monday, or at least part of Monday. When, exactly, did you notice it was missing?"

"About noon on Tuesday."

"Did you lock up when you left Monday evening?"

"I dropped the board across the doors, but most anybody could fish somethin' between the doors and knock the board up out of the arms."

"I think we'll stick to the times when the shop was open," Mitchell advised. "Tell me who came into the smithy from Monday morning until noon on Tuesday."

Tolson's bushy eyebrows sucked to the center of his forehead, and a frown transformed his face into a fearsome spectacle.

"Nobody came in Monday mornin' except William Sharpe. He dropped off a broken wagon wheel and left. He never took it though. I talked with him the whole time, and he never went near them tools."

"Who else?"

"Henry Mason. He brought in that foundered mare."

"What time?"

"Around noon…maybe a little after."

"Then?"

"Nobody, until around three, or three-thirty. Sort of crowded up about then."

"Name 'em off."

"Well, Doc Wadman come first—wanted that fat roan re-shod. Jake Farney come next—returned a hammer he borrowed, but I hung that on the wall myself."

"Anyone else?"

"Becker come in—told me somebody complained about one of my cows bein' loose. Said he sent somebody out to collect the critter and take her back to my farm. Said he promised the boy two-bits, and I was to pay it to him."

"That all of 'em?"

"Miller come in. Paid me for fixin' a bridle. That feller is just about worthless…." Tolson clamped his jaws shut. "Sorry. I got no call sayin' that—Nephi Clarke come in too, and the boy come for his two bits."

CHAPTER 32

Utah Territory
Ogden—September 1868

*B*y eleven a.m., Mitchell sat outside the county courthouse. The morning sun was already nearing its apex high above the Wasatch Mountains. Mitchell leaned back, resting against the weathered wood of the bench beside the courthouse door. A few, scattered trees shaded the courthouse and the surrounding property. One of them, a decent sized elm, had been planted in precisely the right place, protecting the bench and Mitchell's head from the blazing torch overhead.

Quietly, he fanned himself with the yellowed envelope containing Melinda Tolson's letter to Dr. Harold Wadman. It had taken nearly two hours of pleading, cajoling, and finally threatening bodily harm, before the county clerk deemed it wise to search the files of 1862 for the record of Melinda Tolson's disappearance. Mitchell had quickly read the report and pocketed the letter. Outside the courthouse, he had settled on the bench and read the two terse sentences that made up Melinda's only communication.

> *I'm sorry I took your horse. Here's fifty dollars to pay*
> *for him and the saddle.*
>
> M. Tolson

Mitchell unfolded the brittle paper and looked at the note again. No salutation—nothing to indicate the girl's location or condition. Why? He wondered. Why would a woman who cared enough to write to a near stranger and pay for a borrowed horse never write to her own father?

As far as Mitchell was concerned, no one could hold a grudge for six years. No.... Melinda Tolson had never written anyone. The letter *had* to be a forgery. Of course, he had no proof. But the possibilities were intriguing. *Someone* had written the letter. And it certainly looked like a woman had penned the note and signed Melinda's name. After six years, it was unlikely that he would ever discover the author's identity, but the purpose of the forged missive seemed clear enough. Someone wanted Harold Wadman to believe that Melinda Tolson was alive and doing well in Denver. Perhaps it was true, and a friend had written the note and sent the money, but Mitchell found that hard to believe. It seemed more likely that someone had sent the letter to end the questions about her disappearance and halt the search for Alfred Tolson's daughter—and it had worked. The county sheriff had dropped the case the day the letter arrived.

"Mind if I use some of that shade?"

"Go ahead," Mitchell replied as Mort settled himself on the other half of the bench.

"Got me a newspaper," Mort announced, rattling a worn copy of the New York Times. "Says here that thirty-thousand people died in Peru last month.... Big earthquake it says."

Hard for me to imagine three-hundred people," Mitchell replied. "Thirty-thousand.... That's a dang big bunch."

"This ain't exactly accurate," the old man confided. "There's five of 'em didn't die in the quake."

"Guess they're lucky to be alive," Mitchell replied.

"Oh, they're dead all right," Mort protested. "Shot 'em myself."

"You were in Peru last month?"

"Spent two weeks in Lima."

"And you're here in just three weeks?"

"I had me some stops along the way."

"Wondered what held you up," Mitchell admitted. "Three-thousand miles.... That's only a day's walk for a Nephite."

"I ain't no Nephite," the old man growled.

"That's why it took you so long to get here," Mitchell retorted. "A real man could have done it in a couple of days."

"Listen here pup...."

"Look at that," Mitchell interrupted, pointing at the old man's newspaper. "The democrats want to put the southern states under presidential edict."

"What?"

"Congress will never stand still for that," Mitchell announced, ignoring the mutterings of the old man. "It'd give the president too much authority... disturbs the balance of power. Besides, those folks down south will be mighty unhappy if the Federal government starts throwing more of its weight around. They ain't got a bean left between 'em down there, but I'll bet they've got some fight left in 'em."

"Dang it, Mitchell!" Mort howled. "I brung this paper over here so I could sit in the shade an' do some readin'. You're takin' all the fun out of it."

The old man slammed the paper shut, stood and stomped away. Mitchell watched Mort's retreating back, wondering how anyone could ever take the old man seriously.

"Mort!"

The old man stopped and looked back.

"Who killed Melinda Tolson?"

"I ain't allowed to tell you that, Danite, but when you find 'im, I'll collect 'im right quick.... An' happy to do it. I like Melinda. She's a nice little gal."

The old man turned and walked north, toward the Fife and Douglas smithy.

"I ain't no Danite," Mitchell muttered angrily.

"An' I ain't no Nephite!" Mort bellowed, half a block away.

"Strange old man, isn't he?"

Mitchell turned at the sound of a woman's voice.

"Very strange," he replied. "Do you know him,"

"I met him once," replied a tall, slender woman, "several years ago." Her voice was gentle, and low, as though it was unnatural for her to vocalize her thoughts with any degree of certitude. Her blue eyes glanced nervously to either side then back to Mitchell's face. She lowered her eyes quickly, avoiding contact with Mitchell's searching gaze.

"Have we met?" Mitchell asked, searching the woman's face. He couldn't remember her, and surely he would have remembered the striking features of such a handsome woman.

"No," she replied, "but I've talked with Sister Mitchell. She said you might be interested in a property I would like to sell."

"Sister Miller," Mitchell acknowledged.

"Yes."

"Sarah seems convinced that your property would be an excellent investment."

"Sister Mitchell is a very astute woman," Deborah Miller replied quietly.

Mitchell watched the slight quiver of the woman's tightened lips, and suddenly realized that the woman was neither meek, nor submissive. She was terrified. "Is there something wrong, Sister Miller?"

"Just feeling a little ill," she replied.

"Is there anything I can do?"

"No. The doctor gave me something, and it seems to help."

"Please, sit down," Mitchell advised, taking her by the elbow and helping her to the bench.

"I'll be fine," she said after a moment.

Mitchell stood as she opened her handbag and withdrew a several sheets of folded paper.

"This is the deed to the property my father left me, and some instructions for finding his claim."

"Sister Miller," Mitchell objected, "you shouldn't just hand these things over to someone you don't even know."

"I don't believe you're the kind of man who would cheat me, Brother Mitchell. Besides, they're properly recorded in my name. My father made sure of that, before he died. I want you to hold them for me."

"But why?"

"If my husband discovered that I own that property, he would do just about anything to get his hands on those papers."

"And you want me to make sure he doesn't get them."

"Exactly."

"Are you still interested in selling the property and the claim?"

"Certainly."Deborah Miller glanced quickly up and down Main Street.

"Sister Miller, I get the feeling you are afraid of something."

"My husband is a brutal and vindictive man, Brother Mitchell, and I am terrified of him."

"You think he'd harm you?"

"I know he would."

Mitchell looked from the woman's down-turned eyes to the blond hair braided down the middle of her back. "Maybe you should leave before anything happens," he suggested.

"I don't know," she replied.

"Do you have family or friends who would take you in for a while?"

"No family," she answered. "When my parents joined the church, their families disowned them. I've never had contact with any of them. My parents tried to patch things up, but nothing came of it. My mother always said there were just too many angry words between them."

"Friends?"

"A few," she said quietly. "I'll look into it, but I'm not counting on it," she concluded, shaking her head. "Once the land is sold, I can handle things on my own. I would prefer it that way, in fact."

Mitchell contemplated the papers in his hand. "I can't promise anything," he cautioned.

"I understand."

"We can look at the property in about three weeks," Mitchell confided. "That's the best I can do."

"I understand."

"Dang it, woman... stop saying that. You're making me feel guilty."

"I'm sorry." She lowered her head.

"Look," Mitchell insisted. "You're ill. Let me take you to a doctor."

"I don't think a doctor can help," she answered.

"It won't hurt to try," he argued.

"I think Vernon is poisoning me," she moaned suddenly.

"Are you sure?"

"No," she admitted.

"Then what makes you think he's poisoning you?"

"His first wife died of poison," she answered lamely.

"And because you're feeling ill, you think he's trying to kill you." Mitchell suggested.

"It sounds ridiculous, doesn't it?"

"Some."

"I never believed Ruth killed herself," she offered. "It seemed too unlike her."

"Yet you married Miller anyway."

"I knew it was a mistake from the day we were married. Until then, Vernon was a paragon of virtue... a gentleman, well positioned in the church, a businessman.... How was I to know that beneath all that was something loathsome?"

"I suppose you couldn't."

"No, I couldn't."

"If Ruth didn't killed herself, who did kill her?"

"Vernon must have," she replied.

"But you don't *know* that," Mitchell argued.

"No, I don't, but I've seen her journal. She was unhappy and she had decided to leave Vernon."

"Her journal?"

"Yes. I found it behind a loose board in her sewing room."

"And you think Vernon poisoned her because she was going to leave?"

"Yes."

Mitchell shook his head thoughtfully. "I've heard this before," he protested.

"But you don't believe it," she accused.

"From what I've heard of your husband, Mrs. Miller, he might have killed her. Does he know you've read Ruth's journal?"

Deborah Miller retreated against the back of the bench, her face pale. "No, I've only told you today, and I mentioned it to Mr. Clarke yesterday at the mercantile. We got talking about the ear-cuffs, and I mentioned that she had written about speaking with him the day she died," she admitted quietly. "At least he was willing to take the time to help me. I've been a mess worrying about what she wrote of Vernon, and Mr. Clarke took the time to fix me some tea and talk me through it. Vernon was very upset that I was at the mercantile and I started feeling ill right after he chastised me."

"All right," Mitchell growled a moment later. "It's obvious that you're terrified of the man, and you're ill. Are you able to think clearly?"

"Yes."

"Good, come with me," he demanded.

CHAPTER 33

Utah Territory
Ogden—September 1868

*T*wo hours later, Mitchell stood outside the White House Hotel. In his pocket was a copy of Deborah Miller's letter to President Young, asking for divorce from Vernon Miller. The original was already on its way to Great Salt Lake City. Mitchell had no idea how long Brother Brigham might take to make his decision, but he knew that as the former territorial governor and President of the Church, Brother Brigham's word would be binding. He had no doubt that President Young would grant the divorce, especially with his own letter and Dr. James Conway's statement attached. It was Conway's statement that gave Mitchell a moment's pause on the hotel's veranda.

"Among other things," Conway had assured him, "the woman has been beaten, and often. In fact, judging by the marks on her wrists and the cuts on her back, I'd say she had been strung up and whipped. She'll have scars for the rest her life."

"What about poisoning?" Mitchell had asked.

"I'm no expert on poisons," Conway answered, "but I'd say she's been given arsenic."

Mitchell looked westward, down Fifth Street, imagining that he could see the stockade at Fort Buenaventura among the thick trees lining the banks of the Weber River. He knew it was his imagination, but the thought of that small Fort, hidden among the trees, gave him the urge to saddle the dun and ride to someplace where there were no people—someplace that hadn't yet suffered the taint of civilization. He couldn't do it, and he knew it. But that knowledge only tamed the urge, and had no power to extinguish it. At the sound of boots and spurs on the veranda, Mitchell turned to watch the approaching county deputy.

The tall young man held out a hand. "Robert Wheeler," he said.

"Collin Mitchell."

"Pleased to meet you." The deputy retrieved his hand and pointed toward one of the tables. "Shall we sit while you explain what's going on?"

"Sure," Mitchell replied, "but there ain't much to explain." He took a seat at one of the tables.

"The sheriff got your complaint, but all I've got is a warrant from the county court for Vernon Miller on a charge of assault," Wheeler replied. "So, what can I expect? Will this guy come along peaceable?" Wheeler pulled out a chair and straddled it.

"I don't know," Mitchell answered. "He might, but I don't think he'll like it."

"They never do," Wheeler answered.

"I half expected Deputy Becker," Mitchell confided.

"Becker quit, Sunday night," Wheeler replied. "Never said word. Just dropped his gear and walked out."

"Seems a little strange," Mitchell observed.

"Strange ain't the half of it," Wheeler responded. "He's been off his feed for two or three weeks. Got so no one wanted to work with him. Now, I've got more than I can handle."

"He was a mite cantankerous," Mitchell suggested cautiously.

"A *mite*! He's just plain ornery. I guess he figured the County wasn't payin' 'im enough. I heard he had a business deal that was gonna make him a rich man."

"Those deals don't come along every day," Mitchell offered.

Wheeler frowned and shook his head. "I'm not sure I'd want in on any deal Becker and Gilson was hatchin'."

"Gilson quit to?"

"So I heard. Now, I got to collect Miller then check on some complaints about stolen property."

Mitchell sat quietly, wondering what type of business deal Becker and Gilson had going.

"This Miller fellow... think I can find him at his house?" Wheeler asked.

Mitchell shrugged. "I really don't know much about the man."

"I'll go at it a bit careful then," Wheeler concluded. "Wouldn't want to get shot by accident."

"You wouldn't want to get shot on purpose either," Mitchell observed.

"Reckon not." Wheeler looked closely at Mitchell. "You in town on account of Miller?"

"No."

"Just wondered. Didn't seem likely that they'd send a territorial deputy just to arrest a fellow for assault."

"They didn't," Mitchell confided. "I ain't been a deputy for a while now. But I *was* sent to check on a girl who disappeared about six years ago."

"Melinda Tolson?"

"Yes. Seems like everyone knows about her leaving town," Mitchell responded.

"Most folks don't believe she ever left town," Wheeler observed.

"What do they believe?" Mitchell asked.

"They believe a lot of things," Wheeler answered. "All of it's hogwash... except the one tale... that's true."

"So tell me some of the tales," Mitchell prompted.

"Well.... One of 'em is that she was pregnant and when Tolson found out; he went nuts, killed her, and hid the body somewhere. Other folks say Reynald did it for the same reason."

"Do you think she ran off to Denver?" Mitchell asked.

"I knew that girl," Wheeler said quietly. "She was head strong, but she would never run off. I think she saw or heard something, and someone was afraid she would talk."

"I think you're right," Mitchell confided. He took the ear-cuff from his pocket and laid it on the table. "Ever see that before?"

Wheeler took the ear-cuff and examined it closely. "Nope. What is it?"

"It's an earring."

"Think it belonged to Melinda?"

"Right now, we think it was taken from the mummified remains of a woman," Mitchell responded.

"That's sick."

"Yes, it is."

Wheeler stood and rotated his chair until it was under the table. "I'd like to talk about this again," he said.

"Suits me," Mitchell agreed.

"I'll let you know when we have Miller," Wheeler promised.

"His wife will appreciate that."

"He really took a buggy-whip to her?"

"Appears so," Mitchell answered. "Looks like he tried poison too."

"That ain't good...."

"That bothers me, though," Mitchell admitted.

"How's that?"

"I just can't figure why Miller would suddenly poison his wife.... Seems a little impersonal for a woman-beater."

"I see what you mean," Wheeler acknowledged. "Feller like that is more likely goin' to whip her to death."

"That's what *I* thought."

"So, how'd she get the poison?"

"I don't know."

Mitchell watched the deputy collect a grulla mare from the rail at the south end of the veranda, pull himself into the saddle, and ride south on the dusty Street. Within minutes the deputy turned east and disappeared from view. Mitchell forced himself from the chair and stepped to the edge of the veranda.

It was a hot, windy day. Dust swirled in the streets, and the few souls who braved the stifling heat soon clustered together wherever they found a spot of shade. Such days were a misery for most folks. No one could stay indoors for long. Shops were cool enough in the early morning, but by noon a smart woman could close up her house and bake bread on the kitchen table. Mitchell had never seen it done, but it was a local yarn—spewed forth like the parable of frying eggs on a rock. Still, it was plenty hot as he stepped into the violent glare of the afternoon sun. He unhitched the dun and pulled himself into the saddle. A moment later, he stood in the stirrups, cussing himself.

"Why didn't you find some shade?" he growled at the animal. He reined the dun to the west and headed for the trees and the river. "Saddle's hotter than a Mexican bean," he muttered. "We'll go down to the river for a spell, find some shade and cool off."

The dun seemed to understand and started off across the street at that dead-headed pace. Suddenly, halfway across the wind-blown town, Mitchell reined the gelding south, through the alley were Reynald had died and into the empty field behind Farney's store.

"Still lookin' for Reynald's killer?" Farney called from the back door.

"Still lookin'," Mitchell confirmed, riding into the field. "Where's your dog?" he called over his shoulder.

Farney lifted both hands in the air and shrugged. "She run off. Probably over to Clarke's place. She runs back to Mama whenever she gets loose."

Mitchell smiled and wondered where Sarah's Lady-dog would run off to if she ever needed a place to go. Goodwin's barn was probably the closest thing to a home the long haired little mutt had ever seen before sharing a steak with Sarah.

He reined the dun to a halt and sat quietly, searching the dry, grass-covered field. The field had seen little use, except as a dumping ground for the odds and ends of broken furniture, tools, and empty crates that had migrated farther from the shabby, gray buildings that spawned them. Mitchell ground-hitched the dun and began a slow walk through the tall grass. When he reached the place where he had found Tolson's knife, he paused.

"Crap!"

He stared at the remains of a narrow, overgrown pathway. For an instant, he felt like kicking himself. When he had found Tolson's knife, he had been so intent on looking for some direct link to Reynald's murder that he had missed the path entirely. Leaving the dun, he stepped onto the overgrown path and followed its faint, half-revealed traces.

Thirty feet into a patch of shoulder high sunflowers, all fully bloomed and heavily laden with seeds, the trail split, one branch leading south while the other turned to the east. Mitchell ignored the eastern branch. It could only lead to Young Street, and not a single building occupied that side of the block. Instead, he turned south and walked toward the buildings that lined the southern edge of the block, facing Fifth Street. A hard-packed path led straight to the back door of Joseph Morlen's saloon, but not before it passed a large, weathered shed. Mitchell glanced at the shed, started to pass, and then suddenly stopped.

The pathway was dry as a bone and hard enough to reject nearly any track, but the soil on either side of path was soft—soft enough to hold tracks—tracks of a pigeon-toed horse.

"Milo...."

Mitchell turned from the path and followed Milo's tracks until they disappeared at the rock-hard ground surrounding the shed. The shed was a simple yet solid structure—bark-stripped logs overlaid with rough-hewn planks and chinked with mud... and the smell of smoke.

Smokehouse.

The door, ten rough planks of various widths, swung easily on new leather hinges. Ducking his head, Mitchell stepped inside and surveyed the little building. It was actually quite large—nearly twelve feet on a side as far as he could guess—and everything inside was blackened from years of use and smelled heavily of smoke.

An hour later, baked by the September sun and no more enlightened than he had been an hour earlier, Mitchell mounted the dun and headed back to the hotel. As far as he was concerned, he had just wasted an hour tromping around in someone's weed patch. Yet, he couldn't help wondering what Mort was up to. Milo's tracks were cropping up all over the county. The old man wandered the country like a stray cat.

In the middle of the block, Mitchell reined the dun to a halt. A dead stop wasn't much slower than their previous speed, but the arm-waving stable boy had an easier time of the run from Farney's store to the point where the dun stood with its head hanging.

The kid took hold of the left stirrup. "Two fellers was lookin for you over at the hotel stable, he gasped. "One of 'em looked like a gunfighter.... All duded up an' such. The other feller I ain't never seen before.

"Tow-headed feller—got a plug of chew in his mouth all the time?" Mitchell asked.

"That's him."

"Gilson."

"Yeah. That's the man," the boy answered. "The other feller came back later and left a message. Said if you was wantin' to find that body, you should meet him at the cemetery at five this afternoon."

"The cemetery?"

"Yep."

"And where would I find the cemetery?"

"Go back a block north of First Street then east—up the hill about a quarter mile. You can't miss it."

Mitchell tossed the boy two bits. "This feller who left the message, how was he dressed?"

"Kinda rough lookin'—like he just come in from owl hootin'."

"Packin' a six-gun?"

"Yep. Tied down on his right leg. But he had another one. I seen it in the pocket of the duster he was wearin'."

"That's good to know," Mitchell replied. "One more thing," he added. "You know that pigeon-toed critter my wife rides?"

"Sure do."

"Did a scruffy-lookin', old coot ride out on him in the last day or so?"

"Milo? Nope. He's been at the stable, eatin' like he was starved."

"Could anyone take him out at night?"

"I reckon they could," the boy answered, "but I ain't around at night to see 'em if they do."

"Reckon not," Mitchell replied.

"He don't look like he's been rode none," the boy interjected.

"Thanks," Mitchell answered.

He looked north, noting the quietude of the late afternoon and the people moving slowly along the boardwalks. Nearly a block away, Harold Wadman left his office, mounted his horse and rode west. On the opposite side of the street, Nephi Clarke raised a hand as Wadman passed then turned his attentions to the two black dogs trotting playfully at his heels.

For a moment, Mitchell kept the dun standing in the middle of the street. The boy's message didn't feel right. It was possible that someone wanted to tell him where to find the missing body, but if the kid had told the truth about Gilson's partner, it seemed mighty strange that the fellow had delivered the message after Gilson was gone. Gilson should have been chomping at the bit trying to show off for Becker. It was possible that the fellow really knew something, but a meeting at the cemetery was an odd way to pass on simple information. Something wasn't right. He could feel it—a sense of foreboding so strong it made the air about him feel lifeless.

"Reckon something about meetin' that feller don't set right with you either."

Mitchell started at the voice near his right-hand stirrup.

"Didn't spook you none, did I?"

Mitchell glared at the Pratt kid. "You been hangin' around Mort too much. He likes sneakin' up on folks and scarin' the bejeebers out of em'."

"Guilty conscience, my Pa says."

"Conscience my ass."

"Yeah. I didn't believe it neither. Had a pup once.... sweet little thing—never done nothin' wrong—'bout jumped out of her skin every time I sneaked up on her. Reckon *she* didn't have no guilty conscience."

"Reckon not."

"You goin' up to the cemetery?"

"Figured I might."

"Kinda coincidental. I was just goin' up there myself."

"You were, eh?"

"You bet. Thought I'd take some flowers up to some of the family."

"Thought you Pratts were all down south."

"Some, but we got kin up here too."

"Maybe so. Where's your horse?"

"Over to the barber shop. Sister Mitchell told me to get my hair cut and have 'im shave me whilst he was at it. I protested some, but she told me to get it done or cut a switch. I reckon I cut enough switches; so I let the barber have at it." The kid laughed and doffed his hat. "What do you think?"

Mitchell studied the barber's handiwork for a moment. "Reckon I'll find someone else when I need shearing," he muttered. "Put that hat back on you head. You'll scare decent folks."

"Hell, they'll see this fine lookin' head, and that barber will be the richest man in town."

"More likely they'll hang the poor sot as a warning."

Daniel Pratt dropped the battered hat back on his head. "Ain't no pleasin' some folks," he muttered.

"Find your horse," Mitchell advised. "I ain't waitin' for a baldheaded kid to keep up."

CHAPTER 34

Utah Territory
Ogden—September 1868

*T*he September sun was half-way down the western sky when Mitchell nudged the dun through the gate of the city cemetery. Less than a mile north of the hotel, on the foothills rising quickly to the tilted rocks of the mountains east of town, the graveyard lay in the lengthening shadows of pines, elms, and shrubbery. A cool, fitful breeze tugged at the trees, robbing the place of any warmth shed by the lowering sun.

Mitchell walked the dun northward, noting how the place was divided into long rectangular sections, like a small city block. In the distance, between two small headstones, a crow stood pecking at the ground. Mitchell watched as the bird raised its head, squawked at the sky then bent once more to peck at the mounded soil beside a new grave.

The dun plodded calmly into the mixture of sunshine and shadow, but Mitchell felt a growing sense of unease. The Pratt kid was nowhere in sight. He'd left the kid at the fence, but the boy had jumped the whitewashed pickets and disappeared in the tangled mess of Russian olives lining the western edge of the cemetery.

The thought of the kid worming his way through a jumble of three-inch thorns gave Mitchell the chills, but the kid had insisted that the cemetery was like a huge bowl surrounded by high ground, and the best vantage points were to the northwest among the trees, near the Pingree family plot.

Mitchell didn't have a clue what the place looked like, or where the Pingree plots were. He knew the kid was a good shot, and having him hidden in the trees watching for trouble should have been a comfort, but the uneasiness grew stronger as he walked the gelding deeper into the graveyard.

The place wasn't much to look at. It covered an area the size of two city blocks with random patches of weeds, flowers, trees, and shrubs scattered everywhere. It was obvious that the caretaker couldn't keep up with the place, and an abundance of toppled headstones and ruined crosses gave mute testimony that the kids in town were not always home before dark.

Somewhere near the center of the bowl, Mitchell reined the dun to a stop. He waited quietly, listening to the crow. Fifty yards to the northwest, a man with a rifle stepped from the cover of a few small trees.

"They said you'd come," he called out, pointing the rifle in Mitchell's direction.

Mitchell flinched at the sound of the man's oily voice. He knew instantly that this was one of the men Mort had been hunting—a skin walker.

That designation held little meaning for Mitchell. He had thought of skin walkers as natives who were thought to be shape changers with evil intent toward those around them—men who could shift their form into that of animals as a way of going about some evil purpose unseen.

The man lifted the muzzle of the Sharps to waist level.

"I didn't think you'd be that stupid," he said darkly. "They said you would be difficult to kill."

The wind tugged at the man's coat, flapping the tails fitfully. Mitchell felt a calmness touch his mind, though the whisper of danger urged him to run.

"You never know," He replied, easing his hand to the butt of his Colt. He had expected something of the sort, but there had been a faint hope that the fellow really knew something of value. "You don't really know anything about Melinda Tolson, do you? You have no idea where her body is."

"Never heard of her," the man called out. "But I figure there's plenty of bodies hereabouts," he added. He took several slow, deliberate steps toward Mitchell. "You can take your pick, if you're lookin' for a body. Myself...I prefer them alive and willing."

Mitchell ignored the remark and strained to see the breech of the man's rifle, hoping he had forgotten to cock the thing. Fifty yards wasn't that far, but the bushwhacker was closing the distance, and Mitchell knew that the fellow would shoot when the distance was right.

The man waggled the barrel of the rifle. "Climb down," he demanded.

"Reckon I'll pass," Mitchell answered. "Looks like you plan on talkin' with that Sharps."

"Don't matter none. I don't miss."

"Do I know you?" Mitchell asked. He'd never seen the man; at least he couldn't remember meeting him, and with the ever-growing influence of the dime novel, it seemed as though every would-be gunman in the territory was tying a gun to their leg. This one was no exception.

"Could be," came the reply.

"But it sure looks like you plan to shoot me."

"I been paid."

"Mind telling me who paid you?"

"I don't think the lady would be too happy if I done that. Right purty little gal though."

The gunman stopped at forty yards and rested the forearm of the Sharps against the trunk of a small tree. Mitchell kicked free of stirrups and threw himself from the saddle as the sound of the Sharps boomed across the cemetery. He hit the ground rolling as the gunman shagged a pistol from his belt and fanned the hammer. Sand and gravel erupted in Mitchell's face as he snapped two wild shots at the gunman. Wind gusted, tearing the smoke from the muzzle of the Colt. He stroked the hammer back, but stiffened as something hard struck the back of his skull, and the world went black.

Susan took a seat in a chair beside the sitting room window and looked westward toward the lake. The sky had changed from a clear, heat shimmering blue to a dirty, dust filled gray. Across the street, the trees surrounding the courthouse thrashed wildly. "Collin told me he had arranged for Mr. Farney to make the dining room furniture," she said.

"Mr. Farney?" Sarah asked. Her own chair faced the window where she could see the dust in the air and hear the pulse of sand and grit on the windowpane.

"Jake told Collin he could make everything," Susan replied.

"Mr. Farney does excellent work," Deborah Miller offered. She had taken a chair facing the outer door and now sat somewhat stiffly, her hands folded primly in her lap. Sarah could see that the woman struggled to remain calm, but her sudden removal to the hotel and her fear that her husband would suddenly break down the door and drag her home to another beating made her eyes dart to the door at every sound from the hallway. They knew precious little about her life with Vernon Miller, but it was obvious that her marriage had been a truly hellish experience. Sarah had no desire to learn the details of that experience; yet she knew that sooner or later Deborah Miller would need to talk and that Susan and she would probably be the recipients of that confidence.

"I wonder if Collin plans to haul that furniture to Idaho Territory," Susan remarked.

"It *would* seem more sensible to cancel the order until we have a house to put it in," Sarah replied.

"I would carry it to California on my back, if I had to," Deborah said softly.

Silence held the room for a moment. Sarah and Susan looked guiltily at one another.

"You're right," Sarah admitted finally. "We should be grateful Collin cares enough to offer us new furniture."

"I've never had new furniture," Deborah confided. "Vernon had the house and all the furniture when we were married."

"This will be a new experience for us too," Susan explained. "The house in Salt Lake belongs to a friend. We only rent it."

Deborah glanced at the door again. "Will Brother Mitchell be long?" she asked.

Susan frowned. "He is taking a long time," she agreed pensively.

In the darkness, Mitchell felt himself fall deeper into an oblivion that gradually filled with the ethereal glow of an early morning sunrise. The sun was low in the east, just below the skyline, and in the valley below, a thick mist rose upward, boiling over the edges, writhing into the upper meadows.

With the eerie quality of a dream, a wraith-like Mitchell watched a roan gelding break through the brush and lunge into a long, narrow clearing. A much younger Mitchell walked the animal slowly into the open. To the west, aspen covered a gentle slope, hedging the clearing. To the east lay a tangle of brush that consumed everything in sight.

For the watching Mitchell, all was quiet. No birds fluttered through the aspen, no insects buzzed within the thick brush, and nothing moved save the coiling threads of mist. The younger Mitchell took off his hat and brushed a sleeve at the sweat on his face, and the watcher felt an ache in his skull, dizziness, and nausea.

Somethin' dead over there....

The watcher heard the thought as though it was his own and smelled smoke and a stench that assailed his nostrils.

Rotting meat and hide....

An odor he couldn't forget—and the stink of maggots was a taint in his mouth begging to be heaved into the grass.

The younger Mitchell walked the roan deeper into the clearing. Near the center, a small stand of aspen stabbed like a finger into the belly of the meadow. Now, the buzz of flies drifted on the air.

Dead pinto—white and black—body's all hunched-up in the trees....

He turned the gelding toward the trees, changed his mind and rode to the lower end of the clearing. He stopped the horse, dismounted and examined the trail. The tracks of the pigeon-toed horse left the clearing, turned to the north then inexplicably returned, followed by two new sets of tracks. There was a noise behind him, the crackle of boots in the grass and the dry snap of a twig, and the younger Mitchell turned cautiously.

"I'm glad someone finally came along."

The watcher felt tears in his eyes, remembering....

The young Mitchell stared at the red-head walking toward him. She was a tall, slender, almost gangling girl dressed in a man's clothing. Instantly, he liked the sound of her voice, the shape of her face, the way she walked. For a moment he thought there was blood on her shirt, but the thought passed. Her shirt, torn and oversized, was only coated with the red dust of the mountain.

She reached his side and held out her hand. "I'm Sarah Flitton," she said, smiling in a way that grabbed at his heart.

The watcher sighed and felt drawn like a wraith, following the younger man and the woman who rode clinging tightly against his back, her arms tight about his chest.

They started down the slope, into a narrow canyon tumbled with rock. The mountain drew close on either side, and soon the trail was lined by scattered aspen and undergrowth that brushed at their pant-legs. The gelding fought his way through the brush, picking his way through slapping branches until Mitchell felt as though he had been beaten with a stick. And it was late afternoon when the gelding finally broke out of Wheeler Canyon at the edge of the muddy waters of the Ogden River.

Mitchell shifted uneasily in the saddle, and the gelding stepped wearily onto a muddy rut that served as a trail leading down into the newly settled town of Ogden, State of Deseret. The gelding ignored the fact that it was a Mormon settlement, but Mitchell took a moment, sucked in a chest full of air, and thanked God it was Mormon air.

The walls of the canyon pressed close on both the north and the south, and the trail leading down into the canyon was choked tight with willows and rock. The narrow gorge was nearly impassable. The gelding was tired, and there was no doubt in Mitchell's mind that they would spend a sleepless night down in the brakes. Already the shadows of evening were creeping upwards on the strangely folded rock, and the lowering sun cast a red-orange glare that retreated swiftly from the power that filled the shadows.

Mitchell shivered at the feeling. Suddenly, he felt as though ghosts of the past wandered among the tilted rocks, or stood at the river's edge and peered toward the mouth of the canyon. He eased himself from the saddle and walked the gelding thirty yards from the trail. He helped the girl down then tied the animals to the nearest tree.

The watcher remembered—the rut was a road now—had been for nearly ten years. Willows and brush had been cleared, but the rotting remains of an old buggy were still at the base of the cliff, a buggy that had once been shiny, new and black.

He remembered the girl had seen four men shoot down a farmer, and she had run her father's horse and buggy hard, trying to get away, down into the brakes. The buggy had broken down, and somehow, she had gotten away and made it to the clearing where he had found her. And like a fool, he had brought her back. And the killers had found them there.

The watcher's head hammered where the pistol had cracked him on the skull. He felt dizzy, and he heard horses coming down the trail. The younger man was suddenly gone, and the watching wraith felt the softness of the girl's hand in his own.

From a coat pocket, he pulled a Colt's pocket pistol and slapped it in her hand. "Take this and get in the buggy."

The girl stared at the pistol, anxiously. "You expect me to shoot someone with this?"

"Only them," the wraith answered. "Don't be shootin' *me* by mistake. Old maid of nineteen might have trouble findin' another handsome fellow to marry."

He held the gelding close and pulled a worn Sharps from its scabbard. He could sense the girl crouched in the buggy, the barrel of the pocket pistol resting on the edge of the open window. Only thirty yards separated them from the killers and Jack Kendall was with them. The men were moving, forcing their way through a stand of aspen. Suddenly, he *knew* they would not pass. He could feel it just as sure as he felt the gelding's breath on the back of his neck.

Blast....

"They're in the trees!"

The wraith felt himself raise the Sharps as the five horses turned. A bullet whined overhead, and a sullen *boom* filled the canyon. He leveled the Sharps and snapped off a shot. A horse went down screaming, and the rider lay still. The wraith dropped the Sharps at his feet and drew the Navy. He fired quickly—three shots as fast as he could settle the sights on man or horse. Suddenly, the smell of sulfur was thick in the air. Another man was down, cursing and coughing blood. The wraith fired again. Another horse collapsed, throwing its rider at the wraith's feet. The man rolled to his knees, and the wraith fired into his body. The man hunched up, but pulled the trigger.

Fire and smoke exploded in the wraith's face. He felt the impact of the bullet, staggered, and struggled to bring up the pistol.

"Forget it...." Kendall hissed. He was on the ground. He took three quick steps, and pointed the fancy Colt at the wraith's forehead. "It's empty, Mitchell. But mine ain't." He cocked the hammer. "Thought I killed you back in them mountains—even dumped you in a ravine. I'll do it right this time."

"I don't think you will." The girl's voice sounded faint after the deafening blast of gunfire.

Kendall was fast. He turned and fired. His shot splintered wood, but the girl's shot took him in the chest. He stumbled and dropped at Mitchell's feet.

Then, Sarah was out of the buggy. The wraith struggled to his knees, but he saw the blood on her.

Get back..... They're not all down....

His thoughts screamed. But his mouth made no sound, as the girl grabbed up the reins of Kendall's horse and struggled into the saddle.

The wraith saw her blood on the horse's side. One good kick, and Kendall's horse was out of the clearing. He heard a man bellow, and suddenly the canyon was filled with the sound of wind, the rushing of water.... and the smell of smoke.

CHAPTER 35

Utah Territory
Ogden—September 1868

Mitchell opened his eyes to the dimness of the hotel room and a throbbing skull. Sarah shifted in the chair beside the bed and laid one hand on his arm.

"You're awake," she murmured softly. "Doctor Conway thought you would come around soon."

Mitchell let his eyes search the room and caught Susan as she quietly crossed the room to the bedside. "My head feels like someone hit it with a hammer," he complained sluggishly.

"A pistol barrel," Susan informed him quietly.

Mitchell frowned and raised himself into a sitting position. "Smoke," he muttered.

Susan leaned over and took him by the hand. "What about smoke?" she asked softly.

"I don't know," he answered. "I was in the brakes, by the river.... Sarah shot Kendall, and I smelled smoke."

Sarah frowned at the mention of Kendall. "You were hit on the head, dear. It must have brought back those memories, but that all happened a long time ago."

"You were at the cemetery," Susan offered. "We got worried and started looking for you. The Grange boy said you went up to the cemetery, so we went there to find you.

"We heard shots while we were coming up the hill and when we got there, we found Daniel and Sarah's Lady-dog digging like two crazy gophers. Daniel told us that one fellow shot at you then another hit you from behind. He was stuck in the trees. All he could do was fire a couple of shots at them when they dumped you in an open grave and started filling it in. You were lucky you didn't suffocate, before they got the dirt off of you."

Sarah took a tighter hold on his arm. "You gave us a fright anyway," she accused disarmingly.

Susan looked closely at Mitchell's face. "Deborah Miller seemed *extremely* concerned," she said quietly. "Is that something *we* should be concerned about?"

Mitchell frowned. "Deborah's a nice girl," he acknowledged reluctantly, "but the two women I've got are all I'll ever need to be a happy man. I ain't interested in acquiring another."

"Ain't, ain't a word, Brother Mitchell," Sarah advised stiffly.

Mitchell flushed and shook his head. "There's no need to *Brother Mitchell* me. I've got no intentions on the woman."

Sarah smiled sweetly. "Just making sure you understand *our* feelings on the subject," she warned.

"My head hurts," he muttered. "I'd like to know who hit me."

"Daniel says there were two men, but he was too far away to see their faces," Susan said. "They ran off when he started shooting."

"I saw that fellow with the sharps just fine," Mitchell insisted dryly. "I'll recognize him if I see him again."

"Deputy Wheeler came by about an hour ago. He hadn't heard what happened, but he came to let us know that Vernon Miller is dead," Susan reported.

"How did that happen?" Mitchell asked grimly.

"Deputy Wheeler said that Mr. Miller saw him coming and ran. He must have heard that he was going to be arrested. The deputy tracked him down, but Mr. Miller tried to jump his horse over a fence. The horse shied and threw Mr. Miller. He broke his neck."

Mitchell was quiet for a moment. "Too bad he didn't spend some time in jail first," he responded stiffly.

"So, what do we do now?" Sarah asked quietly. "Deborah may not want to sell her land, now that her husband is gone."

"We'll see what she wants to do," he answered.

"What about Melinda Tolson and Lester Reynald?" Susan asked.

"I'm not sure," Mitchell responded." I'm convinced that Melinda Tolson is dead, but there are pieces to this puzzle that don't seem to connect."

Sarah looked over at her sister. The younger woman nodded her assent. "Maybe we have two puzzles," she suggested pensively.

Mitchell waited quietly while the woman gathered her thoughts.

"Your Uncle, William, sent a telegram earlier this week. As soon as we read it, we suspected that someone wanted us all dead," she said, explaining the contents of the telegram. "We think they're here, in town and responsible for all the trouble we've been having."

"That's one puzzle," Susan interjected. "They want the silver mine. They left Uncle William for dead, and they think they can have it all by killing us too.

"That means that everything else must be part of a different puzzle," Sarah added, "including a connection between the disappearance of Melinda Tolson and the murder of Lester Reynald. All of it must fit together somehow," she insisted.

Mitchell shook his head. "It must," he agreed, "but how?"

A sudden rapping on the door interrupted their thoughts, and Mitchell watched in fascination as both women conjured Navy Colts from their clothing and disappeared into the sitting room. Moments later, they returned with the Pratt kid in tow.

"I went back for your pistol," the kid said excitedly. He dropped the 1862 navy Colt on the bed beside Mitchell.

The fluted cylinder captured the dim lamplight and threw it back in a scatter of subdued sparks.

"That ain't all I found though," he announced cryptically.

Sarah took the boy by the arm and gave it a good squeeze. "Tell us what you found," she insisted.

"Just that mummy you been lookin' for," he replied nonchalantly. "I got it in the wagon out in front of the Hotel. Mort's keepin' watch on it. Says he don't want it disappearin' again."

Mitchell grabbed the Colt and threw off the blankets. "Where in the world did you find her," he demanded, reaching for the trousers Susan offered.

The Pratt kid grinned.

"She was in that hole where those fellows tried to bury you," he replied thoughtfully. "I saw your pistol layin' in the bottom of the hole, and when I jumped down to get it, I landed right on top of somethin' all wrapped up in a canvas. I looked inside, and there she was. Mort helped me get her in the wagon, and we brung her back here."

Mitchell shook his head in disbelief, and when he was ready, they trooped down the stairs to where Mort waited with the wagon.

Mitchell stared at the dark hair and the blackened, dried out features of the woman's face. Instinctively, he knew it was not Ruth Miller. He looked at Mort, who sat quietly on the steps of the Veranda. "It's Melinda Tolson, isn't it?" he said.

Mort nodded glumly. "Yep, It's Melinda."

Mitchell frowned. "I guess I'm not surprised," he admitted tiredly. "I was hoping she was still alive though."

"Been dead a long time," Mort advised reassuringly.

Mitchell shook his head wearily. "I'm going back to bed," he muttered. "I'm too tired to think right now."

At the steps, he paused, looking down at the old man. "You smell smoke?" he asked.

"Been smellin' it for six years," the old man replied somberly.

Mitchell paused and pondered the wagon and its unhappy load. If the death of Melinda Tolson and Lester Reynald were connected, they were connected by some circumstance that had not changed in six years.

Melinda Tolson had been killed. Her body had been hidden away. And Lester Reynald had been killed when her body had been rediscovered. To Mitchell, it seemed only logical that someone wanted the killing of Melinda Tolson to remain a secret and had killed Lester Reynald to keep it that way. The question, however, remained. Who was the killer and why had he killed the girl?

CHAPTER 36

Utah Territory
Ogden—September 1868

Mitchell woke to the sound of wind and the hiss of sand on the window panes. Beside him, Sarah moved drowsily and threw one arm across his chest.

"Don't step on the dog," She murmured softly. "She was out on the Veranda earlier, barking at everyone; I let her in so you could get some rest."

Vaguely, Mitchell recalled the early morning barking of the Lady-dog and the half-remembered dream of a woman trapped in a smoke filled room. Suddenly, he knew how Melinda Tolson had died, and who had killed Lester Reynald.

Two hours later, Mitchell and Wheeler slid their chairs back from the table and stood as Susan came hurriedly onto the verandah.

"You won't believe it," she said breathlessly. She pointed down Main Street and shook her head. "I was down at the millenary, and who do you suppose came in and bought a yard of plain white cotton?"

"I haven't a clue," Sarah answered.

"Your Mrs. Richards, of course. And when she left the millenary she met Mr. Jensen, whom we haven't seen in several days—and who is now limping most noticeable."

"Your hat pin!" Sarah exclaimed.

"Quite possibly," Susan agreed. "When I mentioned that Mrs. Richards was very involved with the suffrage movement, half of the women in the shop looked at me like I was daft. When I questioned them, they told me that

Mrs. Richards has nothing to do with the suffrage movement and has been in town only three weeks."

"Uncle William's thieves," Sarah announced decisively.

"I believe so," Susan replied.

"Can you prove any of this?" Wheeler asked cautiously.

"If Mr. Jensen is the man who attacked me in the stable, he may have a very infected wound in his right thigh," Susan responded.

"That should give me enough reason to go after Mr. Jensen," Wheeler concluded thoughtfully, "but I don't see what I can do for you, Mitchell. All you have is the body of a girl who's been missing for six years and some odds and ends that point to no one in particular. If you had a witness to any of it, I might be able to tie it together and go after your man. As it is, you don't have anything definite that points to him."

Mitchell frowned and shook his head. "I think I realized that," he answered reluctantly. "I can't prove a thing, but I know he poisoned Ruth Miller, and I know he killed that girl and hid her body in Nathan Calder's smokehouse until he took it out to the burial mound and switched it with the remains of Two Bears' wife.

"I have no idea what drove the man to do such a thing, but once it was done, he thought he was free and clear—until Groesbeck brought the body back to Reynald who thought it was just the mummified remains of an Indian woman.

"It must have shocked the hell out of Reynald when he recognized that ear-cuff and the body of the girl he had wanted to marry. Coincidence or not, he ran from the shop straight into the knife of Melinda Tolson's killer. And the only proof I have is that the dog *didn't* bark."

Wheeler frowned. "There's still nothing I can do. Dogs can't testify in court. If they could, we'd probably all go to jail for something or other."

Mitchell was quiet for a moment, starring into the distance toward Ben Lomond Peak. "There's nothing you can do," he concluded grimly. "But there's still one thing I can do."

Wheeler shook his head and glanced at the two women who sat stiffly, hands folded in their laps, starring grimly and unhappily at the table top.

"I don't think I want to hear any more, Mitchell," he warned. The deputy slapped his hat on his head and stalked to his horse. A moment later, he rode away, visibly upset.

CHAPTER 37

Utah Territory
Ogden—September 1868

*T*he Pratt kid stepped into the dimly lit shop and searched for his target. He didn't know why Mitchell had sent him on this errand, but he knew he was about to put the fear of God into a man he'd never met, and it was a job he didn't relish one bit.

A few steps put him close enough to satisfy Mitchell's instructions. Congenially, he nodded to the man inspecting a new bridle. "Heard they found Melinda Tolson's body," he announced casually.

"You don't say," the man replied.

"Yep. I guess they know who killed her too," the kid added. "Same fellow killed that Reynald fellow last week."

"I heard about that," the man answered.

The Pratt kid frowned and looked at the floor. "They know who done it, but they can't prove nothin'. So, I hear they sent a *Danite* to set things right," he concluded reluctantly.

"Danite...."

The Pratt kid watched the man frown, and six feet away, he saw the shopkeeper's face drain of its color.

"God help the man if that's true," the customer acknowledged quietly.

Mitchell stood quietly at the back of Nathan King's dentistry and watched the back of the mercantile. He felt no surprise when Melinda Tolson's killer slipped through the back door, secured saddle bags and bedroll, climbed aboard his horse and headed south as though Satan himself was charging down his back-trail.

"I guess that settles that," Mitchell told the Pratt kid who stood shaking his head.

"He looked down right sick when I said there was a Danite comin' for Melinda Tolson's killer. He sure ain't growin' no moss waitin' around."

Mitchell frowned as he watched the killer turn west and kick his mount into a gallop. "You go back to the hotel and tell Sarah and Susan not to worry," he told the kid.

"I should go with you," the kid protested. "They'll make me cut a switch if I let you go alone."

"I'll make you cut one if you don't go back to the hotel," Mitchell growled. "That Jensen fellow is still around, and I have a feeling Becker and Gilson are up to no good. You make sure none of them bothers my women while I'm gone."

When the Pratt kid was gone, Mitchell climbed into the saddle and headed southwest, toward the crossing of the Weber River and the remains of old Fort Buenaventura.

West of the river, Mitchell heeled the dun into a fast walk. The trail led west, winding through the river bottoms, past the rotting remains of the tumbled palisades of Fort Buenaventura to the steep slopes leading to the top of the sand hill.

Mitchell crossed the river and turned the dun south into the trees surrounding the remains of the fallen palisades of the fort. For nearly half a mile, Mitchell followed the tracks of the killer's horse until the dun broke through the trees and into the clearing. Nothing stirred as he scanned the clearing and searched the farthest edges of the surrounding trees.

Nothing remained of the old fort. The trees surrounding the small meadow-like clearing it had once occupied had grown thick with the passage of years. Yet, there was something—a feeling—a feeling of something dark and malignant.

To the west, a tall ridge of sand rose like a small mountain where the river had carved deeply into the sandy bottom of the ancient Bonneville lakebed. Uneasily, he rode across the clearing and onto the trail leading up the ravine on the north of the hill. He was barely in the trees when a hailstorm of lead pounded the brush on every side. Heedless of the tearing brush, Mitchell threw himself from the dun, scrambled into the deadfall at the edge of the trail and fired at his assailants.

Moments later, the gunfire died as suddenly as it had begun. Immediately, the sand hill smothered the sound, and the roar of gunfire dwindled to a whisper in the distance, shrouding the ravine in an uneasy silence. Mitchell pressed himself deeper into the cover of oak-brush and rocks.

Gilson's voice bellowed from a nest of rocks just forty feet away. "I think I hit him!"

Mitchell lay motionless, waiting. Quietly, he checked both revolvers—just one round in the navy—three in the army, and the dun was fifty feet away. He'd never reach his saddlebags or the powder and lead he needed. Gilson would pick him off like a jackrabbit.

Gilson had the better position. Lying behind a heap of small boulders on the north face of the hill, he had a near-perfect view of Mitchell's brushy hideout.

"Can you see him?"

The voice was farther away—nearly fifty yards upstream. Mitchell shuddered uncontrollably at the sound of the man's voice. Oily smooth, it was pleasant enough to the ear, but like a wood rasp dragged across unprotected flesh, the voice tore at the soul, leaving agony with its passage.

Samiel The name whispered in Mitchell's head, conjuring scenes from a half-remembered nightmare.

"No!" Gilson called to the man hidden in the trees. "He's down in the rocks. I can't see anything but the backside of a rock pile."

Mitchell kept his head down, brushing at spots of blood where splintered rock from Gilson's last shot had pelted him in the face.

"You alive, Mitchell?" Gilson hollered.

Mitchell ignored the question. "You just keep wonderin' what I'm up to, you back shootin' skunk," he muttered under his breath. Quietly, he left the cover of brush and rock and moved toward Gilson's rock pile.

"Becker!" Gilson's bellow filled the narrow ravine, but lacking the volume of the gunshots, it dwindled among the trees and died.

"He took off," the other voice called back. "Took his horse and ran off."

"Gutless dog," Gilson snarled. "Keep your eyes on Mitchell."

Mitchell stopped and stood still. The brush was barely knee high, but he dared not move. A man poked his head from behind a tree, glanced at Mitchell's last location then pulled back quickly.

"Don't see anything," he called out, "a boot maybe... but he ain't movin'."

"I killt 'im." Gilson answered. "So much for all that garbage about ridin' with the angel of death and livin' to a hundred and ten! Pour some lead into 'im, Jensen!"

With a clatter of boots on the rocky talus, Gilson lunged from behind the nest of boulders. He took three steps down the hillside, both pistols firing into Mitchell's abandoned lair. Six rounds slammed into the brush covered alcove, filling the air with a thick sulfurous fog.

Silence followed the gunfire, pressing as though every bird, every insect, waited for a resumption of the man-made thunder. Mitchell stood quietly, waiting for the smoke to clear, waiting for Gilson to turn ever so slightly and see him standing in the open. Time grew sluggish, caught in the lazy dissipation of the smoke, trapped in the motionless silence of the ravine.

Suddenly, Gilson was facing him, his guns cocked and ready to fire. Smoke bloomed at the muzzles. Lead tugged at Mitchell's shirt and white-hot pain slashed at his upper arm, but his own revolver thundered, shrouding the air between them with smoke.

For a moment, Gilson stared at Mitchell. His face grew slack as he looked down at the small hole in his shirt. His eyes seemed to widen, and the barrels of his pistols drooped toward the ground. His knees locked, and for a moment it seemed as though he would topple like a felled tree and slide down the sandy hillside and into the shallow waters of the river. Instead, his knees buckled, and he sat down heavily, stabbing the barrels of both pistols into the sand.

Mitchell stepped forward, covering the distance between them in ten long strides. Gilson looked up. Blood covered his lips.

"It was ninety-three," Mitchell said dryly. "Mort told me 'pneumonia at ninety-three'. Don't reckon a bullet will ever do the job."

Gilson coughed then sagged back on his heels and toppled over on his side. Mitchell knelt beside Gilson's body and pried the pistols from his fists. With a twig, he dug the loose dirt from the barrels and blew them clean. The forty-four caliber Army Colts were half loaded. Mitchell holstered his own weapons and looked toward the trees where Jensen had been hiding.

Jensen was gone, but the sound of breaking branches gave the man away as he ran west through the thick oak brush. Mitchell turned away from the dead man, leaving the body where it lay. It wouldn't take long before heat, bugs, and wild animals reduced it to a scattering of rags and bones. Right now, he was more concerned with running down Melinda Tolson's killer, and to blazes with Gilson and Jensen.

Quickly, Mitchell forced his way out of the brush. The gelding shied, nearly breaking the reins from a tangle of trees as Mitchell burst from the brush under the animal's nose and grabbed the headstall.

"Easy," he crooned, sliding his hand down the startled animal's neck. The dun threw its head back, rattling the bit in his teeth. "Settle down, you bonehead," Mitchell snarled. He grabbed at the saddlebags and dumped powder and lead into the empty cylinders of both pistols.

CHAPTER 38

Utah Territory
Ogden—September 1868

*T*wo hours later, the girl's killer spotted him and kicked his horse into a gallop. For three miles they ran, with the dun slowly closing the distance on the fat, out-of-shape animal the killer rode. Finally, the animal gave out.

The horse staggered and fell, tossing Nephi Clarke like a rag in the wind. The killer hit the ground, rolled to his feet with an agility that took Mitchell by surprise and ran like blazes. Fifty feet away, he yanked a pistol from his belt and turned. Twice, smoke and flames roared from the pistol's mouth.

Mitchell heard the angry sound of lead cutting through the air then the hard click of the pistol's hammer on a fired cap. "Give it up, Clarke!" he bellowed. "It's empty, and you got nowhere to run!"

"Go to blazes!" Clarke screamed as he turned and ran again.

Suppressing the urge to shoot the man in the back, Mitchell kicked the dun into a lope. "Run the skunk down," he snarled at the animal.

The dun stretched out, closing the distance. Clarke dodged like a rabbit through trees and brush then suddenly launched himself into the air. Mitchell dragged at the reins, and the dun crow-hopped to a stop at the edge of a twelve-foot drop. In the creek below, Clarke swam strongly toward the opposite bank.

Mitchell searched the bank for a way down, but the sides were steep, and the narrow banks of the creek were choked with brush and rock. It was as though Clarke had picked this spot knowing the only way down was a jump into the muddy water below.

Clarke reached the shallows, stood, and waded toward shore.

"Dang it," Mitchell muttered. "I ain't letting him get away."

Angrily, he turned the gelding for a run at the bank and slammed to a halt. The dun fought the rein and tried to rear back, but Mort held the animal's headstall in a death-grip, while the pigeon-toed Milo stood like rock with the dun's chest pressing his shoulder and the animal's head straining across the saddle-horn.

"Don't jump him in there, Danite. There's a better way across." The old man released the dun and quietly turned Milo to the north. "There's a shallow place—up around the bend," he called over his shoulder. "We'll cross there."

Mitchell nudged the dun and caught up with the old man. "Were the blazes did you come from?" he demanded.

"Been waitin' here."

"You been waitin' everywhere," Mitchell grouched.

"Reckon so, but I got plenty of time."

"Well, I don't. That buzzard is headed for that farm, and this animal is tired. If Clarke steals a fresh horse, I'll have to chase him across half the territory."

"He ain't headed nowheres," Mort replied.

"What are you talking about?"

"Quicksand," The old man answered.

"Quicksand?"

"Yep. He'll be knee deep about now."

The old man gave Milo a touch of the spur and led the way to the crossing. Minutes later, they crossed the creek and turned south.

"See," Mort insisted, pointing toward a distant, struggling figure. "I told you he weren't goin' nowheres."

"Good," Mitchell responded. "I'll drop a rope on him and drag him out."

"Let's see if he'll fess up, before we do that" the old man argued. "Then you'll know if you got it figured right."

"I'd rather drag his sorry ass back to Salt Lake City and let them give him the firing squad."

"Aw, for Pete's sake...give him a chance to talk. You know you ain't gonna get 'im in no court anyways."

Mitchell grew silent as they moved closer to the struggling Clarke. Finally, they dismounted on the upper bank.

"Got yourself in a fix, ain't ya," Mort observed.

"Pull me out," Clarke demanded.

"Reckon not," Mort replied. "We want to know what you done with that girl's body."

"I don't know what you're talking about."

"You killed that Tolson girl," Mort accused.

"Tolson's girl ran off," Clarke snarled. "Everyone knows that."

"Reckon not," Mort disagreed." Mitchell found her dress and a few other things that prove she never left town alive."

"We have Ruth's diary," Mitchell said quietly.

"That woman was a lying whore!" Clarke screamed.

"You killed both of them," Mitchell accused, "You poisoned Ruth because she suspected something, and later, you killed that girl and had someone mail the letter and the money from Denver."

Mitchell watched the water creep higher on Clarke's shirt. The killer was only three feet from shore, but the water was a foot deep, and Clarke was already buried to the waist in the muddy creek bed. He lunged, but the mud held him tightly and dragged him deeper into the creek. The man would certainly drown before he disappeared in the quicksand.

"Pull me out and I'll tell you what happened." he said suddenly.

"Why did you kill her?" Mitchell replied.

Clarke glanced down at the rising water and seemed to panic. "It was an accident," he argued. "Miller recognized those ear-cuffs and said something to the girl the night she ran off from her father's place. I saw her and followed her. She had Wadman's horse, but I caught up with her at Reynald's place. I pulled her off the horse and tried to explain, but she started fighting. I hit her, and she fell. She just lay there.

"There were people about, and I couldn't just leave her lying in the street. So, I carried her to Nathan Calder's smoke shed and covered her with some burlap sacks then I left and hid the horse at my place."

"You left her body in the smoke house?"

"I didn't dare go back. Calder started using the shed the next day. I could never get near the place. Finally, I went late one night and got the body."

"You took it out to that mound," Mitchell prompted.

"I was digging and opened up an old Indian burial."

"Then, you switched things around."

"I put the Indian woman's clothes on the girl's body."

"Don't stop now," Mort advised. "That water's getting' a mite close."

Clarke raised his chin. "I put the bones under a pile of rocks and buried the dress; then I took the horse out and shot it. Nobody ever found it. Now pull me out!"

Nephi Clarke was buried to his armpits in mud, and the slow moving water lapped at his chin.

"Why did you kill Reynald?" Mort demanded.

"We were in business. At first, Reynald looted a few graves. Later, he started robbing houses when folks were off to a funeral and such. I took the gold and silver and reworked it into my own stuff. Wadman sold any loose jewels in Salt Lake or Denver. We split everything three ways. When Miller's wife recognized a necklace that came from one of the looted graves, she had to go.

After a couple of months, we were all doing ok and decided to shut things down before someone caught on. But Reynald was a drunk. He couldn't hang on to a dime. He was ok for a while, but he was always sour about something or other.

"A few weeks ago, he got mad at Wadman and me and threatened to make trouble. He wanted three thousand dollars to leave town and keep his mouth shut. Neither of us had that kind of money, so we hit a few more houses and gave Reynald everything so he'd leave town."

Clarke coughed and slipped beneath the water.

"I can't let him drown," Mitchell told the old man. He reached out and grabbed a flailing arm, and pulled at the man. The mud fought him as though hungry for the man's life, then suddenly, as Clarke's face broke the surface of the water, the killer's eyes widened in terror.

"No!"

Smoke and flame thundered beside Mitchell, and Clarke's head slammed back into the muddy water.

"Dang it, Mort! Why'd you go and do that?"

"Couldn't just stand here and watch the man drown."

"You Dang near deafened me," snarled Mitchell. "You could have helped me pull him out."

"Reckon not," the old man answered. He turned his back on the bloody water and looked west, toward the lake. "Kind of a portentous place," he said quietly. "Del Thomas will lose a horse in that very spot. Don't reckon you'll ever meet Del, but his grandson will think on you now and then."

Mitchell frowned unhappily and shook his head. "Let's head back to town," he growled. He was tired, his ears were ringing, and he wasn't sure how to handle the strange old man.

"Reckon not," the old man replied. "You go on back to Sarah, and thank her for the horse. She's a fine woman. Tell her I'm goin' to borrow 'im for a spell.

"An' you tell Susan that I said to stop troublin' herself. She's scared stiff she'll die in childbirth. That's why she wants a place in town—figures it's closer to a doctor.

"You tell her and Sarah both that they been fine friends, but I won't come for 'em 'til they're both old and ready to come home."

"Childbirth?" Mitchell echoed incredulously. "I've seen that woman steady as a rock with lead flyin' everywhere!"

"Go figure," the old man answered.

Mitchell glared at the bloody water. "How am I goin' to explain about Clarke?"

Mort looked down at the pistol in his hand. With a wink, he tossed it high into the air. The Colt flipped end-over-end and dropped with a solid *plunk* in the center of the slow moving water. Ripples spread outward, multiplying.

"Time is a mighty big pond, boy. Everything we do makes ripples. Trouble is folks can only see what's on the surface. They never notice how deep the water is—and like that pistol, not everything is movin' in the same direction."

"You ain't makin' any sense," Mitchell muttered irritably.

"Reckon not," the old man admitted. "You just forget Clarke. You never done nothin' to him, and I reckon no-one is goin' to ask you about him."

"I wouldn't be so sure of that," Mitchell advised.

"You don't have much choice," Mort replied. "Just tell anyone who asks that I shot poor Mr. Clarke and held you at gun-point while I made my escape."

"Your gun's in the crick," Mitchell said, glancing toward the water.

"Maybe," Mort replied. "Maybe not."

Mitchell turned back and found the muzzle of the old man's pistol pointed directly in his face.

The old man smiled. "Like I said.... Time is a twisty sort of thing." Mort backed away, dragging Milo with him. "I'll be seein' you, Danite. I got to be in Paris France tonight, but I'll be back in a week or so. Maybe you could take me elk huntin' when I get back. I ain't never hunted elk before." The old man shrugged. "Besides, you and me...we got a skin walker to catch."

CHAPTER 39

Utah Territory
Ogden—September 1868

*I*t was late evening when Mitchell eased back into the comfort of a chair on the hotel verandah. "I didn't use him up," he said quietly. "I was going to bring him back and hope they could send him down to the point of the mountain or something, but Mort shot him before I could drag Clarke out of the mud."

Sarah smiled and laid her hand gently on Mitchell's arm. "We didn't think you would kill him," she said disarmingly. Mitchell touched her hand gratefully. "I only had that Pratt kid say that stuff about Danites to see what Clarke would do. I figured he'd run if he was guilty and thought there was a Danite coming to use him up. Wadman rode out of here as soon as he heard there was trouble and no one's seem him since," he added.

Susan scooted her chair closer, and Mitchell wrapped an arm around her. "Deputy Wheeler came by and told us that Mr. Jensen and Mrs. Richards have cleared out too," she murmured softly. "He's sending word to Salt Lake so everyone will be watching for them. Deputy Wheeler thinks the County Sheriff will find them unless they just ride straight through the valley without stopping."

Mitchell felt the hair bristle on the back of his neck at the thought of the soul wrenching nightmare calling himself Jensen.

Sarah smiled coquettishly and leaned against his free shoulder. "Now, tell us what gave Mr. Clarke away. No one who knew him would have ever thought he was a murderer."

Mitchell laughed softly. "Once you made me realize that we were looking at two puzzles, things began to make more sense," he replied. "All I had to do was give my poor fuzzy brain time to sort it out.

"We had a knife that pointed at Tolson," he admitted. "But Tolson never seemed like the type who would sneak up on a fellow and stab him to death. Then there was the burial. There was a broken shell necklace under a body that should have been *wearing* the necklace. I never understood that, until I started thinking that the body in the burial might not be Two Bears' wife.

"The skeleton near the mound had been tampered with. It was just a pile of disarticulated bones. No one buries their dead that way, and with that dress buried so close, I had to wonder if the bones were those of Melinda Tolson. But Nathan King made me doubt that possibility when he told me he'd never seen that dished out shape on the front teeth of any white folks, especially Melinda Tolson.

"For a while I felt so mixed up, I had no idea how any of those things might connect, or if there was any connection at all. And I had no idea what to think of those ear-cuffs. There was no way Two Bears was lying about the ear-cuffs. He knew his wife had never been buried with them. So, that mummy was no Shoshoni.

"At first, I thought it had to be Ruth Miller, but there was no reason for her body to be buried in that mound. Melinda Tolson was a different story. Something about the mummy upset Reynald so badly he became ill and tore that ear-cuff right off the body. I decided fairly soon that he recognized either the ear-cuff or the body. That meant the mummy was probably Melinda Tolson.

"I'm only taking a guess at some of this," he continued, "but it seems to fit well enough with the things we know for certain. Ruth Miller's journal helps fill in the gaps a little.

"Clarke gave Ruth Miller a pair of silver ear-cuffs and made her think he wanted to marry her. Then, one day, she saw a bit of jewelry in Clarke's shop. Clarke claimed he had made it, but Ruth commented on how unusual the little necklace was and how it was identical to one Elizabeth Tuner had owned. That day, she wrote how agitated Clarke became when she picked up the necklace to look at it closer. He literally snatched it out of her hands.

"She had a cup of tea with Clarke before she went home. Her last entry mentions the necklace and how oddly bitter the tea tasted. She died that evening, and was buried a few days later."

"He poisoned her," Sarah concluded grimly.

"Maybe Vernon Miller killed her," Susan suggested. "It's hard for me, even now to see Nephi Clarke as a murderer."

"Clarke admitted it," Mitchell said quietly. "He wasn't quite the gentleman he led everyone to believe."

"So he was a thief as well as a murderer, and he killed her so no one would ever know he had stolen that necklace from Elizabeth Turner," Sarah said accusingly.

"They were worse than thieves" Mitchell muttered grimly.

"Grave robbers," Susan muttered her voice thick with disgust.

"Reynald and Wadman arrived in town about a year before Ruth Miller died," Mitchell continued. "Wadman set up his office and Reynald built his shop within weeks. Reynald came from Salt Lake City, but Jake Farney remembered that Wadman came to town with nothing but a beat up old hat and the clothes on his back. Both of them arrived about the same time Jean Baptiest disappeared from Fremont Island."

Sarah nodded. "He was the grave digger at the Salt Lake City Cemetery," Sarah answered. "Back in sixty-two, some fellow got himself shot and the sheriff had him buried in the city cemetery. The fellow's brother came along and had the body exhumed to move it to a family plot. I guess they found the coffin broken up and the body stripped.

The brother accused the sheriff of taking poor care of the remains. But the sheriff knew things had been done right, so they went to see Baptiest and ask him some questions.

They found the back room of his house full of burial clothing, shoes and other things he'd looted from the cemetery. People all over the valley wanted to lynch Baptiest, but they tried him, convicted him, and sentenced him to life in exile on Fremont Island, where no decent soul would ever come in contact with him again.

"Whether they had any connection to Baptiest or not, we'll never know," Mitchell said quietly. "But Clarke killed the girl and buried her body in the Shoshoni burial mound. Groesbeck dug it up and brought it back to town. Reynald mentioned the mummy to Wadman and when Clarke heard where they got it, he couldn't think of anything except getting rid of the body again. It became an obsession.

"But nothing' made any sense until I realized that Jake Farney's dog always ran off to Nephi Clarke's place, 'cause that's where home was. No one else could have gotten near that alley without the dog making a racket, and that would have warned Reynald. But it was fairly obvious that Reynald had been killed without the slightest warning. "

Mitchell looked out across the verandah. Over the Great Salt Lake, dark clouds churned with rain, rolling eastward with the winds, bringing a chill to the air. Or perhaps the chill had come with the thought of another killer who roamed the territory like a malignant plague—a killer chased amid the blowing sands and rain by an old man—an old man who knew everyone's name and thought he was the angel of death—an old man riding a pigeon-toed horse.

Author's Note

This story and its characters are fictional. It is a mingling of three genres, historical, mystery, and western. The historical facts are as accurate as I could make them and still allow enough flexibility for a very limited interaction between historical individuals and fictional characters.

Susan and Sarah Flitton were real Mormon pioneers, although neither was ever involved in plural marriage or any gunfight that I am aware of. They were, however, part of the inspiration for this story, and I have taken the liberty of using their names for two of my main characters.

Susan Flitton was my 2nd great grandmother, and Sarah was her sister. Susan lived into her nineties, and in 1949, the State of Utah awarded Susan a bronze medal for being the oldest living Utah pioneer.

Many of the scenes in this story unfold in settings that have changed greatly in the last one-hundred and forty years. Street names and numbers are no longer the same. The White House Hotel and the Prairie House are gone. Fort Buenaventura has been rebuilt.

Any Latter-day Saint doctrines mentioned in this work are expressed in the context of a fictional character's interpretation, and may not represent *true* LDS thought on the subject.

Mort is a fictional character whom I have yet to meet.

About the Author

J.T. Fleming is a *Magna Cum Laude* graduate of Weber State University with a B.S. in English as well as a B.S. in Anthropology. Mr. Fleming works as a technical writer for an international manufacturing company and has published numerous stories as a community news correspondent with the Standard-Examiner in Ogden, Utah.

Mr. Fleming has written two books in the Collin Mitchell series: *Tracks of a Pigeon-toed Horse & The Obsidian Serpent*. The third book in the series, *Mouriel,* is soon to be released.

Born and raised in Utah, Mr. Fleming is a member of the LDS church and has hunted deer, elk, and gold in the mountains and deserts of Utah and Colorado. With his wife and family, he lives west of the Wasatch Mountains, near the Great Salt Lake.

REVIEWS FOR

J.T. FLEMING'S
Tracks of a Pigeon-toed Horse & The Obsidian Serpent

Unique in its combination of western history from a still little known but vast area called the Utah Territory, and a culture known then as the "Mormons." There is much to learn about this people and these times. This was a wild west still not fully explored on the written page, and few western writers have the background and ability to do this. Fleming writes his characters off the page and into your heart....

With just a touch of mysticism, great descriptions of these lands and the people on them, Fleming combines all this to create one very good story after another. Anyone who loves westerns will really appreciate these books, and it is refreshing to have women characters just as interesting as the men....

Western fans will love this true balance of dialogue, descriptive prose and action. The historical information is skillfully woven into these stories which are filled with humor, sudden fast paced action scenes and a clear love of nature and the out-of-doors. I highly recommend these books and those yet to be written....

Author LINDA DUNNING

(Ghost Lights; Lost Landscapes; Restless Spirits; Specters in Doorways)

I bought this on a chance—one of those 'pick-it-out as you look'. It pulled me in and kept me up late into the night reading. Kept the suspense until the end. A great mystery in the main plot and a secondary plot that had me buying his second book before I finished the first!

cinderpf; Utah

Being an avid reader of all types of books, from J.K. Rowling, to James Patterson and everything in-between, I began this book with high hopes of many evenings of entertainment. I was not disappointed. Mr. Fleming's knowledge of the Utah area I grew up in was evident, and it was obvious he had done his homework.

This book covers the very controversial area of Mormonism in the 1800's, and examines the pros and cons of plural marriage, and a people who were not saints, but very much wanted to be.

I was impressed with the way I was pulled into the story, from page one. I give this a definite thumbs up, and also recommend "The Obsidian Serpent" which continues the story of Collin Mitchell and makes you want for more.

nana211 Oregon